Scream Muddy Murder

OTHER BOOKS BY LESLEY A. DIEHL

A Deadly Draught

Poisoned Pairings

Dumpster Dying

Grilled, Killed and Chilled

Angel Sleuth

A Secondhand Murder

Dead in the Water

A Sporting Murder

Mud Bog Murder

Old Bones Never Die

Killer Tied

Murder Is Academic

Failure Is Fatal

The Aunt Nozzie and Grandmothers stories—The Killer Wore Cranberry: Thanksgiving Anthologies Vols 1-5

Bobbing for Murder novella—Happy Homicides4: Fall Into Crime

Find out More about Lesley at
www.lesleyadiehl.com

Scream Muddy Murder

Book 3 in the Big Lake murder mystery series

Lesley A. Diehl

Scream Muddy Murder
Book 3 in the Big Lake Murder Mysteries
Copyright © 2018 Lesley A. Diehl
www.lesleyadiehl.com
Creekside Publishing

Cover Copyright 2018 by Lesley A. Diehl

Cover design by Karen A. Phillips
www.PhillipsCovers.com

Formatted by Debora Lewis
www.arenapublishing.org

Printed in the United States of America

—◈— —◈— —◈—

ISBN 13: 987-0-9972349-5-4
ISBN 10: 0-9972349-5-4

To all the writers who supported me over the years, too many to name.

You know who you are. My profound thanks.

ACKNOWLEDGMENTS

For information about the Seminole and Miccosukee People of Florida I am grateful to Brent Richards Weisman for his book *Unconquered People: Florida's Seminole and Miccosukee Indians,* 1999, The University Press of Florida.

CHAPTER 1

The rain poured down on the combatants as they took up their stances on opposite ends of the field. One side stationed their men behind the palm trees and live oaks, while the fighters on the other side positioned themselves out in the open, preparing to march straight at the enemy—a foolish strategy, but insisted upon by their commander.

Emily pushed wet locks of hair off her face and prepared to advance with the first wave of troops. She held no weapon for defense; her assignment was to beat her snare drum. She grasped her drumsticks tightly for fear she'd drop one and would be unable to beat out the martial tempo she'd been assigned. Emily's daughter, Naomi, holding the American flag, stood beside her, the two of them dressed as boys from the early nineteenth century, shirts with long, full sleeves and knee britches. Naomi had been smart to tie her blond hair back with a leather thong. Their only concession to modern dress was that each wore a pair of rubber boots. Naomi's sported a yellow duck pattern, Emily's were a nautical blue with a thin red stripe around the top.

"How did we get ourselves into this mess?" asked Emily, attempting to lift one foot out of the mud. Her boot made a sucking sound. "This is as bad as quicksand."

"It was your idea to take part," replied Naomi. "You said it would be fun and a service to the community."

"It would have been fun if it hadn't been raining for three days. The field was so flooded the organizers cancelled yesterday's performance. It's not much better today."

A shot rang out signaling the start of the reenactment of the Battle of Okeechobee, an event held each year at the site of the original battle fought in 1837, a military engagement in the Second Seminole War. Emily started at the sound of the gun and stumbled forward, almost falling to her knees. Naomi reached out and steadied her mother. The announcer thumped the microphone to determine if it was working. It gave forth a screech and again startled Emily, but this time she held her position. With a clearing of his throat and another squeal from the loud speaker, the announcer began his account of the military tactics used by the soldiers of the United States commanded by General Zachary Taylor and the Seminoles led by their chief, Alligator, often called Billy Bowlegs.

"Maybe all this water will shortcircuit the loudspeaker, and they'll call off the event. We could get electrocuted, you know," Emily said, but began marching, careful to avoid yet another hole in the soggy ground. She took up a steady drumbeat. The two women staggered forward, the thick mud making their advancement slow and difficult.

"Having trouble keeping up?" asked the tall man in front of Emily, slowing his pace and turning back to address her. How he managed to look dry and comfortable in all this rain was beyond Emily, but she always found Detective Stanton Lewis the other side of comprehensible in her mind. He was a member of the local police department, and the man who had arrested Emily for murder on one occasion, and on another, kissed her with passion.

"If I'd have known he'd be volunteering for this event, I would have stayed home," Emily said.

"I heard that," replied Lewis, "and I know you don't mean it."

Maybe she did and maybe she didn't. Emily could never tell how she felt about Stanton Lewis. It seemed that whenever they got together two things happened: first there was the verbal battling, and then there was the warmth she felt somewhere south of her waist. He was about the handsomest man she'd ever met, and the most annoying. It seemed he knew the effect he had on her, and he loved to aggravate her by standing too close or smiling that annoying smile with his full, very kissable, lips.

"I thought you and Detective Lewis had worked everything out between you," said Naomi. "I kind of like him, and he certainly likes you."

"For your information our 'date' didn't turn out so well. He fell asleep before anything interesting happened."

"I heard that, too. I was recovering from a gun-shot wound and the combination of painkillers and wine knocked me for a loop," Lewis said.

"Well, why didn't you say so at the time?" said Emily. "I thought you weren't interested in, uh, anything."

"I'm always interested when it comes to you, Emily."

"You never said that."

"I was passed out on the couch."

"See? That's what I mean." Emily missed a beat on the drum, caught herself and took up the rhythm again. Lewis turned again and flashed her another smile, as if he surmised the loss of cadence was because of him. As he turned back forward, he missed a step on the uneven and mucky ground. Emily, seeing he was about to fall, reached out and grabbed his arm. His momentum took both of them down face first into a large puddle of standing water in front of them.

Lewis sprawled on the ground, his nose at mud level, Emily lying on his back. He lay still for a moment, then twisted his head around to eye Emily. "What are you doing back there?"

"I was trying to prevent you from falling, but your big old feet took both of us down."

"You wouldn't be down here with me if you watched where you were stepping. You ran into me," Lewis said.

That's what she got for trying to help him out, the ungrateful....

Emily decided she wouldn't be baited this time by him. "I can't see much because of the rain and my hair is in my eyes. Obviously, you have the same problem."

"You didn't think of wearing a hat?" asked Lewis.

"Let's not quibble about how I'm dressed. I think you're sinking deeper into the mud and taking me with you."

"Maybe if you got off my back, I could...."

Yeah, that was always the way, thought Emily. He thinks I'm on his back one way or the other.

"Move, Emily."

"I can't. The strap to my drum is caught underneath your chest. You move."

Lewis lifted his body to one side of the strap, dumping Emily from the mud-free position on his back and sloshing her into the puddle next to him.

"Just stay put. Don't move from there," he said.

"I'm up to my ears in mud," Emily said.

"Yeah, but if you move you'll be up to your ears in dead body."

CHAPTER 2

"**D**on't you say it," said Emily. "It is not my doing."

She knew he was thinking it, biting his tongue not to say it aloud. She had done it again. Emily Rhodes, that snoopy, sassy, barely five feet tall Yankee gal had stumbled onto yet another body. This was what...number three? Well, to be fair. She didn't stumble onto this one. She kind of slid onto it. With his help.

The enactment was halted while Detective Lewis and a crime team from the police department moved people back to begin their work. Naomi stood with her arm around her mother outside the area cordoned off by the police as the crime scene. Someone had handed both of them a cup of hot coffee, for which Naomi was grateful. Emily would have been more grateful if the cup contained brandy. She was drenched, mud-covered and cold.

"Did you recognize the body?" asked Naomi.

"I wouldn't recognize my own body if I was lying there covered with all that mud. We must have been floundering around in half the swamp back there."

"Emily?" a voice called to her from behind the gathering crowd. "Now who's been killed?"

Emily recognized her friend and former boss, Clara. Clara had set up a law practice in the community, but once had been the bar and restaurant manager at the Big Lake Country Club and had hired Emily as a bartender there.

Clara's question about someone being killed was heard by bystanders who tried to push forward to see what the police were doing.

"You weren't responsible for this one, were you?" asked Clara, who was dressed prepared for the weather in a yellow slicker and knee-high boots.

The people nearest Emily stepped away from her.

"She's just kidding," explained Naomi to the crowd.

"But someone's dead? Is that right?" asked one man.

"Is it a murder?" another woman said, both fear and excitement in her voice.

Detective Lewis stood up and moved away from the body toward Emily, Naomi and Clara. "It's bad enough that Ms. Rhodes seems to have a propensity for discovering bodies, but now her good friend Clara shows up and starts asking a lot of questions that are stirring up the crowd. Can't the two of you stay out of police business? Or do you both like to interfere in my work?"

"Emily was responsible for helping you catch at least two killers that I know of," said Clara. "You'd think you'd be grateful she's here."

"So it is murder, then?" asked a man dressed in military garb and still holding his flintlock rifle. "And our drummer boy is responsible?"

The crowd turned accusing eyes on Emily.

"She's just a little bit of a thing. How did she manage to kill the guy?" a spectator said.

"I didn't kill anyone," Emily said. "Tell them, detective. You were the one who tripped over the body."

"So the cop killed him?" The murmurs from the crowd increased.

"Everyone step back. We need room to work." Detective Lewis tried to remain calm and in control of the crowd. "You two," he said to Emily and Naomi, "go with this officer to the station. I need to get your statements."

"I'll go along," said Clara.

"They don't need a lawyer. I'm not arresting them," said Lewis. A note of defensiveness had crept into his voice.

"Of course not," Clara said with a smile. "I'm going just in case."

Detective Lewis shook his head and muttered, "Every time I try to do my job, I have these three to contend with."

"What was that, detective?" Clara asked.

"Nothing," he said and turned back to the body.

⸙

Of course, it was murder. Lewis knew that the moment Emily rolled onto the body. Why else would the principal of the high school be lying in a mud puddle in the middle of the reenactment scene? Emily hadn't gotten a good look at the body, but Lewis had, and he recognized Leonard Parsons, the man playing the part of General Zachary Taylor for the United States. There was a bullet hole in Parsons' temple. It could have been suicide, but that was unlikely, Lewis reasoned. Why would someone come out into a muddy field in the middle of a reenactment of a nineteenth century battle and kill himself?

Lewis' new partner, Sandy Davis, responded as if he had spoken aloud. "Well, maybe as General Taylor, he realized his military strategy had doomed him and he'd lose the battle. He did the honorable thing and killed himself."

Lewis squinted his eyes at her. "You're kidding, right?"

"Of course, I'm kidding, detective. If I was right about that, he wouldn't have used a real gun with a real bullet in it, and he would be pretending to be dead. It is an event for show, you know." She got to her feet and stripped off her latex gloves. "You know you have no sense of humor, don't you? You're as bad as Donald Green. I've never seen that man smile."

Lewis knew others thought him humorless—Clara had said so many times, but he never used police humor to get around the horror of murder.

He knew many police did, although like Sandy, they were careful not to let civilians hear them in their ghoulish attempts to keep out the awfulness of what one human could do to another.

Sandy Davis had taken the detective exam last month, and Captain Worley had promoted her last week to detective, to be Lewis' partner. So far their relationship seemed to be working out well, certainly a lot better than that with his former partner, Toby Sands. Sands had proven to be a dirty cop, one who worked his under-the-table schemes for money. The fat troll—and Toby looked very much like one with his rotund, body, pinched fat face and the continual smell of chewing tobacco, booze, and sweat that came off him like swamp gas off a gator hole—not only performed his police duties with little skill, but he performed them rarely, preferring to nap in his car under the shade of a palm tree. In contrast, Sandy, a tall woman with a pale freckled-face and a fringe of red-gold bangs and a Prince Valiant haircut, was clean, alert and respectful. She did her job, and Lewis could tell that with a little more experience under her belt she was destined to be a good detective.

Lewis might not like her way of dealing with death, but he'd take that over Toby's dishonesty and unpleasant, wheedling personality any day.

Lewis gave her a long, penetrating look.

"Sorry, detective," said Sandy, briefly touching his shoulder in apology for her macabre remark about the dead man. "I didn't mean to say what I did."

And she was sensitive to the feelings of others, thought Lewis. Maybe too sensitive. She was reading him almost as well as Emily did. When women did that with Lewis, it always made him uncomfortable. He was used to hiding most of what he was experiencing from others. He was nervous around insightful women.

"'Sokay," he said. "Let's get the body to the morgue for the autopsy. We'll know more then. I'll go back to the station to interview Ms. Rhodes and her daughter. You and the officers can continue taking the names of everyone in the vicinity. Anyone here could have killed Parsons. You can start with those acting as soldiers for the United States. I'll get the names of the men playing Seminole warriors. And call in some more officers to do a complete search of the area."

"The entire battlefield?" asked Davis.

Lewis nodded. "As well as the observer stands and concession tents. We'll also need to keep everyone here until we get their names." Lewis was grateful that the rain meant fewer people attended the event, or the police would be interviewing people all night long.

The reenactment had attracted fewer and fewer participants each year. Last year there were only five on each side, and it was difficult to convince spectators that the event was worth viewing with so few combatants. This year, because of a drive to attract more people as actors, local police departments along the Big Lake recruited their officers and employees. The Seminole and Miccosukee tribes also encouraged their younger members to embrace tribal history by featuring information on the Seminole War in history classes and providing students with extra credits for joining the reenactment. It worked to a degree. Now each side had almost twenty people.

"I'll get right on it," said Sandy. "I know you want to get back to the station as soon as possible."

Lewis scrutinized her face. Was she suggesting he was eager to get Emily and her daughter alone because he had feelings for Emily? How could Sandy know that? Sandy's face registered nothing, but he thought he saw one side of her mouth tilt slightly upward. Now how could he have given anything away to Sandy? They'd only been together as partners for a short time. Lewis began to worry that his interest in Emily Rhodes had somehow eroded his ability to keep a poker face. *Women. Always a problem*. The thought of Emily as an aggravation was replaced by his memory of her naked in the shower one night. He couldn't help it. He smiled.

"Is there something amusing, detective?" asked Sandy. "Something I missed about Ms. Rhodes?"

This time Sandy's expression matched what he worried his own had failed to hide: his was guilty knowledge of having Emily tug him by his belt buckle into his bedroom. And Sandy's? She knew something about him and Emily. Or she suspected something.

"Just get to it. We have work to do," Lewis said. Sandy nodded and began walking toward the soldier actors standing at the end of the field.

Lewis kicked at the mud. At least the rain had stopped. If the sun came out, it would be a typical South Florida, muggy day with the temperatures in the high eighties and the mosquitos liberated from the drizzle to feast on sweating bodies. Lewis swatted one of the bloodsuckers off his hand.

Someone tapped Lewis on the shoulder. It was a young man dressed as a Seminole warrior in a long-sleeved, colorful shirt, which hung over the tops of his pants, and a leather belt cinching it in below his waist. He held a rifle in his hand and carried a large knife at his belt. His hair hung below his shoulders. Because his skin was as dark as mahogany and his hair dark as a cloudless night, Lewis figured him to be a member of one of the tribes.

"Was that Principal Parsons?" he asked.

Lewis was surprised at his question. He thought his team had been able to keep everyone away from the body. How did he know the victim was the principal?

The young man replied before Lewis had time to ask him the question. "I could see the hat and the general's uniform even with all the mud, so I assumed.... I'm David Otter. I'm, uhm, on the other side." David gestured to the combatants behind him.

"You knew Mr. Parsons? How? I would have thought you attended the tribal school, not public school."

"I do, but I'm friends with his son. We're in the chess club set up between the two schools."

"Is his son here today?" asked Lewis.

David shook his head and gave a short bark of a laugh. "Not hardly."

Lewis waited for him to say more, but David was silent, his eyes perusing the battle scene, then coming to rest on the place where the body, now contained in a body bag, was being loaded into an ambulance.

"Was he shot?" asked David.

This young man was too curious, and he was making too many assumptions that were on target.

"Why do you ask?" asked Lewis.

"Well, you know. All the guns around here and everything."

"But the guns used for the reenactment don't fire live ammunition, do they?" asked Lewis, deciding to press David for what he knew.

"I guess not," said David, then added, "No, of course not. This isn't real, just a staged battle."

"Not completely," said Lewis. "Someone is as dead as the soldiers that died here over a hundred years ago."

"Zachary Taylor was the man responsible for all those deaths that day," said David Otter, his words spoken with an edge of hatred.

"Do you think one of your members might have used the battle as a way of revenging the death of one of his ancestors?"

David looked startled for a moment, but then recovered his stance of innocent curiosity. "Why would anyone do that? They wouldn't be killing General Taylor. They'd be murdering the principal."

"It does make a kind of statement, though, don't you think?"

David shook his head. "That's stupid."

Now that's more like it, thought Lewis. The typical reaction of today's teen.

"Do you know if any of Principal Parsons' family is here today?"

David replied with certainty. "No."

"Keep what you've guessed about the victim's identity to yourself. I need to notify the family."

David nodded and rejoined his fellow Seminole soldiers.

Lewis would want to question David Otter again, but the conversation brought up an interesting possibility: could the murder be an old tribal grudge finally revenged? Lewis knew the Seminoles had never signed a peace treaty with the United States. Instead, following the Seminole Wars, many tribal members particularly the Miccosukees fled to live in the swamps. Miccosukees and Seminoles had been farmer and cattle ranchers before the whites interrupted their way of life. It was not that the swamps were where Indians wanted to live. They felt as if they had no other choice if they wanted to evade the white settlers and soldiers. As with other Indians viewed as hostiles, those captured were sent to Indian territory in the Western United States. The march west killed many, although some managed to survive. A few prospered and became ranchers again, even owning slaves. Billy Bowlegs, the Seminole leader for this battle, was one of these. It was alleged the United States offered tribe members money to resettle. Billy Bowlegs had at first refused the money, then later took it and moved to Indian territory before the Civil War.

Despite resettlement, thought Lewis, the treatment of indigenous people by the United States government was horrific and not easily forgotten all these years later. Although David Otter had thought it a stupid supposition, Lewis still played with the possibility that a tribe member might decide to right an old wrong by killing off a white man who chose to play the role of General Taylor at the Battle of Okeechobee. But that did seem a stretch. The victim was not the general or even a member of his family, but the local principal. How would the death of Leonard Parsons avenge any past wrongdoing? Unless, thought Lewis, unless Parsons was a relative of Zachary Taylor. Now that would be a coincidence worth pursuing, concluded Lewis. He looked down at his nineteenth century clothing and shook his head. His participation in a battle over a century before had to be clouding his reasoning.

He followed David Otter to the tribal members who were part of the reenactment, took his notebook from his pocket and prepared to take down their names. The looks most of them gave him were not friendly. Was this investigation about to reignite enmities that had been laid to rest with the cooperation past reenactments had encouraged, Lewis wondered? He and his team of investigators would need to step carefully in their work so as not to stir up the barely suppressed feelings of suspicion between many whites and some Indians in the Big Lake area. Unraveling the truth meant not offending the parties involved, a responsibility Lewis took seriously. He knew more than a murder investigation was at stake here.

⚫

Back at the station, Emily and Naomi sat in Detective Lewis' office. The air conditioner blew cool air into the room, making the two women, still damp from the rain, shiver.

The door opened, and Clara entered. She walked over to the AC unit and turned it off.

"We already tried that, but then the air is so still and humid it's almost impossible to breathe," said Naomi.

Clara looked at the coat rack by the door where two jackets hung, one with the letters "Lewis" emblazoned on the back, the other a tweedy, brown and yellow, ugly plaid sports coat. Clara grabbed the jackets off the rack and threw them to Emily and Naomi. "Try these," she said, flipping the AC back on.

When Lewis entered the room moments later, Naomi had the departmental jacket slung over her shoulders while Emily had wrapped the other one around her.

Lewis stopped in the doorway and began laughing when he saw the two women.

"I know it's much too big for me, but it's better than dying from hypothermia in your office," Emily said.

"Oh, it's not that," said Lewis, finally catching his breath with difficulty. "You know that's a jacket Toby left here, don't you?"

Emily's face turned green, and she gulped, then pulled off the jacket and threw it on the floor.

"You could have killed me with that jacket," she said, looking down in horror at it.

"That's a bit of an exaggeration, isn't it? I know we all dislike the man, but...."

"He could have left fleas or worse on it. If I had gotten bitten, I might have contracted some deadly disease like rabies or something."

"You have to be bitten by a rabid dog to get rabies," Lewis said.

"Toby is worse than a rabid dog. I'm not answering any questions until I can go home and shower, then burn my clothes."

When Emily said the word "shower," a red flush worked its way up her neck and onto her face. Lewis noticed it, knew just what she was thinking and began to redden also.

"Honestly," said Naomi, "the two of you do a little hanky panky once…"

Emily held up two fingers.

"…twice then, in the shower, and you'd think you were the only two humans to have gotten soapy and slick together. Now. Did you have some questions for us, detective?"

Lewis nodded.

"Then let's get on with it," Naomi said, "because I'm getting tired and cranky, and I'd like a really stiff drink.'

"We all would," said Clara.

Emily and Lewis nodded.

CHAPTER 3

Emily and Naomi caught a ride with Clara back to the reenactment site to pick up Emily's car.

"Donald is bartending now, but I have to relieve him at six," said Emily, peeking at her watch as Clara drove back to the battleground. "It's already five. No time for other than a quick shower and change of clothes."

"Why not give Donald a call and see if he can take over tonight? You really need to warm up and get some rest."

Emily thought about that. She was exhausted, but the thought of asking Donald for a favor was daunting, given his surly nature. And she'd have to explain why she couldn't come in. He'd have something sarcastic to say about that, she was sure. "*Stumbled onto another dead body, did you?*" he would say. "*And did Detective Lewis arrest you for this one, too?*" Oh, well. It was worth a try. At least she wouldn't have to confront him face to face.

"I'll see what I can do," Emily said.

Naomi caught the note of reluctance in her mother's voice and wondered if she was afraid to talk to Donald. Naomi knew he was a snarly fellow, but she also knew he had a soft spot for Emily under all that negativity.

"Do you want me to call him?" asked Naomi.

"No. It's my job." Emily reached in her purse for her cell to make the call.

"Give me that," said Clara, reaching out to grab the phone. She pulled over to the side of the road and connected with the bar at the country club.

Donald growled an unfriendly greeting. "What do you want?"

"Is that any way to answer the phone?" said Clara.

"Who is this? The caller ID says Emily Rhodes, but you're not her."

"It's Clara. Something has come up. You need to work the bar tonight." Before he could say anything, Clara disconnected and tossed the phone back to Emily. "There. That's done. I'll follow you home. I can heat up some soup or something, then make certain the two of you get some sleep."

"You don't have to babysit us," said Emily. Her phone signaled another call was coming in. She looked at the caller ID. "It's Donald."

"Don't answer it."

"I should explain, or he'll keep calling."

Clara again grabbed the phone, but this time she turned it off.

"Honestly, Emily. You can handle a passel of preschoolers, toss a drunken cowboy out of the bar, aggravate a detective so much he acts like a love-sick teenager, but you can't tell Donald Green 'No.' You're supposed to be his boss, aren't you?"

"Technically, yes," Emily said, "but no one has much luck backing Donald Green down."

"I just did," said Clara.

"You're a lawyer. He worries you'll sue him or something," said Emily.

Clara turned onto the gravel road leading to the parking area by the battleground. An officer stopped them.

"You can't go in here."

"Detective Lewis said I could pick up my car," said Emily. The officer took out his cell, and Emily heard him talk to someone at police headquarters.

"Okay. Go ahead." He gestured them in.

Clara pulled up beside Emily's car.

Naomi had been quiet the whole time, but now she leaned forward from the back seat. "There are still a few cars left in the lot. I wonder who's still here."

The yellow crime scene tape remained in place, flapping around in the wind blowing off the lake. Uniformed police moved in lines up and down the site, searching for evidence.

It looked as if a few spectators still remained on the periphery of the grounds, nosey folks or maybe some reporters, guessed Emily. She watched as a short, round man carrying a duffle bag walked out of the trees on the far side of the battleground and headed toward the road where a pickup truck was parked. It was so old and battered that one fender hung loose, connected to the body of the vehicle by duct tape and some heavy wire.

"Naomi," said Emily, her voice low and shaky. "That looks like Toby Sands."

Naomi squinted her eyes at the figure and seemed to sniff at the air. "It is. No one else looks like an unwashed bridge troll."

"You can't really smell him from this distance, can you?" Clara asked.

"No, but look." Emily pointed as the man stopped a moment, took something out of his pocket and tucked it into his mouth. He tossed the duffle into the cab of the truck and got in.

"It's Toby, all right, and he's still chewing tobacco," said Clara. "What's he doing here? I thought he was in jail."

"Let's go. I don't want him to see us," said Naomi. "I'm sick enough without having to smell that chaw juice."

Emily agreed with her daughter's attitude toward Toby, but she also knew Toby Sands showed up in places he shouldn't, and he always had something illegal up his sleeve. "You go on ahead. I want to know what Toby is up to." She jumped out of Clara's car and started to run down the gravel road toward Toby's truck, but before she could accost him, he started up the truck and pulled away.

Emily ran back to her car. "Get in," she said to Naomi.

"You're not going to follow him, are you?" said Naomi.

"I certainly am. Toby is up to no good, as usual. Detective Lewis should know what it is."

"We're following him," Naomi yelled to Clara who also took up the pursuit of the old truck.

As the caravan of three vehicles turned onto the road, Emily saw Detective Lewis drive into the lot's second entrance located nearer the viewing stand. He looked at her car, seemed to recognize the old red sedan and swung around to follow the truck and two cars. She noticed he had that "now what's up?" look on his face. She gave him a tiny finger wave in her rearview mirror.

The convoy of four headed out of town onto the road leading around the lake to the west and south.

"It looks as if he's heading toward Clewiston," said Emily, easing off on the accelerator and letting a car pass her so Toby wouldn't spot the tail. Emily looked in the rearview mirror, saw Clara and waved. Clara shook her head.

"She thinks we're crazy to follow Toby," said Naomi.

"She's not the only one." Emily checked the mirror again.

"What's up? Does Clara want us to pull over?"

"No. I thought I saw Detective Lewis' police car back there. He's also following us," said Emily.

"Well, good. Let's give him a call and tell him what we're up to. He can take up the tail, and we can go home and get some sleep." Naomi grabbed her mother's phone to call Lewis.

"No! I want to see what Toby is up to, and Lewis isn't likely to share what he learns from the little twit."

"Mom," said Naomi, "I can't find his number in your list of contacts unless... it's not under his name. I've tried 'Annoying,' and 'Source of Aggravation' and even 'Infuriating.' Is it here?"

"Yes," said Emily, her lips set in a tight line. She muttered something under her breath.

"What was that?" asked her daughter.

"It's under 'Sexy.'"

The convoy continued on south, and the sun began to set behind the rim of the Big Lake, creating purples and corals in the clouds sitting on the horizon. As darkness descended, Emily knew there was a chance she would lose Toby. Although there were few cars on the road, the lack of traffic created its own problem. If the car between her and Toby turned off, Toby might wonder why the same three cars continued to follow him.

The turn to the tribal casino was just ahead. This might be where the other vehicle was headed. Maybe Toby was going to take in a little gambling tonight. That would be great. The casino was only a few miles down the road after the turn, and Emily would have the satisfaction of knowing what Toby was doing without having to drive all the way to Clewiston, another hour away. Exhaustion from the day's events was catching up with her, and she yawned.

"Don't do that," said Naomi, covering her mouth as she also yawned.

Toby signaled to turn right, and the car between him and Emily did the same. Where else could Toby be going than to the casino? There was little beyond it aside from a few houses, and then the casino rad joined a back road that turned into gravel and dead ended.

Emily relaxed a bit, knowing she would catch up with Toby soon. *And then what,* she asked herself? Should she confront him and ask him what he was doing at the reenactment? What would he tell her other than he was watching a slice of the history of the area being brought to life. Emily knew better than to believe that story. The only things Toby were interested in were chewing, spitting, drinking and napping. Emily also knew there had to be some reason for Toby to hang around the scene of a murder. He was either involved somehow or he knew someone who was. Lewis knew that, too, and that was why the detective was so close on their tail. The only way Emily would find out what Toby was up to tonight or earlier today is if she played it sly, like she just happened to run into him at the casino. That was going to be a hard sell because she and Naomi still wore the costumes they had donned for the battle. And they were mud-covered. Even slovenly Toby wouldn't believe two women would appear in public looking the way she and her daughter did.

Naomi broke into her thoughts. "What are you going to do, Mom?"

Emily hesitated. "I'm not sure."

She followed Toby's car into the casino lot. Toby drove past the lines of parked cars and proceeded toward the main entrance where he pulled up in front of a woman waiting by the curb. Emily eased into a parking slot and watched Toby lean over and open the door for the woman who was tall and thin and wore her black hair teased into a bouffant style reminiscent of the nineteen sixties. The woman slid in and leaned towards Toby. He kissed her on the cheek.

"Yikes!" said Naomi. "She touched him. Toby's got a girlfriend. Now I've seen everything."

That couldn't be, thought Emily. Who could possibility be so nose numb to make Toby a part of her life?

There was a rap on the passenger side window. It was Clara. Behind her stood Detective Lewis. They both looked as if they had seen an alien spaceship land.

"Did you see that?" asked Clara. Lewis looked as if he couldn't find the words to express his amazement.

"Yep, but we gotta go. They're leaving, and I've got to find out who that woman is. We have to save her from herself," said Emily, as if Lewis would believe her only goal was to rescue someone from Toby's amorous advances.

"Don't bother," said Lewis, watching Toby's tail lights. "He just turned left out of the lot. There aren't many houses down that dead end road. Only one I can think of. It's Toby's old cabin. I'm just as curious as you gals are about why Toby was hanging around the reenactment. I'd like to talk to him, and since I know he's going home and with someone, I think I'll ruin the rest of his night by dropping in on him for a visit."

"We'll be right behind you," said Emily.

"No, you won't be. This is official police business, and I can't have a gaggle of women accompanying me."

"But I was the one who spotted him and took up pursuit. If you hadn't seen my car take after him, you wouldn't know he was at the reenactment, would you?"

Lewis cleared his throat and chewed on the inside of his cheek. Emily knew he was loathe to admit she was right...*as usual*, she added to herself.

He stared off into the night for a moment, then said, "Tell you what. If you want to be helpful, why don't you go into the casino and see—in an unobtrusive manner—if you can find out who that woman was he picked up. He probably won't be eager to introduce me when I burst in on him, so anything you can find out about her would help me."

Clara gave a roll of her eyes, knowing Lewis was trying to put them off, but she said nothing about her suspicions to Emily.

"I don't understand how the casino would know anything about her. There must be hundreds of people who play here every night. Unless she's a regular, why should anyone in there know her?" Clara asked.

"Just find out. And don't follow me." Lewis' tone of voice had the hard edge Emily found so annoying. He used it with her when he didn't want her to argue with him. He turned on his heel and headed back to his car.

Emily looked at Clara. "This is a wild goose chase."

Clara nodded in agreement.

"No, it's not. Didn't you notice what the woman was wearing?" asked Naomi.

Emily and Clara shook their heads.

"It was an apron. A white apron. I could see the bib and ties when she draped it over her arm. She had to be either a cook or a server on the buffet line."

Now all they had to do was concoct a story that would get them her name and something about her. *No,* said Emily to herself, *now they had to find a way to explain why two women dressed as nineteenth century boys covered with mud would be interested in entering the casino.*

The place must have some kind of dress code. Emily took a quick look at herself in the rearview mirror. By now the mud had begun to dry and cake on their clothes and faces. Emily, because she had fallen into the puddle containing the body, was more encrusted than Naomi who was more wet than muddy, but neither of them looked presentable in public. Clara still wore her slicker.

"Your clothes are dry under that, right?" asked Emily.

"What are you thinking?" asked Clara, her forehead drawn together in wrinkles of suspicion.

After using the comb in her purse to detangle her hair and sharing it with her daughter, Emily grabbed a Kleenex from Naomi and they removed as much dirt from her face as possible. After a quick clothing change in the back seat of Emily's car, Clara stepped out still dressed in her boots and slicker. Emily wore Clara's shirt over her boy britches and cinched in with her belt. It fell to below her knees and covered up most of the mud on her pants. Naomi had simply brushed off the dirt clinging to her clothes and pulled her shirt out of her pants and wore it like tunic. They exchanged looks. Their appearance wouldn't get them into a West Palm Beach nightclub, but they might be able to get past the employees positioned by the doors to welcome entering guests as well as check them for suspicious behavior. This was rural Florida, after all.

The employees scrutinized the three women and exchanged curious looks with one another, but no one stopped the trio. Emily caught sight of them in one of the giant mirrors inside the door and was surprised at how presentable they appeared. Dressed oddly, yes, but they had managed to get most of the dirt and mud off the parts of their bodies and clothes that others could see. While Emily had been unable to comb all the caked mud out of her hair, she noticed that it looked as if she was a brunette who needed a better hairdresser and a shampoo.

"Let's make this quick," said Clara. "I'm sweating like a pig with this raincoat against my bare skin. It doesn't breathe. I'm beginning to feel slimy. I might grow mold."

"Check your coat, miss?" asked the woman behind the counter just beyond the entryway doors.

"Absolutely not," said Clara, pulling the yellow slicker more tightly around her. She pushed Emily and Naomi ahead of her and hurried into the hallway that led into the gaming rooms.

"Wrong way," said Emily. "The buffet is the other direction."

"What are you doing here? I thought there was some important reason why you couldn't come into work," said someone from behind them. The voice belonged to Donald Green, the man who worked as her bartender at the country club. The tone contained more than his usual allotment of annoyance.

Emily spun around to face him. "I'm, uh... I, that is...." Her eyes darted around the crowded area as if she was seeking an exit to escape through or some hole she could hide herself in. She looked up into Donald's eyes and saw what she often saw there: his unrelenting disapproval of her. He always seemed to be judging her. Enough, decided Emily.

She glanced at her watch and an idea struck her, the comeback she needed to put him in his place. "It's only eight. Who's tending bar at the country club? Not you. Who?"

He stood unmoving in front of her, not embarrassed by her question. "No one came into the bar for over an hour, so I made an executive decision. I closed down for the night."

Sometimes she wondered who irritated her more, Detective Lewis or Donald Green. Both were handsome men in their own way: the detective tall and muscular with that boyish mop of hair that fell over his forehead and those too-blue eyes of his. And Donald. She had to admit that his lean, hard, suntanned looks were appealing if a woman could see beyond his unsmiling countenance...and all his negative attitudes toward women, especially Yankee, uppity women. Her.

"So I've got a good excuse for being here. You don't. And what the hell did you do to your hair? The color is...well, it reminds me of the color of the lake, kind of rusty brown, like a bass or crappie would find a welcoming home in it. If this is a new look you're trying on, I'd recommend you rethink it."

Emily wanted to jump up and grab his silver ponytail and yank it.

Clara intervened before Emily could take action. "I'm sure you don't mean that, Donald, especially after the day Emily had. Stumbled into a mud puddle and fell onto the body of Leonard Parsons.

Somebody killed him. We're just here because Emily is so distraught she can't sleep. She needs a little time out and entertainment. If you're here to gamble, Donald, you might want to take Emily with you and show her how it's done. She's a novice. Meantime, Naomi and I are going to get a bite to eat at the buffet."

Clara shoved Emily into Donald's arms and steered Naomi toward the restaurant offering the all-you-can-eat buffet.

"But I'm starving," said Emily. She wanted to get into that buffet and ask questions, but it was also true that she needed food.

"Donald and you can try the roulette wheel and then Donald will buy you dinner," Clara called over her shoulder.

"I'll do what?" said Donald.

Clara gave him a wide grin and continued to pull Naomi down the hallway toward the restaurant.

Donald looked down at Emily with the usual frown on his face. "What do you know about gambling?" he asked.

"Only that counting on you to buy me anything is something I don't want to take a chance on."

CHAPTER 4

Lewis hung back a good half-mile from the beat-up truck, not wanting to alert Toby that someone was tailing him. Lewis knew he wouldn't lose him, and as he anticipated, the truck turned in at the drive to Toby's old cabin and drove down the sandy, rutted road, stopping in front of what Lewis remembered to be an ancient swamp cabin. The last time Lewis had seen it was when he had been assigned, much against his wishes, to use Toby as a snitch for the department in a scheme that took Lewis and Toby to Jekyll Island, Georgia. The police department was supposed to pay any expenses Toby incurred in his job of grounds' cleaner at a barbecue festival where he was to get close to the participants to see what he could find out about the murder of one of them. As usual, Toby wheedled money out of Lewis, and the department had not reimbursed him because Toby, true to his bad boy form, had not done his job, but had worked his own crooked deal. Lewis didn't bother anymore trying to keep up with the outcome of the slew of charges against Toby. He was certain Toby hadn't killed Leonard Parsons, but he was equally certain Toby's presence after the end of the reenactment event meant Toby was again working some kind of a scam. Lewis couldn't imagine what, but he was about to find out.

It was a stroke of luck that Lewis had spotted Emily, Clara and Toby back at the reenactment. After he had taken down Emily's and Naomi's stories, he left the station. He knew he had a duty to perform, one that most cops found unpleasant. He had swung by Leonard Parsons' house to notify his wife and family of his death, but his knock on the door produced no answer. The curtains in the front window were partially closed and an orange tabby cat eyed him from its perch in the window for a moment, got up, stretched and returned to its curled position. An elderly woman wiping her hands on her apron answered Lewis' knock when he tried the neighbor next door. She wiped a strand of gray hair back from her forehead, and with a knitted brow that signaled her concern over talking to a stranger on her front steps, asked who he was. Lewis showed her his identification.

"Is there something wrong?" she asked, still not comfortable enough to open the door any wider.

"Do you know where the family is?" he asked, ignoring her question.

"Mrs. Parsons and the two children are out of town for the weekend visiting family. I'm taking care of Turner."

"Turner?"

"Their cat."

"You wouldn't have a number where they could be reached, would you?"

She shook her head.

"Would you give Mrs. Parsons my card and have her call me?" Lewis handed the woman a card. "Thank you, Mrs., uh, I didn't get your name."

And he still didn't get it. The woman closed the door without replying. He shrugged and stepped off the porch and returned to his car. As he drove off, he saw the curtains in her window move. *Suspicious old...,* he started to say to himself then stopped. *If I were a woman her age living alone, I'd be wondering why a cop showed up to talk to my neighbors also.*

Lewis shoved thoughts about his earlier encounter with Parsons' neighbor from his mind and waited in his truck for several minutes until Toby and the woman had entered the cabin and the lights came on. He remained in his car for an additional ten minutes, giving Toby and his partner time to get cozy. He knew it was petty of him wanting to disturb Toby's personal life by intruding on his evening alone with a woman, but Lewis figured Toby had discomfort coming. The man owed Lewis, not only money, but Lewis reviewed in his mind all the times Toby hadn't come through as a partner and the other occasions in which Toby put people Lewis knew and, uh, liked, Emily especially, in danger. Toby might find clemency in the criminal justice system, but Lewis had lost patience with the slimy nature of Toby Sands, ex-cop and con artist.

Lewis closed his car door quietly and walked on tip-toe to the cabin. He pressed his ear against the door and could hear low voices inside. They seemed to be coming from the back of the one-room residence. Lewis smiled to himself. They were probably making whoopee on Toby's rickety old bed. Wanting to upset him, but not eager to see Toby nude, Lewis pounded loudly on the door to startle them, but give them enough time to get decent, if Toby Sands ever got decent.

"Police. Open up!" Lewis turned the knob and leaned into the door. It wasn't locked and opened easily. Toby and the woman were on their knees in front of Toby's bed.

"You have no right to come in here like this," said the woman as she got up and turned to face Lewis. Instead of seeing embarrassment on her face, he was confronted with anger, her mouth drawn tightly across her lips in a thin line and her tall, reedy body leaning toward him like a Florida panther about to pounce.

Toby was the one looking embarrassed. He had shaved off the beard Lewis had last seen on his face. Gone too were the usual tobacco-stained lips and shirt front. In fact, Lewis admitted to himself, Toby looked as if he had bathed. And recently.

Toby seemed to recover himself. He got off his knees, reached out and up, and put his arm around the shoulders of the woman next to him.

"Let me introduce my old partner to you, Melissa. This is Detective Lewis. I've told you about him many times, haven't I? Detective, this is my, uh, friend and spiritual guide, Mrs. Melissa DeVry." Toby's words were civilized, polite, but Lewis could tell from the anger in his voice that Toby wasn't pleased to see his old partner.

What the heck was going on? Lewis removed his hat and nodded to Mrs. DeVry. "Ma'am. Sorry to interrupt, but I need a word with Toby."

Melissa DeVry's stance changed immediately. "I'm guessing from what Toby told me that you need his help again. I'll make some tea. The two of you can talk on the porch. It'll take just a minute. Sugar, detective?"

Lewis could hardly believe what was happening. He and Toby stepped out onto the porch, and Lewis noted for the first time that two rocking chairs, both in good repair, sat there. The floorboards once broken, some missing, had been repaired or replaced. It was like a real home, thought Lewis.

Toby remained silent as he fell into one of the chairs, and Lewis took the other. Toby's round, red face registered worry in the way his little eyes darted around in their sockets.

"What were you doing at the reenactment today?" asked Lewis. "And don't lie to me."

"I was working it, cleaning up the grounds, just like I did for that barbecue festival, lot of good that did me." Toby's body language changed, and he leaned back in the chair, relaxing a bit. Lewis again caught the anger in his voice.

"Run that by me again," said Lewis. "You got a job at the reenactment?"

"Yeah, I did. I'm removing trash from the grounds, you know, food wrappers, paper cups and other junk. It seems that's all I'm good for since you and the department took away my position."

"You earned being fired on your own, Toby. You broke the law again and again. You were involved in a murder. I wouldn't have given you a chance to show good behavior by work as a department snitch, but the captain felt bad for you."

"I came clean on the murder thing. I even turned in the people responsible for it."

"And then you took money from some international criminal to kidnap Emily and her daughter. You couldn't help yourself, could you? Bad is part of your personality."

"I was just going along with Naomi's husband's plan until I got the goods on him and that bad guy named Mr. Smith."

Lewis almost laughed that Toby seemed to believe the man's name was Smith. Toby was a crook, just not a very smart one. Lewis was about to remind him that he also tried to frame Toby's own cousin for a murder, but Lewis could tell by the innocent look on Toby's face that he was wasting his breath.

"Tea's ready," called Melissa. "Do you want me to bring it to you or will you have it in here? I think the mosquitos are beginning to bite, so the two of you might want to come in."

"I can easily check on your story about working the reenactment, you know," said Lewis.

"Check away," Toby replied.

Melissa appeared in the doorway. "Toby's not a liar," she said.

"Since when?"

"Since I introduced him to God. He's a new man. Look at him and look at what he's done to this place. Why it's a lovely little home now, and Toby's hard working, not that he wasn't always. He was done wrong by you and by others, but he holds no grudges."

Lewis could see Toby's clothes were clean and pressed and that he had made repairs to the cabin. There were screens on the windows, the floor had been swept, and no dishes sat dirty in the sink. The last time Lewis had been at the cabin, it looked as if pigs would have been embarrassed to live there.

"I think I won't have time to stay for tea. Thank you." Lewis tipped his hat to Melissa and turned to go.

"And if you're wondering about what we were doing when you broke in here, Lewis, we was praying, asking for God's blessing," Toby said.

Lewis tried not to let skepticism or shock show on his face. They may have been praying as Toby said, but what did Toby want God to bless? Another devious plan to make money illegally? Who would Toby draw into his con this time and who would get hurt?

Lewis got into his car and watched the two of them standing with their arms around each other in the doorway of the cabin, the light from within illuminating Melissa's skinny frame next to Toby's rotund figure. The back lighting made it appear that Toby wore a halo. Lewis' mouth dropped open in amazement at the image. He blinked, and it disappeared.

As for Melissa's comment about Toby not holding grudges. Lewis knew that was a lie, and he knew Toby was itching for a chance to settle the score with him, because if there was anyone Toby blamed for all his bad luck, it was Lewis. Oh, good old Toby was playing a new a part, but it was the same old play. Lewis wondered if Melissa believed Toby, or was she a part of yet another of Toby Sands' schemes? Toby was probably working at the reenactment as he claimed, but as Lewis stepped on the accelerator and spun his tires backing out of the sandy drive, he was convinced Toby was there for more than just the minimum wage he would get from the work. Was he involved in the murder, wondered Lewis? Probably. Lewis just had to figure out how Toby could make money from the death of Leonard Parsons.

As he pulled out of the drive and onto the road, his cell rang. It was a number he didn't recognize.

"Detective Lewis? This is Winona Parsons. I'm Leonard's wife. I understand you stopped by the house earlier. Is there something wrong?"

"Are you home now, Mrs. Parsons?"

"No, I'm in Orlando with my parents."

The neighbor had known how to contact Mrs. Parsons but hadn't shared that with him. Lewis sighed deeply. He wasn't about to inform this woman of her husband's death over the phone. He'd have to drive to Orlando. Tonight. This kind of notification wasn't something that could wait. Enough people had recognized Parsons by the uniform he wore at the reenactment. Although the authorities wouldn't release the name of the victim until the family was notified, Lewis didn't want her finding out about his death through the grapevine.

He knew telling her there was something important he needed to talk to her about wouldn't allay her fears about a contact from the police, but it was all he could say for now.

"I see," she said, her tone to Lewis' ear containing more of a note of resignation than of continued fear or worry. It was as if this weren't the first time she'd had bad news from the authorities. What was that about, he wondered.

Lewis blew by the casino, thinking he should stop to see what Emily, Naomi and Clara had found out about Melissa DeVry, if anything, but he was in too much of a hurry. Even with his flashers on and going over the speed limit, it would take him at least two hours to get to Orlando. The day had begun in a driving rain, which stopped in the late afternoon. For that Lewis was grateful. He was tired, but he had that tingling feeling in his head, which was always present in the early stage of a murder investigation and sustained him through fatigue, too much coffee and too little food. He liked it better than the sense of failure, which set in when he had no leads or all of his work on a case led nowhere. He reminded himself he was just beginning to work the case. There was no reason to be other than optimistic about the outcome.

The rain began again and chased him into the outskirts of Orlando.

⚬

"Have you ever gambled?" asked Donald, sounding as if he hoped she would answer, "just the slots." Emily knew he wanted to send her off with a roll of quarters and let her entertain herself while he applied what he considered his considerable gambling skill to Texas hold'em. Emily chuckled to herself. It might be fun having him teach her about cards and see how embarrassed he was doing it in front of the other gamblers, old friends of his, she was sure. It would make him look so lame. Everyone would think she was his girlfriend. Horrors.

"No. I mean I've played the slots, but I'd prefer to..." she said.

"Okay then, get yourself some quarters. The machines are that way. I'll be in the back room. I'll meet you here in an hour or so." He tossed her a twenty.

"But I..."

Donald flapped his hand at her in a dismissive gesture and strode off. Emily stood in the middle of the hall incubating a slow steam of anger. Oh well, she thought, he's paying to lose my company.

She slid into a seat at a slot machine when a woman abandoned it. Emily began to play with little focus on the machine. She was more interested in the people in the casino. She saw faces she recognized from the bar and some folks from her own RV park. The latter acted as if they didn't know her, especially Mrs. Frye and Mrs. Wattles, who never approved of Emily's choice of bartending as a profession. She smiled. *I guess they don't want me to know they've got the gambling bug.*

She pulled the handle for the last time and was about to leave the machine when lights began flashing and bells and whistles along with music played loudly.

The woman next to Emily leaned over and said, "You won, dearie. How much?"

Emily was in shock. The noise and light show continued while people gathered around her. Everyone seemed happy for her good luck.

A hand grabbed her from behind and whirled her around. "That's my machine, ya thief." Emily looked into the face of the woman who had earlier left the machine. What Emily remembered as a woman in her forties dressed in a silk dress with artfully applied makeup now changed to a wild-eyed, purse-swinging harridan.

"You left the seat," said Emily.

"I left it to go get more money. You coulda seen that." The woman reached toward the machine and began scooping quarters out of the bin. "Now back off. I'll take my money and find another machine. This one is played out."

Emily knew her jackpot wasn't much money, maybe a hundred or so dollars. She could have let the whole incident pass, but the entire day with all its humiliations suddenly came down on her.

"It's my money." She grabbed for the bucket the woman had dropped most of the money into. And missed. Quarters flew into the air and onto the floor.

"Now look whatcha done," yelled the woman, diving for the quarters laying nearest to her.

"No, you don't," said Emily, who piled on top of the woman.

"Cat fight!" someone yelled, and soon more people were watching Emily and the other woman fight on the floor. They rolled around with each other, and there was a lot of hair pulling and yelling, but neither woman landed any damaging punches.

"Your hair smells like a swamp," said the woman.

"Yours looks like a palmetto patch," countered Emily.

"I just got it done," said the woman, grabbing Emily's leg.

"Fire your hairdresser. She's got no talent," said Emily, kicking at the hand on her leg.

"Break it up, you two," said a man dressed in the uniform of a casino employee. "And the rest of you, there's no side betting allowed in the casino."

Neither Emily nor the woman seemed to be seriously injured. The casino employee pulled them to their feet and held them back from each other.

"People were placing bets on which one of us would win the fight?" asked Emily.

The casino employee nodded.

"So who won?" asked Emily's opponent as she and Emily were escorted off to the casino office. "And what about my money? She took it." The woman grabbed for Emily's arm to begin the confrontation again.

"Oh, stuff it, ya old bag," said Emily who stepped in front of the woman and let go with a punch in her face. Emily's aim was bad enough that the blow missed her nose, and brushed by her ear, but the force was enough to drop the woman to her knees.

Someone yelled out again, "Catfight!"

CHAPTER 5

Emily let the authorities in the casino know that Clara and Naomi were in the buffet restaurant. The casino sent someone to find them. Until then Emily and the woman with whom she had the argument sat in an office eyeing each other across the room. The woman held an ice pack on her nose. She seemed more subdued than she had when she and Emily confronted each other on the casino's floor.

"Now what did you do?" asked Clara when she and Naomi entered the room.

"I didn't do anything," said Emily. "Why would you think any of this is my fault?"

"Any of what?" asked Clara.

The casino official explained the argument, ending with, "Then this woman," he pointed to Emily, "hit the other one and barely missed breaking her nose."

"I'm going to sue. My lawyer should be one his way," said the woman.

Clara gave Emily a look of warning which said, *Don't say anything.*

"Good. We can talk when your lawyer arrives. Until then let me introduce myself. Clara pulled out a business card, which she presented to the casino official and another to the woman. "I'm Ms. Rhodes' lawyer."

The woman looked Clara up and down taking in her yellow rain slicker and boots.

"You could have fooled me. You look more like a crabber."

Emily appeared about to speak up, but Clara squeezed her shoulder with such force that Emily could only emit a tiny squeak.

"And your name is?" asked Clara in a business-like manner, but holding out her hand in a friendly way. "Are they taking care of your nose? Do you need to see a doctor?"

The woman introduced herself as Mrs. Anthony Griswold. Clara's face registered recognition at the name of a well-known rancher in the area.

"I'm going to sue the casino, and your client for every penny she has." She sniffed and turned her head to one side as if she could no longer bear the sight of Emily and Clara.

Clara leaned down and whispered something in the woman's ear. Mrs. Griswold's head snapped around and up. She looked into Clara's eyes and stammered, "You wouldn't dare."

"Oh, yes we would," Clara said. Her eyes so warm and friendly just a moment ago now as cold as steel.

Clara turned back to Emily, "Of course, my client would like to apologize for inadvertently stumbling into you and, uh, contacting your face with her fist."

Emily gritted her teeth together and started to speak. "I will..."

"You could be arrested for assault, Emily," Clara whispered in her ear.

"I don't care," Emily said, rising out of her chair.

"And then," continued Clara, "you would be taken down to the police station and there you would again confront Detective Lewis. Would you like that?"

Before Emily could form a response, Clara smiled at the casino person who watched this interchange with almost a smile on his face. "Will that work for you?" she asked.

He nodded.

"Emily?"

"I'm sorry we collided, and my fist landed on your face," Emily said. It was difficult to hear her words, spoken as they were through lips that barely moved.

Mrs. Griswold nodded.

"So I guess that's that," said Clara, herding Emily and Naomi out the door.

"What about the money? I want my money," Mrs. Griswold said with a whine in her voice.

Clara grabbed Emily by the collar of her shirt just as she stepped back into the room and made for Mrs. Griswold, her arm cocked and her fist raised.

"Let her have the money, Emily. Just forget about it," Clara warned in a whisper. "We got off easy." Clara wanted Emily out of hitting range before another incident occurred, so she didn't tell her that the casino would have notified their own tribal police to handle the situation and not send Emily off to the city police. What Emily didn't know, Clara could tell her some other time. For now, she wanted to get food in her friend and have Naomi drive her mother home to bed.

Clara gave a sigh of relief as the three of them started toward the hallway that led to the exit, but she hadn't counted on Donald Green.

He leaned against the wall outside the office. "What did she get herself into now?" he asked.

"You owe me dinner," Emily announced and started off toward the restaurant.

Donald followed her muttering under his breath. Clara and Naomi followed. Emily made a beeline for the buffet, heaped food on her plate and then chose a table in the back of the restaurant by the kitchen doors.

"I hate sitting by the doors," Donald said, joining her. "The waiters rush in and out banging the doors open and closed, sometimes hitting the table." Naomi and Clara sat down across from him. "I'm not buying you two dinner. That wasn't the deal."

All three women ignored him. He signaled the waiter and ordered off the menu. His food arrived as Emily was finishing hers.

"Did you find out anything?" asked Emily of Clara and Naomi.

"Find out about what?" asked Donald.

"Never mind. It's girl stuff," Clara said. "Just shut up and eat your food."

"Now, isn't that nice. You use me for a meal ticket and then discard me." Donald gave Naomi a smack on her fingers when she reached over and grabbed one of his French fries.

"Well?" insisted Emily.

"Nothing. We were too starved to ask any questions and when we finished, a casino employee told us you were in some kind of trouble."

"I heard she broke some woman's nose," said Donald between bites of his burger.

"She and I had a disagreement over the slot machine, and I temporarily rearranged her makeup," Emily said, her tone of voice defensive.

"I was right, then. You broke her nose. Is she going to sue you?" Donald asked.

"I hope not," Emily said in a small voice. "What did you whisper in that woman's ear that made her reconsider suing me?"

"I told her I'd let her husband know she was at the casino gambling away his money."

"How did you know that?" asked Emily.

"I took a wild guess, knowing Mr. Griswold is known to be as tight as a Victorian corset. Now, if you're finished with your food, it's way past time I got you and Naomi home. You both sound exhausted. Neither of you should be behind the wheel,"

Clara said. "We'll leave your car here, and I'll drive you. You can get a ride from Donald tomorrow to pick it up on the way to the country club."

"I'm fishing tomorrow. I've got no time to be giving taxi rides." Donald tossed his napkin on the table and got out of his chair. "You're not the only one who's tired. I worked for you today while you were playing soldier."

"Don't forget that you've got the afternoon shift at the bar," said Emily to Donald's retreating back.

He muttered something and was gone.

"I can drive Mom's car," offered Naomi. "If you're worried, Clara, you can follow us home."

"This roast beef is wonderful," said Emily, picking up her plate and heading into the kitchen.

"What is she up to now?" asked Naomi.

"She's your mother. You've seen her in operation before. Lewis asked us to find out about the woman Toby picked up outside the casino earlier. I'll bet she's in there interrogating the wait staff and the kitchen help."

The kitchen doors opened a few minutes later and Emily exited, escorted by a smiling man wearing a chef's hat. "I'm so pleased you like the prime rib. How thoughtful of you to seek me out to compliment me. Perhaps you'd like a second helping? And a special dessert on the house?" he offered.

"I don't usually have beef, but I ran into one of your staff who was just getting off work earlier, and I asked her what she would recommend on your buffet line. She chose the prime rib. She said you had a way with meat," Emily said, matching his wide, ingratiating smile with one of her own.

"Someone you know?" asked the chef.

"No one I knew. I took a chance when I saw her apron. I thought to myself, who better than one of the kitchen help to know what's good? She was tall, thin, late forties with a beehive hairdo."

The chef shrugged. "Who could that be?" He turned toward one of his sous chefs.

"That must be Melissa DeVry," one of them said. "I didn't know she was such a fan. She's only been working here for a month or so."

"Oh, Melissa DeVry. Is she one of the DeVrys from Orlando?" asked Emily, hopeful of pumping someone for information by acting as if she knew the family.

"I don't think so," said Emily's server, waiting to present someone at the table with the bill. He would have given it to the man except for his rapid departure earlier. Seizing the opportunity to impress Emily and perhaps add to his tip, the waiter continued, "She's from Arcadia. My mother said Ms. DeVry's family works a traveling salvation show around here. Mom said her father had a run-in with the law, spent some time in state prison where he got religion and became a lay preacher when he got out. I think they've set up this week near Clewiston." He might have said more about the family, but the chef shoved him to one side.

"You might want to try my shrimp scampi. It will be on the buffet next Sunday."

"Right. Right," Emily said in a dismissive tone. She reached beyond the chef, grabbed the waiter by his sleeve and steered him away from the others.

"Do you know what he went to prison for?" asked Emily of the waiter.

He shook his head. "If it's important, I can take your number and have my mom give you a call. Mom would know."

"Good idea." Emily asked for a pen and wrote her name and number down on a napkin. "Thanks." She started toward the restaurant's exit.

"Uh, the bill?" asked her waiter.

Emily swept her hand toward Clara. "She'll take care of it."

Clara did. "Put it on Donald Green's account."

The waiter nodded.

In the wake of their exit, confusion registered on the chef's wrinkled brow. Poor fellow, Emily thought. He didn't know if he had been complimented or insulted. Emily sighed and felt some guilt at having used him, but then she shrugged her shoulders and admitted not all of the exchange was a lie. The beef was good. Besides, she found out what Lewis needed, so really it was his fault if anyone's feelings were hurt.

※

Emily fell into a deep sleep while Naomi drove. Clara followed them as far as the gate to the community, gave a honk of her horn and a wave, then turned back toward town.

Emily awoke with a start when the horn interrupted her dream.

"We're home," said Naomi pulling into the drive, "And it looks like Vicki has been waiting for us."

The shade on the house next door moved a bit, and Vicki, Emily's neighbor, opened the window and said, "I've got pie."

As tempting as that sounded—and Vicki's Key Lime pie was the best in the area—Emily was too tired to eat, but she knew the offer was less about the pie and more about what Vicki had heard through the grapevine and wanted to share with Emily. Emily never worried about anyone sneaking around her house or breaking in because Vicki kept a close eye on the place. The woman seemed to know everything about the goings on in the community.

"Come on over," said Emily, "but save the pie. I just ate and I'm stuffed."

"I'll bring a few pieces and you can have them for breakfast tomorrow. Be over in a jiff," Vicki said.

Emily flopped down on the couch and propped her feet on the coffee table while Naomi headed down the hall toward the bedrooms. The park model trailer Emily owned had two bedrooms and one bathroom. Emily slept in the bedroom with the king-sized bed, while Naomi had the other, smaller room. Emily's gaze followed her daughter's retreat. If she had the energy, she would have dragged herself into her own bed, but Vicki's knock at the door reminded her Vicki wanted to talk.

"You look terrible," said Vicki, depositing the pie on the kitchen counter.

"Thanks. I can't say the same for you. You look as if you just got back from some kind of party."

"There was a dance at the club house." Vicki, a tall, Nordic blond who looked as if she had just stepped off the stage after playing a Valkyrie, wore a black and white patterned skirt and a black knit top. Her face was flushed with excitement, and Emily knew it wasn't from the fun she had at the dance, because the dances held in this over-fifty-five community were pretty tame; two Elvis songs in one night was about as wild as it got. Vicki knew something interesting was up.

"So?' said Vicki. "Tell me all about it."

"The reenactment?" asked Emily, knowing that wasn't what Vicki meant.

"No, silly. The murder."

<hr>

Detective Lewis made good time to the outskirts of Orlando. Now all he had to do was find the residence where Mrs. Parsons was staying with her children. He plugged the address into his GPS and hoped it would be more accurate here in a city than it was out in the country around the Big Lake. The device directed him to a gated community on the western side of the city. Mrs. Parsons had notified the security guard at the gate of his impending arrival, and he passed through after showing his ID.

The light on the front porch of the condo was on. All the other places were dark with the exception of a few upstairs lights flickering in bedrooms of those who tuned into the late-night television programs. Lewis looked at his watch. It was midnight. He rang the bell, and the door was quickly opened as if someone had been waiting next to it. The woman who stood in the entryway wore no makeup, was of medium height and had straight brown hair cut below her ears. She wore a white shirt and a pair of jeans. The only thing remarkable about her was her eyes: they were turned down at the outside corners, giving her a look so filled with despair it was as if she had seen only grief in her life.

"Come in, detective. You must have something important to tell me if you've driven all this way and at this time of night."

There was no fear or anger in her voice at his appearance. It was as if she knew why he was here.

"What did he do this time?" she asked.

Lewis was momentarily speechless. "I'm not certain what you mean."

"Just tell me." She gestured toward the couch.

Lewis removed his hat and sat. There was no sign of anyone else in the house. "Perhaps you'd like someone to be with you."

"No. It's not..." she began, then made a dismissive circling gesture with her hand.

"Your husband is dead, and it looks like murder."

Mrs. Parsons sank into a chair across from him. He found it hard to read the look on her face, but it didn't resemble the expressions of disbelief, grief or numbness he'd grown accustomed to seeing when someone was told of the death of a family member. It was more like surprise followed by relief.

"Are you certain you don't want someone to be with you? Are your parents home? This is their place, correct?"

"They're out of town."

"And your children? I was led to believe they were here with you."

"They're sleeping."

She began to pull at the fabric on the arm of the chair. Perhaps shock was setting in.

"I'm so sorry for your loss. Can I get you anything?"

"No." She got out of the chair and turned her back on him, walking toward the window overlooking the street. When she turned back toward him, she was smiling. "You mean, can you get me a glass of water?' She began laughing, a laugh that built into a crescendo. He expected it would be punctuated by gulps of air and sobs, but instead she stopped abruptly. "That felt good." Her face was now devoid of expression. "And now, detective, thank you for your time. I'll be back in town by noon today. If you need to talk with me then, you can get in touch with me at my home. I'll give you my cell number." She walked to an entry table, extracted a pen and paper and wrote her number on it. Lewis could see her hand was steady as she wrote.

She swept her hand over her forehead. "I should get some sleep. There are so many arrangements to make."

He had been dismissed. He considered telling her he had a few questions, but he decided to wait until tomorrow.

She accompanied him to the door. As he walked down the sidewalk to his car, he paused for a moment and turned back to the house. She stood in the window silhouetted by the room's light. She gave him a tiny wave, then placed her hand over her mouth. The shock was setting in. Well, he decided, a good cry might help her. He started back down the sidewalk, then looked back for a moment. He had to be mistaken, but as nearly as he could tell, she wasn't covering her mouth to hide her distress, but rather to hide another bout of laughter. He could hear it follow him until he got into his car.

⬦

Emily awoke the next morning with pie crumbs on her lips and the taste of Key lime in her mouth. Vicki's pie plate was gone. She could hear Naomi in the shower.

"Did you have pie for breakfast?" yelled Emily when she heard the water stop.

"Yep." Naomi emerged from the bathroom, toweling her hair dry. "So did you, but you had yours a little earlier than I did. You and Vicki must have stayed up until one or two this morning. How does she know so much about what goes on around this place? She knew more about the murder of Parsons than we did, and we were there. As usual, you discovered the body. She knew that, too."

"She was wrong. Lewis discovered the body. I rolled onto it."

"Why is it you find it necessary to get so physically close to murder victims? First you fall on a dead rancher in a dumpster, then you pull a barbecuer out of a beer cooler truck, and now you roll into a puddle with the high school principal like the two of you had been in a mud wrestling contest." Naomi seemed to realize after she had spoken how insensitive the mud wrestling comment was given that Parson was dead. Her hand flew to her mouth. "Sorry about that," she said.

Emily screwed up her face and gave her daughter an anguished look, then dropped her head into her hands. "Am I being punished for something?"

Naomi rushed over and put her arms around her mother. "No, no. It's a run of bad luck. It'll end." Naomi added under her breath, "I hope."

Emily ran her fingers through her hair, catching a few pie crumbs in them as well as a lot of dirty gunk. "Ugh, I really need a shower. I meant to take one after Vicki left, but I fell asleep on the couch."

"The way you look I think you fell asleep on your slice of pie. I'll make a fresh pot of coffee. This one is from when I got up around seven."

"What time is it now?" asked Emily, looking at her kitchen wall clock, which she'd neglected to insert a battery in several months ago so it wasn't working.

"It's after nine. Tell me where you keep the batteries, and I'll fix the clock." Naomi dumped out the cold coffee and turned on the faucet to fill the coffee maker. "Oops."

"What?"

"The water is off again. I'll give Vicki a call and see if she knows when it will be back on."

Emily wanted to cry. Her hair was stiff with enough dried stuff from the battlefield as well as pie crumbs that she was lucky she wasn't outside where the mocking birds would build a nest in it and feed their young. And she smelled bad, really bad.

Naomi ended her call to Vicki and said, "It will be on again in two hours."

"I can't wait that long. I'm already late opening. C'mon." Emily dragged herself to her bedroom, grabbed clean clothing and a towel out of the linen closet. "I'll go to the country club and use the showers there."

"Don't do it, Mom."

"Why not?"

"I don't think the golf leagues need to see their favorite bartender looking as if she spent the night sleeping in an alley somewhere."

"Let's try Clara then. If I don't get this mud out of my hair and off my body, the fire ants and a few other creepy crawlies will set up home."

"I thought mud baths were good for your skin."

"Only if it's clean mud." Emily paused a moment, thinking about mud that wasn't found in a swamp, wondered what spas used in a mud bath, and decided she never wanted to subject herself to one, clean or not.

CHAPTER 6

"Water off again?" asked Clara opening the door to her friends. "One of you smells like a swamp in the middle of a hot July."

"That's me," said Emily, holding up her hand. "Can I use yours?"

"In exchange for what?" Clara asked.

"I stopped next door before I left and Vicki gave me two pieces of Key lime pie for you."

"Give," said Clara, grabbing the plate from Emily's hands. "You want some?"

"Nope. I had enough last night."

"Hmm," Clara said, "it looks to me as if most of the pie was used to gel your hair."

Emily ignored the remark and headed off to Clara's shower. Maybe she'd take a bath instead, she thought, spying all of Clara's bubble bath and other bath oils. She ran the water, added enough fragrance to deodorize a cow barn and sank into the water. It reminded her of the time she and Detective Lewis got all soapy together. She sighed and slid further down into the tub.

The next thing she knew, someone was banging on the door and the bath water was cold.

"Just a minute," she called.

"Get decent. We've got visitors," she heard Clara reply.

She tied her hair up in a ponytail, threw on clean clothes and wondered who was visiting Clara and what they could want.

The first thing she noticed when she entered the living room were two pairs of legs stretched out in Clara's recliners: Donald Green was sporting alligator boots; the other plain old cowhide kickers were Detective Lewis'. *Not now,* she said to herself. *I just want some time with women, friends who won't subject me to sarcastic remarks about finding dead bodies, people who might like to talk about food or clothes, girl stuff.* She was about to turn around and head back into the bathroom, but Naomi slipped around her and blocked the way. *Wait a minute. Whose side was her daughter on?*

"The detective wants to know what you found out about Toby's current squeeze, other than she's one woman with really bad taste in men," said Naomi.

"That's about it, detective," Emily replied, fiddling with her ponytail. *I should have blow dried my hair and at least put on lipstick.* "What are you doing here, Donald? I thought you were fishing this morning."

"They aren't biting."

"So you decided to come over here and bother us. How did you find us anyway?"

"I had coffee with Vicki. She baked some fresh muffins, too. She said the water was off, so I figured you'd come here." He shifted back into the recliner as if he intended to stay the day.

"I suppose you wanted to let me know that, because of the bad fishing, you could cover my shift today," Emily said, crossing her arms and daring Donald to say more.

He did.

"You look just fine. Why can't you cover the early afternoon shift and the late one too?" Green asked, reaching out for his coffee cup and the plate with a slice of pie on it.

"You're going to die of diabetes if you don't stop eating so much sugar," said Emily.

Donald grumbled something under his breath.

Clara watched the exchanges between Emily and Donald with a smile on her face, amused by the interplay. And the men, themselves? The air hung heavy with testosterone. "Try being a little generous, Donald. Emily had a bad day yesterday what with her finding that body and having a fight in the casino," said Clara.

Clara threw fuel on the fire because she knew mentioning the fight between Emily and Mrs. Money Grabber from the slot machines was sure to get Lewis' interest.

She was right. Lewis leaned forward in the recliner and asked, "What fight? What woman?"

"She's not pressing charges, so forget it, detective. It's not your business. Now, I'd like to go because it appears my help isn't coming into the bar today. I've got a double shift staring me in the face and no sympathy from you-know-who, despite how bad yesterday was," Emily said.

Clara suppressed a laugh. She could enjoy the sass Emily dished out to Lewis and Donald because she knew her tiny Yankee friend gave as good as she got. The gal had moxie.

"You were supposed to get some information for me," said Lewis. "C'mon. I'll drive you to the club."

"And pick me up later tonight?" Emily asked.

The expression on Lewis' face said it all. He hadn't thought through the ride issues and hadn't intended to serve as her chauffer to and from the club.

She smiled and tapped her foot on the floor. "Well?"

"Uh, sure," he said.

"Or you can just forget it. We can talk some other time, tomorrow, maybe."

"I've got a murder to solve," Lewis said, in a snappish tone. "I need answers now."

Emily gestured toward the door with one hand, bowing from the waist and giving a sweep of her other hand as if she was a gentleman gesturing his lady out the door.

Lewis pulled himself out of the chair. "Didn't even get a cup of coffee," he said, settling his cowboy hat on his head.

Emily stuck out her tongue at his retreating back and said to Naomi, "Take the car, honey. I'll give you a call if my ride home falls through."

Clara followed Emily and Lewis outside, not wanting to miss what she was sure would be more repartee between the two. She shook her head. It was so clear that Lewis had a real thing for Emily. Emily sometimes seemed blind to Lewis' feelings, which he tried hard to hide, and was successful only with Emily and perhaps himself.

Clara thought she heard Lewis say something.

"What was that?" Emily asked.

He opened the door of his car and gave her the same gesture and bow she had given him, "Madam's car awaits."

They drove off. Clara let out the guffaw she'd been holding in.

"You think that's funny?" Donald said, standing at her side.

"I do. I also think it's even funnier when you get involved. You know Lewis likes Emily, and Lewis knows you like Emily. Emily thinks both of you find her annoying..."

"I certainly do," insisted Donald. "A real sassy little blond thing."

"Well," said Clara, "at least this time you didn't refer to her as a 'little Yankee gal.'"

Donald gave her a glowering look. "Any more coffee?"

"Nope. I've got to get to work. You want coffee, try the diner downtown. Maybe you can get Naomi to join you."

"Why would I want to do that?" he said.

Clara slapped him on the back. "Why indeed?"

As Lewis drove her to the club, Emily played with her hair, then reached into her purse and applied eye shadow and lipstick.

"You don't have to get all dolled up for me, you know," said Lewis.

"It's not for you. It's for my bar clientele. Don't be so vain. It's not always about you."

Lewis bit back whatever he might have said, and they rode several miles in silence.

"So?" Lewis asked.

Emily sighed. "I don't know much about the woman except that her name is Melissa DeVry."

"I already know that."

"She's the daughter of a man who spent some time in prison, but now he's found Jesus and is running a revival scheme. He's set up a tent near Clewiston."

"'Scheme'? Emily, you are so cynical."

"So are you. How many ex-cons do you know who claim to have found God as a way of convincing the parole board they've reformed?"

"Most of them." Lewis pulled into the long drive leading up to the clubhouse. "Anything else?"

Emily said nothing.

"Okay then. Here's a warning that you probably won't heed, but just because you..."

"Just because I fell onto yet another dead body doesn't mean I have any right to insert myself into this murder even though I have helped you solve two other murders."

"You're not listening to me, are you?"

"Did you find Toby and Melissa, you know, uh, were they doing anything interesting when you arrived?"

"They were down on their knees..." Lewis said, then stopped.

"Yes?"

"They were praying."

"Get out!" Emily said, laughing and slapping him on his shoulder as he parked the car.

"Ow. Woman you've got a mean streak in you." Lewis got out of the car and started to go around to open the door for Emily, but she beat him out of the car and headed toward the clubhouse, leaving him behind. He pushed the car door closed and started to leave, when Emily turned and walked back toward him.

"I've got a lead on how to find out more about Ms. DeVry," said Emily, gazing up at Lewis, her blue eyes wide with a look of pure innocence. It was a look she knew she did well and one Lewis couldn't resist.

"Yeah?"

"Stop by the club after lunch when things slow down here. I may know more by then."

"Emily," he said, a note of warning in his voice.

"I'll be working all morning so what trouble can I get into here?" she said, batting her eyes at him.

If Lewis had gotten a good night's sleep, he might have followed her and lectured her again on not intruding on a murder investigation, but Lewis was bone tired after his drive to and back from

Orlando. If he didn't get a few hours of sleep, he'd be useless to this investigation. He had Mrs. Parsons to interview today as well as David Otter, the young man who was a friend of the Parsons boy, the one he had met yesterday at the reenactment. He got into his car and slid down in the seat. He could fall asleep right here, but he knew he should go home, get a few hours of sleep, shower and then be back here to see what Emily was up to. He groaned to himself. It was his fault she was showing more than scant interest in this case. He had stupidly asked her to find out about Melissa DeVry. He groaned again, started the engine and slammed down on the accelerator spewing gravel. He'd better keep his wits about him or he'd be picked up for driving while stupid.

⬖

Emily entered the club to find about ten golfers standing in front of the locked bar.

"Hot day, huh, guys?" she said, opening the door to let them in. "I've got cold ones in the cooler but nothing on ice yet." Here in rural Florida Emily had learned that a beer couldn't be too cold, and there was nothing colder than beer on ice.

Spring was coming early this year, and the heat and humidity was descending on Big Lake country fast despite the past few days of rain. Thunderstorms didn't take the humidity out of the air as they often did up North. There was no escaping the tropical heat.

Anyone other than Emily opening the bar late would have been the brunt of some unkind remarks, but everyone respected Emily and knew her small size was no reason to disparage her. The gal could deliver a good enough punch to lay out any golfer, rancher, cowboy or bass fisherman on the barroom floor. It was the surprise of having someone so tiny deliver such a blow, not the power of it. Oh, she was nice enough about anyone getting out of line with foul language or fighting, but she warned you only once, then you found yourself out in the parking lot. Quite a gal.

She passed out beers to the golfers and again apologized for not opening on time and not having the beer on ice. "It's on the house, fellas," she said. She quickly hauled cases of beer out of the back cooler and put them in the metal tubs to ice, sliced up limes and lemons and set out the cherries and olives, did a quick wipe down of the bar, checked her inventory, then leaned into a back shelf holding the liquor bottles, and she stifled a yawn.

Her cell rang. The voice at the other end was unfamiliar to her.

"My name is Cosey Franklin. My son works as a waiter at the casino. He said you might be interested in knowing more about the DeVry family, although I can't imagine why."

"Oh, yes. Thanks for getting in touch. I'm doing some, uh, some work for the, uh, the Christian Leadership Mandate, and I understand the family has set up a temporary revival group near Clewiston.

We'd like to get in touch with them. Is there a permanent address and phone number you know of for the group? I can't find anything in the phone book."

"Oh, you won't find anything permanent on those folks. They move around a lot." Mrs. Franklin gave a snort and added, "Crazy lot of buggers."

"I understand from talking with your son that you know Melissa, is that right?"

"I went to school with her. She was a sweet girl then, very shy because her dad was in prison, but since he got out and set up his so-called church, Melissa has become a real pain in the you-know-what. Now I'm not one to judge other people's choice of what to believe, but that church of her father's? Those people are plain loony."

"Do you stay in touch with her?"

"I tried to, but all she'll talk about is praying and bringing your troubles to God. The problem is she's not really talking about troubles. She's talking about money. Bring your money to God, every dang day."

"I guess the church needs money to operate."

"Operate? Operate what? They do services under a ratty old tent and that's about it. And I think there's something funny going on, too. You might think I was just being prejudiced against her daddy, but he did his time. Now he should do some good, not pretend to heal folks and take poor people's money. You ought to go on out there and see what's happening. It can't be good."

By now Mrs. Franklin seemed to have worked up a good head of steam. Emily could hear sputtering through the phone, and Mrs. Franklin's voice had risen an octave or so. Emily held the phone away from her ear. The woman was shouting loud enough that it sounded as if Emily had put her on speakerphone.

When she paused to take a breath, Emily interrupted her. "You've been very helpful, Mrs. Franklin."

There was a pause, and she began speaking again, this time in a more controlled manner. Her voice was lower and the words came out slowly. "Sorry I got in such a dither. I really liked Melissa. I felt sorry for her with her daddy being in prison and all. Now she's different. I guess she felt she didn't have any choice other than to follow her father's preaching after her husband left."

"She was married?"

"Probably still is. Her daddy ran the poor man off. Said he was evil. The man was also a preacher, but he was some kind of a liberal sort, maybe Unitarian, although we don't get many of those around here. I'm not fond of them either. I don't even think they believe in God, but he was a fine man, kind. The problem was he was part Seminole. Melissa's dad couldn't tolerate that. So sad."

Emily heard sniffles. "I didn't mean to bring up bad memories for you."

"Well, bless you, honey. I know you didn't. You were just doing your job. What organization was it now?"

Emily couldn't remember what she had said. "Uh, never mind that. Sorry I intruded. I have to go now. Thanks for the information." Emily hung up. She felt guilty that her intrusive questioning had been responsible for creating that roller-coaster of feelings for Mrs. Franklin.

Her cell rang again, again registering a number she didn't recognize. She hoped it wasn't Mrs. Franklin asking her for the organization's name again. Christian Leadership Something. What the heck? Mrs. Franklin probably wouldn't remember it either, and she had been cooperative. Emily answered.

"Hiya, Honey. Remember me? It's Daisy."

"Daisy DuBignon St. Simonton!" Emily said. Of course she remembered her and her husband, Rodney. She and Naomi had met them on a vacation in Jekyll Island, Georgia, while playing golf.

"How are you?"

"Why don't you see for yourself? We're right outside the window."

Emily looked out. Sure enough, the St. Simontons' red Cadillac sat in a handicapped slot near the door to the bar. In it sat Daisy, her dark auburn hair tied back in a silk red and yellow scarf, large sunglasses covering her eyes. She was a tall woman, short of six feet; her husband before his crippling illness had been taller than she was. Now he spent most of his time in his motorized wheelchair. Emily had never heard either of them complain. They just seemed to enjoy their life and lived it to the limit. They were a fun-loving couple who embraced adventure, even if it meant a romp slightly the other side of legal. They lifted her spirits.

Emily dropped her phone and ran for the door, banging it open and running out to the car. She threw her arms around Daisy and kissed Rodney on the cheek.

"You came all the way down here to play golf?" asked Emily.

"Well, that, and to see you," said Daisy, getting out of the car and opening the trunk to extract Rodney's wheelchair. Emily helped Rodney out of the passenger's seat, and she and Daisy assisted him into the chair.

He powered the chair toward the far door leading to the entrance to the pro shop. "I'll see if we can get a tee time for later today," he said. Several of the golfers at the door heard him. The surprised looks on their faces said they didn't expect a man in a wheelchair to be playing golf.

Emily looked at Daisy, and they exchanged smiles. "How much money do you think Rodney will take off the guys here today? Or have you warned everyone about my husband?" asked Daisy.

"I haven't said a word. No one gave me a heads up when I bet against him, and he whooped my bottom on every durn hole." Emily also recalled how Rodney took more than a few pool games off several young, full-of-themselves guys in a local bar. He was a gentleman about it, but there was a twinkle in his eye that said fooling arrogant young bucks was the best way to make some money.

"That's a lot of miles just to play golf on a mediocre course and have a chat with me, interesting as I am."

"Speaking of that. Run across any dead bodies lately?" asked Daisy.

Emily's smile left her face and was replaced by a look of despair.

"Oh, honey," said Daisy. "I'm sorry. I was just kidding. How many bodies can one woman stumble over? Haven't you had your share of them?"

"More than." Emily looked upset for only a moment before she recovered herself and said to Daisy, "I'll tell you all about it. In fact, I've got a great lead that I need to follow up on."

"Another body then? Oh, good. Can we help?" asked Daisy.

"Of course. Detective Lewis doesn't..."

Daisy interrupted. "So how is that handsome detective of yours?"

"I'm just fine, ma'am," said a voice from behind Daisy and Emily. Neither of them had seen the detective arrive in his cruiser, get out and approach the building.

Emily gulped. Had Lewis heard what she said about a lead?

"Well, isn't this fun?" Daisy said. "Just like the last time we chased the bad guys together."

CHAPTER 7

"The way I remember working with you on a case was you and Emily intruding into my territory." Lewis grinned at the two women. "Your husband was a big help, however."

"That's because he spied on us and told you what we were up to. He's learned not to do that," Daisy said.

Rodney zoomed up behind them. "Tee time at two. We've been put into a foursome, so there's fun to be had."

Emily knew the fun he spoke of was taking a few dollars off the other golfers assigned to the foursome. Rodney rolled up to the detective and shook his hand, then spoke in a whisper. "Daisy has set a limit on my bets, and I'm not allowed near any dead bodies Emily stumbles over."

Lewis and Rodney had a chuckle over the memories of Rodney serving as lookout while Emily and Daisy searched the trailer of a murder suspect.

Emily and Daisy shot glares at the two men.

"Sorry to interrupt the reunion, but Emily and I have some unfinished business to attend to," said Lewis.

"Still trying to work out who washes whose back first?" said Daisy, referring to the time Emily and the detective got caught in a storm and sought shelter in his condo.

Emily blushed.

"No. I asked her to find out something about someone who might be of interest to us in my current murder case. She hasn't let me know what she found." Lewis let out a sigh. "I'll probably regret asking her to help," he muttered.

"Let's all meet for drinks later then and catch up," said Rodney.

"I apologize but I'm at the very beginning of this case, and I've got some leads I need to follow up on today."

"Nice seeing you, detective. Too bad we can't get together. We'd love to hear about the case," said Daisy.

"I'm sure Emily will fill you in," he said with sarcasm in his voice.

He pulled Emily to one side and asked what she had found out about Melissa DeVry.

"What's it worth to you?" she asked.

"Fine. Keep it to yourself, and when I find out more about this case, I'll keep that to myself."

Emily knew she should not play games with him. He always won. She told him what she had found out by talking with the waiter's mother.

"Uh, huh," he said, paused for a moment and then left the bar.

He'd never tell her anything about the case. She knew better than to believe sharing information with him would result in his doing the same with her. In frustration, Emily tossed the bar rag toward the sink and narrowly missed hitting Daisy, who smiled a knowing smile.

Lewis drove to the Parsons' residence feeling a small sense of victory that he'd wrangled information about Melissa DeVry out of Emily. *As if he'd tell Emily anything about this case.* There was probably no connection between Toby, the murder of Mr. Parsons and Melissa DeVry, so Lewis decided to put off following up on the DeVry family for now. He would keep an eye on Toby, however. He didn't trust the guy.

There was something about his meeting with Winona Parsons last night that continued to bother him. How members of a victim's family dealt with death was never predictable, and sometimes odd. Take the woman who, on hearing of her mother's murder immediately grabbed her cell phone and booked a cruise to the Caribbean, then threw up on Lewis' shoes. She turned out to be innocent of any wrongdoing in her mother's death, so Mrs. Parsons' response was unusual but not something Lewis was immediately suspicious about...yet.

He'd asked his partner Sandy Davis to meet him at the house because he wanted her to talk with the daughter while he spoke with Mrs. Parsons and with her son. He thought it odd that none of the family attended the reenactment yesterday. He wanted to know why.

Davis had beat him to the house.

"Detective," he greeted Davis as she stepped out of the car. "Anything I should know about from your interviews?"

She shook her head. "Everyone seemed to be focused on the beginning of the battle. There was a lot of smoke and the sound of weapons. No one registered much of anything other than the ongoing conflict. We can do follow-ups, but nothing looks promising. We haven't found the weapon used or any other significant evidence at the site. What about you?"

He shook his head, then shared Mrs. Parsons' reaction when he informed her of her husband's death. The two of them approached the door to ring the bell.

"Nice house," said Davis. "Does the wife work as well?"

"No." Lewis pushed the bell. The sound of voices came from within, but no one answered the ring. The volume of the voices increased until it was obvious that an argument was going on.

A door slammed and Lewis and Davis saw someone run from the back of the house, across the lawn and off into a neighbor's yard.

"That looked like a teenage boy," Davis said. "Do you want me to see if I can catch him?"

Lewis nodded, and Davis took off in pursuit. Was it someone who had broken into the house?

Rumors of the murder had already circulated in town. Unscrupulous characters might have tried to burglarize the house, assuming the family wouldn't be there but at the funeral home making arrangements for the deceased. Or perhaps it was the Parsons boy, but why would he be running off?

The door opened and Winona Parsons stood there, her face lined with worry.

"Was that your son?" asked Lewis.

"My son?"

"Mrs. Parsons, I think you know what I mean. Someone just fled out the back door."

She nodded and opened the door wider to let the detective in.

"What's going on here?" asked Lewis.

"He didn't want to talk to you, so he left when he saw you get out of your car."

"Why didn't he want to talk with us?"

Mrs. Parsons seemed to pull herself together. The expressionless mask she wore last night when Lewis first met her returned to her face. "Why don't you ask him?"

This is going to be one heck of an investigation, thought Lewis. *I'm only day one into the case and already none of the people I need to interview wanted to cooperate.*

Davis returned empty-handed. "Lost him."

"Perhaps my partner here can have a few words with your daughter," suggested Lewis.

"She's not here," said Mrs. Parsons.

Lewis silently ground his teeth together. "When might we talk with her?"

"Not anytime soon. She's gone with her grand-parents to California. She's enrolled in a private school there."

Lewis tried not to show his frustration. "Can we sit for a few minutes?"

"I can't imagine why you want to talk with me or any members of my family, detective. We weren't at the reenactment yesterday so I can't see how we can be helpful." She had given no indication last night or today that her husband's death had impacted her in any way, but suddenly she played the grieving family card. "My children have just lost their father. Why are you bothering us at this time?"

"To catch your husband's killer, we need background information on him. You've lived here for less than four years. Where was he before he took the position here?" Although she hadn't offered him a seat, Lewis sat on the couch and signaled Davis to take a seat beside him. He wanted to let Mrs. Parsons know he and his partner weren't going anywhere until she'd answered his questions.

"He worked farther north of here," she said vaguely.

"What community was that?'

Mrs. Parsons pressed a hand to her mouth and tears welled up in her eyes. Maybe it was just now hitting her that her husband was dead, thought Lewis.

"We liked it there," she said.

"And he left there for this position. When was that?" asked Davis.

"I don't remember the year."

There was something the woman wasn't telling them. Lewis could just feel it.

"Why did he leave there?" Lewis asked.

She cleared her throat and wiped the tears from her face. "It wasn't a very good fit for him. You can check with Mason City. They will tell you. They gave him a great recommendation." She rose from her chair. "If that's all for now, I really must...do things."

"I'm going to ask you to accompany my partner here down to the county morgue. We need an identification of the body."

Her face turned white, and she reached out for a chair to steady herself.

Lewis extended his hand to her, certain she was going to fall, but again she recovered, and the momentary expression of anxiety slipped from her face.

She again gave him a blank look. "Of course. I'll get my purse and car keys."

"Detective Davis will drive you there and back. Unless there's another member of the family who can do the identification," Lewis suggested.

"No. No one."

"Mrs. Parsons, do you have any idea where your son would go when he ran off?"

"None. He likes to be by himself."

"But he does have friends. I met one yesterday. David Otter. Could he have gone to his house?"

"I don't recognize that name. I don't' know where he went. He sometimes goes off like that."

"And you don't seem to be concerned, either, do you?" Lewis heard Davis mutter under her breath, too soft for Mrs. Parsons to hear.

What an odd family, thought Lewis. The daughter is sent off to the grandparents, the son runs off to someplace, no one shows up to see the father take a primary role in an historical enactment, and the mother's reaction to the murder is all over the place: grief, anger, lack of feeling, lack of concern about the death of her husband, resolute vagueness about being questioned. It's like trying to pound my way through a concrete wall: I'm stuck on this side while the answers reside on the other.

Lewis mentally shrugged off the lack of information he'd obtained. There were other ways to find out about Mr. Parsons. He decided to try one of them. David Otter seemed approachable yesterday. He might be more willing to talk about the Parsons family.

Emily's cell rang just as she finished up serving a round of beers to the men's golf league from a nearby over-fifty-five community.

It was Clara. "When do you get off today? I need to talk with you."

"As soon as Donald puts in an appearance, I can leave, but I'm not certain when that will be."

"Call me when he arrives. It's important."

Donald pushed through the door to the bar several minutes later. "Well, I'm here. Do you want me to work?"

"Of course I do. I'm dead on my feet."

He growled something under his breath and began restocking the beer in the ice tubs.

"Thanks so much, Donald," Emily said, tossing her apron into the laundry bin behind the bar. She gave him a friendly pat on the shoulder, taking him by surprise.

"What do you want now?" he asked in his usually surly manner.

"Nothin', darlin'," she said, giving him her best Southern drawl. "I just sure do appreciate all your help."

"Are you being sarcastic?" he asked.

"Nope." Emily loved to mess with Donald every now and then, and being nice to him really confused the heck out of him. She dashed out to her car, then remembered she had no car. Detective Lewis had given her a ride to the course and had offered to pick her up this afternoon. She knew he wouldn't remember. She dialed Clara.

"I'm free and stuck at the course. I ran into Daisy and Rodney St. Simonton who are in town and playing a round today. We're supposed to get together when they finish, but until then I'm stuck here. I know Naomi is home, but I hate to bother her. I'm hoping she's napping. She needs her sleep, too."

"You mean your detective isn't going to pick you up?"

"What do you think?"

"I think he's got other things on his mind. I'll be right there. I'll give you a ride home. I've got something you should know. I should have told you sooner."

Clara disconnected before Emily could ask her what she was talking about. She ran back into the bar and left a message with Donald for Rodney and Daisy telling them she'd meet them later at the Biscuit, a country western bar and restaurant in town. Donald grumbled his compliance without looking up at her. He's such a lovely man, she thought. The only woman he treated well was Vicki, and that was because she fed him and could ignore his surliness.

"Well, what is it?" asked Emily as she and Clara sped out the country club drive and turned onto the road leading into town.

"I know the Parsons boy," she said.

"That's not something I need to know, but it could be something Lewis might be interested in."

"Don't tell me you aren't going to get involved in this case? Who stumbled onto the body? I mean literally."

"I'm not interested in every dead body I discover." Emily thought about what she had just said. "I mean, of course I'm curious, but it's Lewis' job."

"That never stopped you before," Clara said, turning into the community where Emily lived.

"I don't have my gate card. Hit the buzzer, and I'll wave at Darlene in the office to raise the gate and let us in."

As they pulled into her driveway, Emily asked, "So how do you know the Parsons boy. What's his name?"

"It's Owen. One of his teachers, Veronique Boudreau, who's a friend of mine from our high school days, remembered how much I love to play chess. The kids in high school wanted a chess club, and she volunteered to be the teacher in charge of it, but she admitted to me that her skills at the game aren't as good as mine, so she asked me if I would help her out. Principal Parsons okayed it. His son Owen is a member of the club."

Naomi wasn't in the living room or the kitchen when they arrived, so Emily checked the bedrooms. The house was empty. "She must be at the pool, maybe taking a soak in the hot tub. Coffee?" Emily asked.

"Yoo hoo," called a voice through the door. I've got a treat." It was Vicki with a lemon Bundt cake.

"You're better than a St. Bernard in an avalanche," said Emily. "I'm starved."

The three women tucked into the cake and coffee with oohs and ahs at its moist texture.

"How do you make it so moist?" asked Emily.

"Simple," said Vicki. "I'll give you the recipe."

"Don't bother. Just bake it every now and then. We'll be right over when we smell the lemon," said Clara.

Naomi pushed through the door.

"Lemon cake," said Emily.

"Oh, no. thanks. I'm not hungry."

"She turned down my offer of chili earlier today. She must be sick," said Vicki.

"You told me you had pie for breakfast at seven this morning, but you're not hungry now?" Emily said to her daughter.

"Did I?" Naomi replied. "I've got to change clothes. I've got a date."

"With whom?"

"Don't worry, Mom. It's with my gal friends down here visiting their family. I'll be out of the shower in a jiffy."

"Who would turn down my chili and then this cake?" asked Vicki, her voice filled with hurt.

"She's both tired from yesterday and excited about seeing her friends, so don't take it personally." Emily licked the crumbs off her fork.

"I never heard of someone too tired and excited to say no to my cooking."

Emily decided it was best to change the subject. "Clara was telling me about her work with the chess club at school."

"Actually, it's a cooperative effort between the school here in town and the tribal school. Neither institution had enough interested students to put together a large enough club for competition with other schools in the area. Now we have a strong group of students. Owen Parsons is one of the best players, and his best friend, David Otter from the tribal school, is almost as skilled."

"Parsons is the name of the guy who was killed yesterday, isn't it? One of the women I play bridge with said he was an odd duck," said Vicki.

Emily shook her head. "Is there anything that goes on around here that you don't know something about? And you're only a winter visitor."

"But I'm a great listener," said Vicki.

"You mean, a great eavesdropper, "said Emily. "I see how you listen in on conversations at the country club, the restaurants in town and when we shop in the outlets up in Vero Beach. You probably know more about people in this three-county area than the police around here do."

"I'd tell her anything at all if she'd promise to move in with me and cook," said Clara.

They all had a good laugh at that. And another piece of cake. Just a tiny sliver for each one. Naomi burst back into the room fresh from her shower and said she had to go. She and her friends were driving to the coast for Thai food.

"Something considered so foreign around here that they believe it's made with guinea pigs," said Vicki. Naomi turned green at the comment and Clara and Emily looked shocked.

"I'm simply reporting what I heard some women say the other day in the fast food place," Vicki said.

Naomi waved good-bye and slammed out the door.

"I'm so glad she found friends around here her own age, so she doesn't have to hang out with us old ladies," said Emily. "Oops, I've got to get cleaned up, too. I'm due to meet the St. Simontons for drinks and dinner. You two want to come?"

"I've got to get back to the office. I've got paperwork staring at me," Clara said.

"Hubby and I are going to the potluck at the clubhouse here," said Vicki.

"We can talk later, and you can fill me in on what you know about the Parsons boy," said Emily, showing Clara out and waving good-bye to Vicki.

"How about coffee tomorrow at the diner, unless you don't plan to come into town?" said Clara.

"I'll see you there around eight," said Emily.

She jumped into the shower. When she got out to towel off, she looked in the medicine cabinet for body lotion, then spied an empty container of it thrown into the waste can. *Darn that daughter of mine*, said Emily to herself. *Why didn't she tell me we were out?* Something else in the waste can caught her eye, something she hadn't seen for many, many years, but still recognized. A pregnancy detection stick. *Darn that daughter of mine.*

CHAPTER 8

It was afternoon by the time Lewis left the morgue after Mrs. Parsons identified the body and he filed the proper paperwork. It seemed as if police work was more about pushing papers and sitting in front of his computer than it was actual work in the field. Lewis knew the captain wanted him to apply for his position when he retired in several years, but Lewis was in no hurry for that day to come. It meant he'd never get outside the office and perform the job he knew he was good at and trained for. He had the ability to lead the men and women on the force, but it wasn't a position he longed for. Maybe he could take an early retirement before the captain took his and avoid the temptation of higher pay for riding a desk.

Lewis was no more successful this afternoon in getting answers from Mrs. Parsons than he had been earlier in the day. While he had a reputation around the station for being good at interviewing witnesses and family members and also suspects, he couldn't find a way into that woman. He tried appealing to her sense of loss, her feelings of anger and her concern for her children. Nothing provided him with a crack in her façade. Whatever secrets—

and his instincts told him there were some—she was holding inside, she kept to herself.

"No, she couldn't think of anyone who would want him dead," she had said, although Lewis wondered if she wasn't happier he was gone. She acted like a woman for whom a huge burden had been lifted. As the hours went by, Lewis seemed to sense in her a freeing up of some kind of awful affliction, as if she had been told she had a terminal illness, but then experienced a miracle cure. The stiffness with which she held herself seemed to relax, her hands which she held clasped tightly in her lap eventually loosened, and she even lifted them to her hair and smoothed it back.

"I must look a mess," she said, unexpectedly, a small smile coming to her mouth.

"Have you heard from your son?" Lewis asked.

She shook her head.

"Are you worried about him?"

Lewis received the same head shake.

"Is there somewhere he might have gone? A friend he might have sought out?"

"I don't know of any friends. He was a loner."

"I talked yesterday to David Otter who said he and your son were friends."

"Who?"

"You don't know that name?"

Again she shook her head.

Detective Davis drove Mrs. Parsons home after Lewis finished his interview with her. Lewis watched through his office window as they left.

Maybe, he thought, Sandy might get something out of Mrs. Parsons in the car. He wasn't counting on it. The secrets in this family and how they might be related to Parsons' murder would have to be revealed through another source. Mrs. Parsons wasn't talking, her son had fled and her daughter was unavailable at this time. Lewis thought again of David Otter who claimed to be the Parsons boy's friend. He wanted to follow up with David soon. Maybe he should do it now, instead of talking with people at the high school.

When Lewis jumped into his car he noted that it was after three in the afternoon. He guessed that school had let out and all the students would be gone by the time he arrived. Afterschool activities would be in swing, however, but since he didn't know if David Otter would be a part of any of these, he decided to put off his attempt to find the young man today at the tribal school. Instead he headed to the public high school. Maybe he'd get lucky and find Owen Parsons had fled to school and was seen there by teachers or by the assistant principal. He checked his notebook for the man's name. He never signaled ahead his intent to discuss a case with a source or a witness. He liked to take the party by surprise to observe the reaction to his probing.

Assistant Principal Harold Bundy was still in his office. Lewis found him packing up his possessions, and Lewis noted his dress shirt fitted him tightly across a muscular chest and his biceps bulged against his shirt sleeves. The man must have spent considerable time in the gym to perfect that build, thought Lewis. He was a handsome man with high cheekbones and a strongly sculpted chin. He wore his brown hair longer than Lewis would have expected of someone in the position of a school administrator, but times had changed since Lewis was in high school when anyone in a position of authority wore his hair short. Lewis sighed and bushed his hair back from his forehead. He needed a haircut, and he was feeling old. At Lewis' rap on the doorframe, Bundy called "come in" without turning around.

"I don't mean to interrupt your work." Lewis presented his identification and introduced himself.

"I figured someone from the police would show up today, but I expected you earlier," Bundy said.

The implication that Lewis was somehow slow to do his job made him bristle. "There is a family involved. They come first, even in police work."

"Of course," said Bundy, his eyes warming at the mention of the family. "How is Mrs. Parsons doing? I thought my wife and I would drop by tonight."

"She's coping," said Lewis. "Packing up your office to move it?"

"I thought I'd get things rearranged now, so that we could reestablish a schedule as soon as possible," Bundy said, clearing his throat.

"You'll be the new principal then?" asked Lewis.

"It will be temporary until we find another person to fill the position. I called the school board today, and they told me to go ahead with the move."

Interesting, thought Lewis. The guy was certainly eager to take over the dead man's job and his office. Hmm. He called the board and not the other way around. A real eager beaver.

"Will you apply for the job?" asked Lewis.

"Certainly," he said in reply, as if Lewis had asked the most obvious of questions.

"Can we talk in your office...one of your offices?" said Lewis.

Bundy signaled Lewis down the hall and into the principal's office as if to impress upon Lewis his new identity with its improved status. Lewis took the move as Bundy's necessary play in a game of one-upmanship with Lewis.

"So, tell me a little about Principal Parsons. How long has he been here and where did he come from?" Lewis would recheck all the information he obtained through Bundy by asking the same question of others at the school as well as ask for school records. Or subpoena them if necessary.

Bundy leaned back on the desk and appeared willing if not eager to talk about the former principal. He said Parsons had taken the position about three years prior, having come from another principal job.

"Mason City is a much larger school. The pay had to be more also. Why would he take this job?" asked Lewis.

"He wanted to raise his children in a smaller place, one without gang issues, drugs and other crime."

As if any town in America could get away from the real world of crime. How well Lewis knew that, but he nodded and made a note in his book. He looked at Bundy and let the silence stretch between them.

"He was highly recommended. The school board supported hiring him unanimously."

"What did you think of him?" asked Lewis.

"He was very task-oriented. The office and the school ran very efficiently."

"Meaning he spent all his time behind his desk and not in the halls with teachers and students."

Bundy gave Lewis a half-smile. "Principals differ in how they run a school."

"But that's not the way you'll do it, is it? And that's not your preference for how a school should be run."

"No, but I'm a different kind of person."

"Did you know the family? Mrs. Parsons and the children?"

"Not well at all. Well, I did have some issues with Owen, the son. He was a troubled boy when he came here. I think he's better now. He's made friends."

"So, because his father was the principal, any issues with the children would have landed on your desk?"

"Yes."

"But you never conferred with either of the Parsons about their son?'

"No."

"That's hard to fit with your philosophy of being a hands-on kind of administrator."

"There was no need. Owen joined a few clubs and settled down soon."

Lewis left after several more questions. His cop instinct told him this guy was hiding something about Parsons also. The teachers he encountered as they were leaving to head home knew little about Parsons, saying he conferred with them in monthly meetings but they never saw him much on a day-to-day basis. Was that just an administrative approach as Bundy seemed to want Lewis to believe, was Parsons lazy or uninterested in the job or was there something else going on with Parsons? Who knew this man? *Maybe I'll have to talk with members of the board. They hired the guy. They must have known what they were getting. Or I'll have to visit his old school.* Lewis knew little about teaching other than what he'd experienced when he was in school. That was a long time ago. Who did he know who had teaching experience? He wasn't interested in the classroom aspect of education. He wanted to know how schools operated. He got in his car and realized Emily had left the headband she used to hold back her hair on the seat earlier today. He tried to tell himself her experience in a preschool setting wasn't relevant to his case, but he failed. It was the best he could do right now. Perhaps she knew someone he could talk with, anyone other than her. She made him tongue-tied, got him feeling all lusty and male with her innocent blue eyes, then made him angry with her nosiness. The woman had an opinion on everything, but mostly on how he conducted his cases. *I should talk to anyone but her*, he thought.

※

Someone else apparently thought Emily might know a thing or two about kids. The phone was ringing as Emily pulled into her drive after her evening with the St. Simontons. She struggled with her key in the door as the ringing stopped and her cell buzzed in her purse. She extracted the cell and heard Clara's voice at the other end of the call.

"You sound out of breath. Did I catch you with company?" Clara asked, a suggestive note in her voice.

"No. I pulled into my drive and heard the landline ring."

"That was me, too."

"This must be important."

"You asked me about Owen Parsons earlier?"

"And."

"Can you come over here?"

"What's up?"

"When I got home late from the office, Owen was sitting on my front steps waiting for me. We've been talking. You're the one who knows about kids...."

"I worked with preschoolers, not teens, Clara. You were a mother. You got Darren through adolescence."

"I was a lousy mother. He got himself through adolescence, and not very well," Clara said, making reference to Darren's history with drugs while in high school.

"Okay. Sit tight. Challenge him to a game of chess until I get there. I swore I'd stay out of this murder investigation, and you're pulling me into it."

As she got back in her car and thought about the phone call, Emily realized she was being unfair to Clara accusing her of dragging Emily into Lewis' investigation. Lewis already had done that by asking Emily to learn more about Melissa DeVry. He certainly didn't intend that she follow up on what she learned about Mrs. DeVry on the phone, but that wasn't Emily's nature. She tried to convince herself she was just sniffing around the periphery of the case and only because she couldn't believe Toby Sands could have a lady friend. She had to know more about her, and while she and the St. Simontons were talking tonight, an absolutely brilliant plan popped into Emily's head. So it hadn't been Clara who was drawing Emily into the case. She had to admit she herself was guilty for hatching a scheme to learn more about the DeVry family. *Besides*, she said to herself, *Rodney and Daisy thought it sounded like fun.*

Driving to Clara's, Emily finally admitted the ugly truth to herself. Like Lewis she knew that if Toby was hanging around the reenactment, it wasn't because he was a history buff. It had to be something criminal. Emily disliked the ugly toad so much she'd go out of her way to see him in jail, this time for good. Legal, schmegal. It was simple for Emily. This was revenge for Toby's collusion in kidnapping her daughter and for trying to help Naomi's husband sell her and Naomi to white slavers. This time she'd get the tubby troll. There didn't have to be any connection to the murder of Principal Parsons. It was enough for Emily to believe that Toby was up to no good.

❈

Emily entered Clara's living room with its dazzling display of Clara's photography on every wall, yet Emily never found the place over-decorated. Instead it seemed as if she was walking into the best that the wilds of rural Florida had to offer: unending pastures with cattle and cowboys, birds wading the canals or flying over the Big Lake at sunset, dawn breaking amidst a steamy swamp, and an alligator rising out of the water with a water hyacinth resting on its nose. Emily looked for the usual feeling of peace that came to her when she entered this room, but the young man sitting on the couch, his hands to his mouth biting his nails, disrupted the serenity usually present. His eyes were a deep blue, but there was no tranquility in them. They seemed to bulge out of their sockets, filled with fear. A chess set sat on the coffee table, but Emily could tell from the position of the pieces on the board that the players hadn't gotten very far into their game.

"Hi," Emily said, holding out her hand. "I'm Clara's friend Emily. I see you're a chess player." She sat on the couch next to him.

"Miz Clara said you knew my father."

"Not well. He was in the reenactment, and so were my daughter and I. I'm sorry you lost him."

"Really? I guess if you can say that you didn't know him at all."

Okaaay, thought Emily.

"You two didn't get along, I guess."

"I hated him. So did my mother, and my sister was afraid of him."

"Clara said on the phone that you ran off when the police arrived at the house to talk with you. That wasn't the smartest move, you know. Cops tend to think the worst of people they're trying to question when they disappear."

"I know stuff about his death."

"All the more reason you should talk to them. Much as you disliked your father, I'm sure you want to find out who killed him, don't you?"

"I think I know who killed him."

Emily caught her breath in shock, but she also picked up uncertainty in his tone of voice.

"You aren't sure though, are you?"

He shook his head and brought his hands up to rub his face.

Clara dropped into the chair across from the couch. "Tell Emily what you're thinking. She's worked with the police here in town on other cases. She'll be able to help you sort this out."

"What other cases?" asked Emily. *What was Clara thinking?*

"You know," said Clara. "the ones where you helped Detective Lewis."

"I never..." began Emily, but Clara gave her an eye roll, signaling to her to be quiet and go along with the ruse.

"You know the ones where the detective had you track down clues."

If Owen Parsons hadn't been so distressed he might have picked up the hidden messages flying between the two women, but he seemed to be wrapped up in his own world.

"If I talk to you, do I have to talk to the police?" he asked.

"If there's anything you know that could lead to finding his killer, you'll have to tell the police."

"Can't you tell them what I say?"

"No, Owen. That's not how it works," said Clara.

"Will you be my lawyer?"

"If we think you need one, we'll work it out," Clara assured him, then turned to Emily. "He's eighteen, an adult, so he can make up his own mind whether he wants to talk with us."

"I was about to ask," Emily said.

"I saw that detective who came to the house today. He's one scary dude," said Owen.

"Yes, he is. And he's pretty smart, too. Whatever you're covering up, he's sure to find out, and that won't help you or your family," said Emily.

Owen looked at her for a long while, then dropped his shoulders in resignation. "Okay. We moved here from Mason City where all my friends lived. I didn't know anyone here. I was kept back a year in school the first year here."

"Why was that?" Emily asked.

"I was disruptive in the classroom. I was expelled for three months for threatening a teacher."

Emily wondered what the threat was all about, but decided she could find that out some other time. She'd gotten him to talk, and she wanted him to keep telling his story in his own way.

She nodded. "Go on."

"I met a guy at chess club when I returned to school. You know him, Miz Clara."

"David Otter," said Clara. "The two of you became good friends and equally good rivals in the game." She smiled. Owen returned the smile with a tiny one of his own.

"I don't know how but David seemed to understand what I was going through. Even though he wasn't in the same school, it made things easier for me. I looked forward to chess club, and David introduced me to his family. They accepted me."

"Your parents must have been relieved," Emily observed.

"They didn't know. I kept them out of my life. Why should I tell them about what I was doing?

They didn't care." The last sentence was said with bitterness in his voice.

Emily was about to say something when Owen interrupted her. "Don't say I was being unfair to them. Believe me. They didn't care. They had their own problems to cope with. Dad handled the situation by avoiding us. He did his job at the school, then came home, went into his office there and read or watched television, then went to bed early, got up again and did it all again."

"That must have been hard on your mother," said Clara.

"You have no idea. At first, she was hurt, then she got angry when she attempted to break through to him. Finally, she acted resigned to the situation. I think she was until just recently. She told me a couple of weeks ago that she wished he was dead."

"So you think..." said Emily.

"She killed him. I don't blame her. I'm glad he's gone too. I would have helped her do it if she'd asked for help, but she didn't."

"Hating someone and killing them are two different things, Owen," said Emily.

He shook his head. "I'm worried the cops will find out she's responsible. She lied to them."

"Lied about what?"

"She told the detective that she didn't attend the reenactment, that she was in Orlando this weekend, but that's not true."

"How do you know?"

"She left the Orlando condo on Sunday morning and went to the reenactment. I saw her there. I followed her in my truck."

CHAPTER 9

Did Owen understand that his confession about his mother being at the reenactment implicated him also? wondered Emily. A boy filled with that much hate...

Emily and Clara exchanged knowing glances.

"You didn't see your mother shoot your father, did you?" asked Emily.

"No, but she took Dad's gun with her. I saw her put it in her purse when she left the house. I tried to follow her when we got to the reenactment, but I lost her in the crowd and the rain made it difficult to see."

"What kind of gun was it?" Clara asked.

"It was a revolver of some sort. I don't know much about guns."

"That's all the more reason for you to talk with the detective and tell him what you've told us," said Clara.

Emily's gaze shifted to the glass-faced gun cabinet on the living room wall. If there was anyone who knew about guns, it was Clara. She was the one who taught Emily to shoot at the nearby range.

"But you're not certain about what kind of a weapon was used, Clara," Emily said.

"You've got an in with Lewis. Ask him," Clara said.

Emily's mouth dropped open. "You've got to be kidding!"

Owen began pacing around the room. "I'm no dummy. I know if I talk to the police they're going to want to see the gun Mom took with her. I could be turning my mother in for murder."

"Okay. I'll try to find out what the police know about the weapon, but regardless of what that turns out to be, you can't keep what you know from the authorities forever. Lewis will find out, and then you could be charged with impeding a murder investigation. Isn't that right, Clara?"

Clara nodded.

"Fine, but how do I go back to my house? My mother will guess something is up," Owen said.

"I'm guessing she'll be too distraught and overwhelmed by your father's death to notice that you're hiding something," said Clara.

"Yeah, you're right. Why should she pay attention to me now when she hasn't given me a notice in months?" Owen's mouth snapped closed in a grimace.

"Detective Lewis will track you down soon, and then you'll have to deal with him. Don't lie to him, but..." Clara said.

"...but maybe don't mention the gun if you can avoid it," said Emily.

"I gotta go," said Owen. "Thanks for the advice." He avoided eye contact with Emily and Clara and headed out the door and was headed down the walk before they could ask him any more questions about the family.

"I don't like where this is going," said Clara. "I have a feeling he's not going home, but will try to hide out. Let's wait for a half hour, then I'll call his mother to see if he's there."

"What will you say?"

"I'll ask for him and, if she says he's not at home, I'll identify myself and say I have a message about chess club. If he's there, I'll tell him I was checking to be certain he made it home. If I have to leave a message with his mother or on the answering machine, I'll say I understand if he can't attend the next chess club meeting because of his father's death. That should work."

"Good."

"Now you better do your part."

"My part?" asked Emily

"Get Lewis to talk about the murder, specifically about the weapon responsible for Parsons' death." Clara's voice held a note of sexual innuendo.

Emily caught on to what Clara was suggesting. "I'm not seducing that guy. Besides he's much too professional to spill anything about a case," said Emily, outraged that Clara thought he would fall for Emily's charms and give away information that only the cops had access to.

"You won't have to seduce him. He has bedroom eyes for you every time the two of you meet. Just say 'yes' when he asks. He trusts you."

Emily slammed out the door with Clara a few steps behind her reminding her that she'd volunteered to help.

"I did not volunteer. You volunteered me," Emily yelled back as she opened her car door.

"Well, giddyap, gal. You're on the hook here to get that detective in a romantic mood." Clara turned back toward the house, but not before Emily saw the smile on her face. She's enjoying this, Emily thought. She thinks it's funny that I might be pushed into getting Lewis hot and bothered enough to spill information about this case. He's not that kind of guy. Besides, he probably doesn't speak of anything when he's engaged in...uh, engaged. He's a man of few words most times. Emily pulled out of the drive and considered the situation. Maybe getting Lewis to warm up wasn't such a bad idea—for her own enjoyment, of course, not to use the man in any other way.

※

Lewis groaned as he sank into bed. He had a number of lines of inquiry he could follow in this case. There was Toby's involvement. He'd like nothing better than to squeeze that fat, little hobgoblin until his eyes bugged out and something close to the truth spilled from his ugly lips. Mrs. Parsons was another issue. She was holding something back, something that had to do with family and perhaps her husband's past position in Mason City. Tomorrow he'd get the report from ballistics and find out the weapon used. He'd probably have to make a trip north to Mason City. Experience told him it was always better to show up in person to talk with potential sources. Seeing someone's face didn't guarantee they'd tell you the truth, or that you could read their expression well enough to determine if they were lying, but there was more information to work with other than words.

Emily knew that. She said children were great observers of adult behavior because their vocabulary wasn't as extensive as their parents' or teachers'. Kids had to read all the cues to understand what adults meant—the way people held their bodies, if they licked their lips, shuffled their feet, made no eye contact or their gaze was too direct. Cops could learn a lot from preschoolers. Dang. Why did he have to begin thinking about Emily? Now he'd never get to sleep. He pounded his pillow with his fist and rolled onto his side. He did this over and over again during the night, but the image of Emily's blue eyes, her delicate but strong hands, her tiny feet and the way her blond hair escaped her ponytail and curled around her ears kept the sandman away until the early hours of the morning. *She's more disturbing to a cop's sleep than any murder case.*

While the dawn found Lewis exhausted, Emily caught a break. A good night's sleep did wonders for the mind, she thought. She shuffled through some old papers including sympathy cards she had received when her life partner, Fred, died of a heart attack several years ago. *And here it is.* She extracted the card and punched the name and address into an online search on her phone, found the number and connected.

"Martin?" she said. "You sound sleepy."

"Emily?" He sounded both groggy and surprised.

"Yes. Hi. How are you? Did I catch you at a bad time?"

"It's kind of early."

"What...?" Emily looked at her watch. "I'm sorry. I thought you'd be an early riser because of your job."

Martin Rudolf was an old friend of Emily's—actually he was an old boyfriend of hers. They had dated on and off before she met Fred and retired from her preschool position. Martin had been the principal in the school system of which her preschool was a part. Although many years had passed since they had last talked, they'd maintained contact through letters and more recently emails, although after Fred entered the picture, their emails were less regular. Emily knew Martin was married when the two of them were in the same school system, but the relationship didn't last long. He hadn't mentioned a woman in his life in the past few years, but Emily wondered if she might have intruded on his personal life. Maybe he was married again, and Emily's call would have been viewed as inappropriate, especially as it was—Emily noted—only six in the morning.

"No, really it's fine. I was up but I hadn't had a chance to make my coffee."

"I can call back later."

"No, no. It's nice to hear from you." His tone of voice said it was really, really nice to hear from her.

Oh, oh, thought Emily. Had she goofed? Did Martin still have a thing for her? Would her call be misinterpreted? She'd better get right to the reason she called.

"You're the assistant superintendent of the school system in Mason City, right?"

"Yes." Now there was suspicion in his voice.

"The reason I'm calling is about someone who once worked in the system, Leonard Parsons."

"Go on." The earlier warmth in his voice was gone, replaced by coldness, and, if Emily wasn't mistaken, the coldness wasn't just because he was let down she wasn't trying to rekindle a fire between them. It was something else.

She hurried on. "He's the principal here, or I should say he was. He was killed this weekend. Maybe you read something in the papers about it?"

"No, I didn't, but, Emily, if you're looking for information about him, it would be unethical for me to talk about him professionally."

"How about personally? You must have known him when he worked in the Mason City system."

There was silence from his end of the call as if he was mulling something over.

"Look, I'd love to get together for lunch or coffee. I know it's been a while, but I can drive up there, perhaps today?" She knew she was rushing him, but she wanted to follow up on the interest he showed early in the phone call. Besides, she didn't have another day off at the bar this week, and there were other avenues of inquiry she needed to pursue.

"Why are you so interested anyway?"

Why was she so interested? Was it because of her curiosity, the fact that Parsons was one in a line of dead bodies she'd stumbled onto, or was she still trying to outdo Detective Lewis? If the latter, what was that all about?

"It's a long story. It's better I tell you in person. *By then,* she thought, *I'll think of a good reason why I'm pursuing this.*

"Sure, why not. Let's do lunch. I've got some time coming to me. How about I drive down to see you today?"

Emily let out the breath she'd been holding and worried that she was taking to conning desirable men out of information about murders by using her charms too easily. *But it's murder, Emily,* she told herself. She shivered at the memory of lying face-to-face with Leonard Parsons' dead body. She shrugged away the image, and she and Martin made arrangements to meet.

And tonight, she reminded herself after she hung up, she, Daisy and Rodney were about to get religion. She hoped Detective Lewis was having as successful a day as she was. She smiled at herself in the mirror, high-fived the image and felt like a million until the water went off midway through her shower. *What was it about showers and her anyway?*

——❈——

Clara's shower was long and hot. She toweled off, dressed and headed to her law office where she was to meet with her dad this morning. Clara had left her previous job as manager of the Big Lake Country Club to return to the law, the profession Clara had once abandoned—she had declared then—for good. Now she shared a small practice with her dad. Of course, while Clara operated out of an office she leased in downtown, her dad Hap continued to run his part of the business from his room at the Blue Heron Retirement Facility. The facility had no idea he was using his room in such a manner. Hap said it was none of their business, his usual approach to anyone who tried to tell him he was doing anything illegal.

"I'll be the judge of that," he'd say, chuckling. "Get it? I'll be the 'judge.'"

Hap had come to Emily's defense when Fred's ex-wife took her to court to sue her for Fred's estate, an absurd and petty gesture on the wealthy ex-wife's part, but in keeping with the shrew's acidic personality. Contesting the will was for spite on the part of the ex-wife, while it was a matter of survival, economic survival, for Emily. Emily never knew whether the outcome of the case was due to Hap's expertise or pure luck, but she had a soft spot in her heart for the old gentleman. She only wished he would stop wearing those white suits he'd un-packed from mothballs. The naphtha was enough to choke an alligator. Maybe that was intentional on Hap's part, keeping the opposition at a distance.

"Dad here yet?" asked Clara, taking the cup of coffee offered her by her secretary and gal Friday, Mona Sparks, or "Sparky" as she was known to her friends. Others respectfully called her Miz Mona. She was in her early thirties with long dark hair and large blue eyes. Clara couldn't have asked for a more efficient secretary nor one who could handle her father's guff without insulting him.

"He called and said he was tied up for a while, but would be over soon," Sparky said.

Clara considered the message. Did it mean he was conducting business of his own or, more likely, was he engaged with one of the blue-haired ladies from the retirement center? He had quite the reputation for amorous cavorting. Just then the door opened and Hap entered with a look on his face so jolly that Clara knew a legal matter could never have accounted for that grin. He sauntered over to his daughter and gave her a hug.

"Spreading the love, are you, Dad?"

He winked and headed toward Sparky's desk.

"Keep your physical self to yourself," Sparky said. "You smell like cheap cologne."

"It's my current squeeze's signature scent," he said.

"It smells like swamp gas," said Sparky.

"Aw, Sparks. You're just jealous." He tossed his straw plantation owner's hat onto a peg on the wall by the door.

"I think it's a definite improvement over moth balls," said Clara. "C'mon in. We need to get started on that estate issue."

"I heard about Leonard Parsons getting offed at the reenactment. I assume our Emily had a hand in discovering the body?"

"More than," said Clara. "In her usual way, she made primo contact with it. Detective Lewis helped."

"Now I assume she'll be helping him find the killer."

"Umm hmm," Clara replied, refusing to meet his eye.

"So you're involved in some way, too? Oh, goody. An inside track. I hate being left out of local criminal matters. We do get our share of deaths at the old geezers' home, but most of them are only the fault of foul play on the part of someone's ticker, not because a resident took a knife or a gun to them. Not that we don't have our share of enmity among the residents, but I guess everyone is just too old and tired to take any kind of action. Except for me, of course. I'm the geriatric version of up and at 'em."

"It's a retirement center or facility, not a 'home.' You're going to kill yourself, Dad, if you don't slow down," Clara warned.

"Yeah, but he'll die in bed, the way a lot of men would like to go," said Sparky, a twinkle in her eye.

"You busy tonight, Sparky?" Hap asked. "My lady love will be out of town, and I'm betting I'll be feeling lonely...and friendly." He waggled his snow white eyebrows at her with a leer on his face.

"You old ram," Sparky said. "I'm forty years your junior."

"I can still keep up," Hap insisted.

"Maybe so, but my fiancé might have something to say about it."

"Bring him along. Maybe I can teach him a thing or two."

"Dad," said Clara. "We've got work to do." She gestured toward her office.

Hap followed, then turned back toward Sparky and said, "This is a one-time offer, you know."

"Just like it was last time," Sparky said. The back and forth between her and Hap was ongoing, and both would have felt slighted if the proposition wasn't extended and Sparky hadn't turned it down.

As Hap and Clara settled at the conference table with the papers spread out before them, the door opened and Sparky stuck her head in. "Oh, I forgot. The Parsons kid called. He wants to talk to you. I told him you were booked solid today, but he sounded distressed. Maybe you can call him back. He left his cell number. It's on your desk."

"Parsons kid?" asked Hap.

"Yeah, he's in the chess club."

"Now I get why you're so eager to get to work and not talk about the murder. I was right. Not only does Emily have her finger in this pie, but so do you."

Clara avoided her father's gaze once more and said, "Speaking of pie, there's some of Vicki's Key lime pie in the office fridge. Want a piece?"

"You can't buy me off that easy, gal. Of course, I want a piece. And I also want to know what's going on in the murder. I never liked Principal Parsons."

"Really, Dad. Tell me more." Clara thought by getting her father talking about Parsons, she could avoid telling him about Owen Parsons' visit last night.

"Not until I get my pie."

She got up to go to the fridge.

"And not until you tell me what your part is in all this." He sat back in his chair and grinned at her.

⸻

When Detective Lewis arrived in Mason City to talk with the school officials there, he found the assistant superintendent, who was the person the school board referred him to, was away for the day. When he pressed them for someone else to provide him with information, he was told everything had to go through the assistant superintendent. Lewis' usual drop-by approach caught him up, and he was left with nothing. He begrudgingly made an appointment with the assistant superintendent for the next day, and headed out on the two-hour trip back to his office, grumbling the entire way. He wasn't getting the rest he needed. Murder investigations always robbed him of his sleep, and if they included Emily as part of the case, it only added to his worry and inability to fall asleep. She's always told him she could take care of herself, but he never believed it. *Believe it, buddy. Who was the one who got shot in the last case? Not Emily.* He rubbed the ridge of scar tissue left in his arm where the bullet had entered, an unpleasant reminder that he had taken a chance he shouldn't have. His stomach grumbled. It would be early afternoon when he arrived back in town. Maybe he should stop at the Biscuit for lunch.

❈

The hostess showed him to a table in the main dining room. A couple seated in the far corner of the room caught his attention. Emily Rhodes and some good-looking guy he didn't recognize. Emily's eyes locked with his. He saw a flush work its way up her cheeks, then she dropped her gaze as if she hadn't seen him. What was the snoopy little gal up to now?

CHAPTER 10

L ewis wasn't about to let this one pass. He got up out of his chair and approached Emily's table.

"Hi there," he said with a smile. "I don't believe we've met. I'm Detective Stanton Lewis." He held out his hand to the other man, who stood, returned the smile, and they shook.

"I'm Martin Rudolf." Rudolf was as tall as Lewis. He was graying at the temples, but he had a full head of dark hair, a cleft in his strong chin and full lips. A good-looking guy. Just the sort Emily would like, Lewis thought.

"You new around here?" Lewis asked.

"Am I under investigation, detective?" Rudolf asked. He continued to smile broadly, but there was a note of uneasiness in his voice.

"Don't be silly, Martin," said Emily. "Detective Lewis is the suspicious type by profession as you'd guess. Martin, for your information, detective, is an old friend of mine. He's just visiting."

"From Mason City, is it?" Lewis said.

The smile was now gone from Rudolf's face, and his eyes narrowed as he took half a step backwards.

"Look, I'm sorry to surprise you this way, but I just got back from there. In fact, I wanted to talk with you, but your office said you were out for the day. I set up an appointment with you for tomorrow, but since you're here...."

"We're having lunch," Emily said.

"So am I. I'll join you." Lewis pulled up an empty chair and watched Emily's face go white with anger. "Or am I intruding?"

"Not at all, detective. Let me lay a little surprise on you then. You want to talk with me about Leonard Parsons, recently killed here."

"Emily told you," Lewis said.

"I did. And for your information, Detective Lewis, I do not welcome your intrusion into my lunch. I fully understand that was your intention, to annoy me, but could you just go away? You can interrogate Martin after lunch."

Lewis didn't let on that Emily had done a good job of putting him in his place, something she was good at. He rose from his chair, tipped his hat to her and returned to his table where he changed chairs so that he was facing Emily and Martin's table. He was only partially annoyed with himself for acting in such an adolescent manner. Making Emily uncomfortable was always fun. He wondered why that was the case, but dismissed any explanations having to do with how he felt about her and bit into his burger, catching the juices with a napkin as they were about to stain his shirt. He congratulated himself on acting so cool. No need to ruin the image by slobbering all over himself.

As irritated as she was at Lewis' intrusion, Emily was rather pleased that the two men clearly didn't take to one another, and she knew the reason had everything to do with her.

"He's staring at us," said Martin.

"Yes," replied Emily, hiding her pleasure by raising her glass to her lips.

"I'm not really comfortable having a cop's eyes drilling holes in me while I'm trying to eat. What is it with that guy, anyway? Are the two of you a thing?"

"Not really." Dragging Lewis into the shower didn't constitute a thing, did it? "Look, let's finish our food and drive out to the boat launch at the lake. Maybe we can see some large gators there."

"So, any of them carry badges?" asked Martin.

Emily gave him a punch on his arm, and they both laughed. Lewis' gaze left his food at the sound and rested again on the twosome. Martin and Emily signaled for their check. Lewis did likewise. The three of them walked out of the restaurant at the same time.

"Nice meeting you, Melvin," said Lewis. "I guess we'll talk tomorrow, although you could stop by my office this afternoon. It would save me a lot of trouble."

"I know, Detective Lyle. I'll see you tomorrow," Martin replied.

Emily and Martin watched the detective get into his car and leave.

"I'm not certain you should have refused to meet with him like that," Emily said.

"Did I refuse? Maybe I didn't understand what he was suggesting just like neither of us heard each other's names."

Emily gave him another playful punch on his well-muscled arm. Martin reached out for her and gave her a hug. Did Lewis see that in his rearview mirror, Emily wondered as her gaze followed Lewis' car down the road.

⚜

"So, Martin, what about it? I know you can't say anything about Parsons' record at your school, and I wouldn't want you to break the law, but is there anything you can tell me about the guy? Someone disliked him enough to kill him. Can you think of anyone who fits that description?"

Emily and Martin walked along the seawall near the boat launch. In front of them the water sparkled in the sunlight, obscuring its usual tea color. A breeze blew off the lake, ruffling Emily's hair and providing welcome coolness in the heat and humidity of midday.

"I don't understand why you're so interested," he said. "I mean aside from falling on the body. I'd think you'd want to forget about the whole thing after an experience like that."

What could she tell Martin? She'd had a few experiences just like that.

"It leaves an impression that's hard to wipe out of your mind." She hesitated. What could she tell him to make him understand her obsession with this case when she had difficulty wrapping her own head around it. "I met Parsons' son Owen. He seems like a troubled boy. I'd like to help him if I can."

"By digging dirt on his dead father?"

"I think he already knows the dirt. I don't, but I think some adult should know what's going on and support the kid. His mother seems to be no help."

"No, she wouldn't be."

"You've met her then?" asked Emily, excited that she might finally get some answers. She turned and faced Martin. "Tell me what you know."

Earlier Martin seemed to be enjoying his time with Emily, but now he looked as if he wanted to run away. *What's he hiding?* She decided being patient with him might work better than questioning him further.

"I'm not sure what I know is even relevant to this case, but if I tell you, I don't want you to speak to the authorities about it because I'll just deny I told you anything. Besides there's no record of it."

"Record of what?" asked Emily.

"Sexual abuse."

Martin's story shocked Emily, not that she didn't know that principals, teachers and others in positions of authority sometimes took advantage of students they should be protecting. What shocked

Emily to her core was that the school system kept silent, filed no charges and let him leave there with letters of recommendation.

"Why would they do that?" asked Emily. "What about the children he abused? Didn't anyone care to help them?"

"I know of only one. Her parent came to us to tell us about Parsons' inappropriate behavior."

"But Parsons broke the law, and the system broke the law in hiding it."

"I know, Emily, but I'm afraid to tell you it's done all the time. Parents are often willing to back off contacting the authorities. They don't want their kids subjected to testifying in court, which is what they would have to do, you know that."

Emily stopped walking and stared out across the lake. Parsons should pay for what he did, violating the trust of the children. Maybe he did pay, she thought. With his life.

"You have to tell Detective Lewis this, you know," she said.

"There is nothing to tell. There's no record to back up my story. For all you know, I've made this up."

Emily whirled on him. "But you didn't, did you?"

"No."

"And you're more involved in this than you've told me, aren't you? I know you and Lewis got off on the wrong foot, and that's because of me, but talk to him. He'd find a way to handle it. And he'll do it legally."

Martin laughed. "Really? Because if it gets out that I told the detective or anyone about this, I could lose my job. I knew about what Parsons did, but a deal was struck."

"A deal?" said Emily, horrified at the use of the word to describe school officials turning their backs on children subjected to sexual abuse.

"A parent came into the superintendent's office. The two men were golf partners, and the parent was also a member of the school board. He said his daughter came to him with a story about Parsons making a sexual advance. I don't know the details, but he said he wanted Parsons fired. The superintendent told him that it was a criminal matter, would be reported to the police, and procedures set up by the school would be followed, but the guy said no police. If the school went to the cops, his daughter would deny anything happened."

"How did you find out about this?" asked Emily, becoming more and more upset with the story.

"The superintendent called me into his office. I think he wanted someone to support his decision to go along with his buddy. I really think he thought he would be protecting the child.'

"Oh, did you? And the super said nothing about your career, about a recommendation for his position when he retired if you went along?"

"You hate me, don't you?"

"That's not even relevant. You and your boss failed to protect the child whose parents entrusted you with her well-being. I'll bet I know how you handled Parsons. You told him nothing would go on his record if he resigned and took a job elsewhere. I'll bet he got a glowing recommendation from you, didn't he?"

"It's over now," Martin said. "If I tried to tell the truth, I'd lose my job and worse. Look what happened on those university campuses. Administrators and others lost their jobs and did prison time. And there was that politician who molested those boys when he was a wrestling coach. And that doctor."

"A lot of people could lose their jobs, and maybe they should," said Emily.

Martin's eyebrows raised in a shocked look.

"You know I'm right. You can't be proud of what the school administration decided to do—or failed to do. People broke the law and put children in jeopardy. Parsons went on to become the principal here without a blemish on his record. You can't honestly believe he stopped being a predator. You know better."

"It's out of my hands. Someone else made the decision to give Parsons a pass and let him move on. I've not heard a word of scandal about him here."

"Really, Martin? If you believed that, why are you trying to justify what happened now? To me?"

Martin ran his hands through his hair in a gesture of despair. "Leonard Parsons was a pig, the lowest of the low. He hurt everyone around him. I'm not unhappy he's dead, and if he was killed because of this, I'm even happier. He deserves what he got. Finally."

"You know that's not the way it should work. The inaction of the school system might have been a factor in his death. The suffering didn't end with his leaving Mason City. His family knows what he did. His son Owen knows. That poor kid."

"That poor kid may have finally taken action. He's a teen now, old enough to fire a gun and take his father's life."

No, no, no. Emily did not want to believe that. Someone else killed Parsons. She had to find out who.

Emily didn't remember much of what else she and Martin discussed. Her mind was too wrapped up with his story. She'd always respected him, but after what he'd told her, Emily needed to reassess Martin Rudolf. His behavior was inexcusable, and he knew it. That's why he minimized the part he played in letting Parsons off the hook.

"So I'll call you about our getting together soon, right?" asked Martin as he gave her a friendly kiss on the cheek.

She shuddered at his touch and stepped back. She got into her car and rolled down her window as Martin walked to his vehicle.

"Talk to Detective Lewis tomorrow," she said firmly.

"Or what?" he asked, both fear and anger registering on his face.

"Or you'll feel worse than you do now, hiding this for so long."

She had always thought of Martin as a kind, caring man. She hoped some of the old Martin remained, but she worried something else motivated his behavior and still operated to keep him silent. Was it only a matter of his losing his job if the truth came out, or had she misjudged the man he was all these years? If so, Emily wondered if she'd pushed him too hard. And she also worried that knowing the truth about Martin and about the kind of man Parsons was put her in a vulnerable position. She shook her head free of her worries. Martin wasn't the kind of man to harm her in any way. Was he? She shoved the story Martin told her to the back of her mind. It was up to him now.

She had a promising evening ahead. Whether she discovered something that helped find Parsons' killer or not, it was always fun to share a caper with Daisy and Rodney. Soul mates of snoopiness, they were as willing to stick out their necks for a good cause or even a bit of fun as she was. This night promised to deliver both. Tonight she would take the first step in finding out who killed Leonard Parsons. She reviewed what she had in mind for Daisy and Rodney.

Detective Lewis drove past the casino, then turned into Toby's driveway. He was in luck. Toby's truck was parked at the side of the house. Would the chubby ex-cop have company this afternoon, wondered Lewis. He hoped for a private talk with Toby without Toby's girlfriend around to interfere.

Lewis' knock on the door wasn't answered. He pounded more loudly a second time. Toby opened the door an inch.

"Oh, it's you. Whadya want?"

"Can I come in?" Lewis asked, shoving the door open with his shoulder. "Or were you busy praying again?" Lewis could see the shack was empty. Toby looked as if he had just gotten out of the unmade bed in the corner. His eyes were blood shot, his hair flattened on one side of his head, and he was barefoot. "Bad night?" asked Lewis, tossing his hat on a nearby chair.

"I work a late shift. A man's got to sleep some-time, and I got someplace to be in an hour or so."

"Work? Where?"

"I do some cleaning at the casino a few nights a week."

"Did your girlfriend use her influence there and get you the job?" asked Lewis. By the way Toby dropped his gaze and shuffled his feet, Lewis could tell he had hit the mark, and Toby was embarrassed that he had to get jobs through her.

"Yeah," he muttered. "So what?"

Lewis looked around the scantily furnished room and took a chair at the table. "Let's chat about the reenactment."

"Nothin' to say. I was hired there to do site clean-up. That's all. I had nothin' to do with that guy's death."

Lewis decided to take a chance. "But you knew Mr. Parsons, didn't you?"

Toby's eyes widened. "Why would you think that?"

"It could be because it's true."

"Yeah. So what?"

"You knew him, and it had nothing to do with working at the reenactment. What kind of business did you have with Mr. Parsons?"

"Protection."

Lewis didn't expect that answer. "What kind of protection?"

"He said someone was trying to kill him. He wanted me to find out who and to stick close to him in case the person tried."

Lewis suppressed a laugh. Toby Sands would be the last person Lewis would select for a bodyguard, but finding someone to do that kind of work would be difficult around here. Parsons couldn't afford to be picky. He probably thought he was hiring a retired cop instead of a dirty cop fired from his job and on probation pending further prosecution of previous criminal activities. The only reason Toby wasn't in jail right now was because he had cooperated with the police on a previous case—*not that he carried out that assignment well*, thought Lewis. Toby had tried to pin a murder on one of his relatives in that situation. Family loyalty, any kind of loyalty, wasn't Toby's thing.

"Not that hiring you wasn't a good idea, "Lewis lied, "but why didn't he bring this to the attention of the authorities?"

"I don't know the details, but he said he preferred to hire private protection."

"And he found you. How?"

Toby threw back his head and chest in an expression of defiance and pride. "I got contacts."

Lewis decided not to explore Toby's so-called contacts, and to focus on why Parsons needed someone to have his back.

"So were there threatening phone calls, letters, emails, what? How did he know someone was after him?"

"Like I said, I didn't ask for specifics, but I could tell he was worried."

Toby wasn't one to explore anything much except for the pay.

"You don't have the legal right to carry. How were you thinking of protecting him?"

"I got my ways. I was trained as a police officer, remember?"

Lewis remembered Toby on the force as his partner all too well. Anytime there was the threat of confrontation, Toby disappeared.

"How long did you follow him? Did you see anyone acting suspicious?"

"I just took on the job Sunday at the reenactment. It was hard to see anything in all that rain."

Lewis waited to let Toby think.

"Well, there was something. It looked to me as if Parsons was arguing with someone just before the battle began."

"Description?"

"I stayed back, not wanting to let the person see me."

"Male of female?"

"I'm thinking probably a woman."

"Hair color, build, height?"

"You were there. No one could see anything in the downpour."

"Why do you think it was a woman then?"

"Cuz she was wearing a rain slicker with a hood. It was blue with all them big yellow flowers on it."

"Sunflowers?"

Toby nodded. "And what guy would wear a slicker like that?'

"Anything else?"

"Yeah," Toby said. "You have no idea how upset I am."

"About what?"

"With Parsons dead, who's gonna pay me for my protection work? I'm out a lotta money." Toby kicked the table leg in anger and frustration. "Ow!" he yelled. "I almost broke my foot."

Lewis left him jumping around holding his foot. As he drove away he shook his head. *Just another job Toby failed at, but in this case, the guy he was hired to protect got killed.*

CHAPTER 11

She put the meeting with Martin behind her and turned up a song on the radio to drown out her thoughts about the conversation they'd had. She had a short shift today, unless Donald got wind of fish biting, then she might be stuck with his shift too. Her grin broadened as raindrops hit her windshield. Good. It was raining. Little chance of good fishing today. She reconsidered what she'd been thinking over the past several months: she should hire another part-time bartender for the club. Donald's first allegiance was to the fish he needed to catch. The job came second, making him unreliable. She'd put an ad in the newspaper tomorrow. If she got lucky, a plucky gal with the right credentials and lots of sass just meant to aggravate a man like Donald would apply. Then Emily and the new hire could gang up on Donald. *Not that I can't handle him by myself*, she thought.

She had successfully shoved Martin Rudolf's story to the back of her mind, but she wasn't so lucky not thinking about what she'd found in the wastebasket this morning. Was Naomi pregnant? Emily hadn't heard anything about a man in her daughter's life. It appeared Naomi was off men for now, needing time to recover from her abusive ex-husband. Naomi was a grown woman, and her life was her own, but Emily worried she might rebound with the first kind, eligible man she met. What she worried about most was that Naomi could end up in the same situation Emily did: having a child and finding it necessary to put the child up for adoption...as she did with Naomi. She never regretted her decision to have the baby, but her circumstances were special. Emily was fortunate in reconnecting with her daughter when Naomi was an adult. Now they had a close relationship, almost like mother and daughter. *It wasn't that close,* thought Emily, *not if Naomi was pregnant and hadn't said anything to Emily about it.*

Her thoughts were interrupted as she spied Donald's truck when she pulled into the country club parking lot. *What was he doing here now?*

"Donald," she said as she entered the bar. "This isn't your shift. You're scheduled for later."

"I was going to play a round, but it's raining too hard, so I thought I'd hang here until you came, and I could spend some time harassing you until my shift."

Emily knew he was joking—if Donald could be said ever to joke.

"Actually," he said, "I was wondering if you had plans after my shift tonight?"

Emily almost fell over in surprise. "Are you asking me out on a date?" she asked.

"Do I look demented? No, of course not. I need to drop my truck by the shop to repair the hitch on it later on, and I need a ride home."

"And then I suppose, I'll have to pick you up at the crack of dawn tomorrow to get the truck, right?"

"No, Miz smarty pants. I got a ride tomorrow. I need a lift tonight. Don't you listen good?"

"Look, I'd be glad to give you a lift, but I'm busy. Isn't there some one else you could ask?"

Donald seemed to roll this suggestion around in his head for a while, then he took out his cell phone and punched in a number, walking out of the bar area so that Emily couldn't hear who he was calling.

In several minutes her cell rang. Vicki was on the other end.

"Did you suggest Donald Green call me to ask me for a favor? I mean, I don't mind baking treats for the guy because he seems so appreciative, but..."

"I suggested he call someone other than me to help him out, but I had no idea he'd get in touch with you. Just tell the old lake rat no."

"I did, but I felt bad. He told me he doesn't have any friends..."

"He doesn't."

"Anyway, I thought I'd offer to make him his own Key lime pie. Naomi's here and she overhead the conversation so she offered to drive him home from the garage when he drops off his truck tonight. She said she'd bring the pie along. Things have a way of working themselves out, don't they?"

"So we're off the hook, but Naomi isn't?"

"She feels the same way I do about Donald. She thinks there's a heart of gold under all that steely exterior."

"You're both wrong. I wonder if he has any heart at all. Do robots come with hearts?"

"The guy has a soft spot for you. You are so mean, Emily Rhodes. Thank goodness your daughter isn't."

"Put Naomi on, would you?"

"Hi," said Naomi.

"Honey, you don't have to be nice to Donald. It won't change him, you know. His personality is set in stone and has been from the time he broke out of his egg or however he was born."

Naomi laughed. "I gather you won't be home tonight then?"

"I've got a date."

"With Lewis?" asked Naomi. Emily could hear the excitement in her voice.

"No. With Rodney and Daisy."

"You three are up to no good, aren't you?"

"Absolutely not. We're following up on a few leads in Parsons' death. I'll tell you all about it when I get home."

"Once I drop Donald off, I'm going to the coast to visit, uh, some friends." Before Emily could ask what friends, Naomi said, "See you tomorrow. Don't wait up for me."

"Naomi, we need to talk," Emily said, but Naomi had disconnected.

"What leads are you following up on?" asked Donald. She hadn't noticed he had come back into the bar and was standing behind her. "I'll bet Detective Lewis wouldn't like you snooping around his case."

"And I don't like you eavesdropping on my phone calls."

Donald's usual ball-bearing gray eyes softened a bit. "I worry about you, Emily. Maybe I could make some arrangements and come along with the three of you."

Emily tried to envision Donald at a revival meeting and failed. "I don't think this is your kind of adventure. You wouldn't fit in well. We're going undercover."

<hr />

Lewis pulled his car off onto a spit of gravel between Toby's house and the casino. The overhanging limbs of a live oak hid most of the vehicle from the road. Toby said he had "someplace to be," not that he was going to work. Lewis wondered where that someplace was. After fifteen minutes, Toby's battered truck appeared, the fender on the driver's side rattling as he hit bumps in the rutted road. Lewis followed, close enough not to lose him, but far enough back that Toby wouldn't notice the tail. Toby pulled into the casino and repeated what he did on Sunday night. He drove to the entrance and picked up Melissa, but this time he didn't pull onto the road and head back to his shack. He turned right out of the parking area, then right again onto the highway to Clewiston. This might be a worthless trip, thought Lewis, but his cop instincts told him that where there was Toby, there was something not right, something against the law going on. Lewis sat back in his seat preparing himself for a long evening and a late night. He sighed, outlining in his head the following day—a meeting with Martin Rudolf and another go at Mrs. Parsons and her son. He also reminded himself he needed to talk with David Otter, the son's friend. He remembered how disparaging Otter had sounded when Lewis had asked him about whether Owen Parsons was present at the reenactment to see his father playing the part of Zachary Taylor. It was clear from Otter's tone that there was trouble between Owen and his father, and Lewis wanted to know what kind of trouble. Enough trouble to turn Owen into a killer?

—❦—

"Donald wanted to come along tonight," said Emily as she, Rodney and Daisy drove the road to Clewiston. "I think he assumed we'd need protection."

"Oh, wouldn't that be wonderful," said Daisy, piloting the large, red Cadillac skillfully down the rain-swept road.

Rodney chuckled. "That would be Donald Green, probably armed with a fishing line with a large hook on the end of it."

"That's about it," said Emily.

"This is better," said Rodney, holding up a large revolver.

"Put that away," said Daisy. "Do you want to get us in trouble?"

"That would be, 'no, I want to get us *out* of trouble,'" said Rodney. "But I'll keep it under cover, in reserve." He tucked the gun away somewhere on his person.

"Okay, now we all know our parts, correct?" Emily asked.

Daisy and Rodney nodded.

"I'll stay out of sight while the two of you make the most obvious entrance you can. You are there to get the head guy's attention. Daisy, are you wearing your diamond rings? Let's see those beauties twinkle," Emily instructed.

Daisy held up her hand and twisted it back and forth so that the large rings caught the fading light from the setting sun.

"See if you can finagle a private audience with him after the performance while I have a look around the area after everyone has left. I'll bet he sees the two of you as ripe for the picking by a revival/salvation show. You want to get as close to the guy as you can, see what he's up to. I'm sure it's not healing or bringing souls to God."

"I'm not quite certain what you expect to find, Emily," said Daisy.

"Toby says he's turned his life around. Who believes that? He was at the reenactment. Lewis told me he was working there. I know Lewis finds Toby's recent metamorphosis as unlikely as do I. Toby's up to something, and it's just too much of a coincidence to believe the murder, Toby's work and his friendship with Melissa and her ex-con father are coincidental."

"But no guns?" asked Rodney.

"No!" said Emily.

"Only if absolutely necessary, dear," said Daisy, reaching over to pat his hand.

Emily wondered what she had unleashed.

"Where are we off to in all this rain?" asked Hap, riding shotgun in Clara's car.

"It's just a hunch, Dad, but Emily told me Toby's new girlfriend is the daughter of that preacher who has set up a revival tent in Clewiston. "He's an ex-con who says he's gotten right with God. I don't believe that, do you?"

"Nope. I always have trouble with folks who like to brag about their relationship with God. But I don't see how this will help Owen Parsons in any way."

"Toby Sands in the place a murder occurs? Toby Sands with an ex-con's daughter? There has to be some connection."

"And Detective Lewis knows all this?" asked Hap.

"Yes, of course. Well, he doesn't know about Owen and his mother being at the reenactment, although I encouraged Owen to talk with Lewis."

"But he won't."

"Of course he won't."

"We're going to get ourselves into trouble," said Hap, the concern in his voice barely covering the glee registered there.

"Maybe."

"Oh, goodie. I am so bored with chasing octogenarian tail around the home."

"That's a horrible thing to say. And it's a retirement facility," said Clara.

"Those ladies refer to me as an old boy toy. Besides, it's boring," said Hap in his defense.

＊

There was parking in the field next to where the tent had been set up, but the ground was muddy, and Daisy worried the car would get bogged down.

"I'll let you out on the road and find someplace better to leave the car," she said. "Emily you scamper out here where it's dark and the parked cars will hide you."

Emily scrambled out of the back seat, and her tiny figure was soon lost to view among the people and cars. Clara helped Rodney out of the car on the road and extracted his wheelchair from the trunk. She knew he'd have no trouble maneuvering the chair up the road and into the tent.

＊

By the time Daisy and Rodney entered the revival tent, the only chairs left were in the back.

"Wow," said Daisy. "I never imagined so many folks wanted to get right with God." People pushed around them, families with children, couples and small groups of individuals, some who wore long, white robes. Babies cried, children laughed and wriggled in their seats, while some adults bowed their heads in prayer. Men's aftershave and women's colognes mingled with the smell of sweat. Although the sides of the tent were open, not a breeze moved through the crowd.

Some people were being pushed in wheelchairs, others appeared to be blind and were led in by a friend or family member. Several individuals with developmental disabilities yelled nonsensical sounds, one young man slapping his head with his hands as his caretaker tried to stop him.

"I suddenly feel lucky, given my motorized wheelchair and my ability to take a few steps with help," said Rodney, "But some of these people are not so fortunate." His face reddened and his mouth snapped shut in an expression of anger. "Call me a man without God, but I can't believe this guy can really heal these people."

Daisy touched his shoulder. "Perhaps not, but maybe he can offer them some comfort by encouraging them to embrace his religious beliefs."

"Oh, you mean the beliefs that say 'Put another couple of fivers in the offering plate'?"

"Rodney!" said Daisy.

"Just saying." He rolled his chair up the aisle as far as he could, but, while some of the folks there tried to give him room to move past them, he and Daisy encountered two white-robed men standing like bodyguards between the stage and the front row of seats. The men were large and heavily muscled, and Daisy spotted an object that looked like a gun causing a bulge in the side of one of the men's robes.

"No room up here. These are reserved seats, pop," said the man whom Daisy thought was packing. His hand moved toward the side of his robe. "Back there." He gestured to the rear of the tent.

There's more than one way to disarm a guard, thought Daisy. She gave him one of her smiles, licked her full, red lips and said in her best southern accent, "Oh, right. We understand, but it's so hard for him to see way back there. Couldn't we just squeeze him in at the far end of this row? I'm not real good at pushing my way into crowds. I promise we won't bother anyone." She reached out and laid her hand on the man's arm. She fluttered her eyelashes and her eyes filled with tears. "Oh, sorry," she said. When one of her teardrops fell on the man's arm, "It's just so hard..." She let her voice trail off as if she couldn't speak. "Sorry," she whispered.

The man gave the other beefy boy a look. The other man shook his head. "Your call, Winthrop, but if the boss gets mad, it's on your shoulders."

"I don't want to get anyone in trouble," said Daisy, now giving full rein to tears. "Winthrop, is it? I'm Daisy," she added. She took a step forward and seemed to stumble on the uneven ground. She fell into Winthrop, and was righted by the man, but not before she assured herself that he was indeed packing.

He gestured Daisy and Rodney to the far right, helping Daisy move Rodney's chair into the end of the line of seats, shoving a thin, elderly man out of his chair and offering it to Daisy. "You're to keep to your seats. Don't be trying to get the reverend's attention. Be quiet."

"Can we at least sing?" asked Daisy.

Winthrop gave her a look to determine if she was being sarcastic, but confronting only Daisy's innocent tear-filled eyes, he replied, "Sure. That's part of the show, uh, I mean, that's part of praising the Lord, isn't it?"

A short, fat man pushed through the crowd, stopping at Winthrop's side. Almost as round as he was short, he also wore a white robe and looked more like a large soccer ball than a human being. "Someone giving you trouble?" he asked Winthrop.

Daisy smiled into her hand. This had to be the dirty cop Emily had so often mentioned, Toby Sands, Lewis' ex-partner. She'd recognize him anywhere from Emily's description. While he wasn't spitting tobacco and he seemed to be sober, no one else could look like the obese ogre Emily described.

"If someone was giving me trouble, what could you do about it, Toby?" asked Winthrop. His partner shook his head again, this time as if he wanted Winthrop to back down.

Toby pushed in close to Winthrop, his stomach poking into the top of Winthrop's leg. He looked like a nasty Humpty Dumpty confronting the Jolly Green Giant. Daisy gulped to keep herself from laughing out loud. She wasn't completely successful. She gave out a small squeak.

"Something wrong, lady? asked Toby.

"No. It's just so hot in here with all these bodies..."

Toby turned his attention away from her and continued to stare at Winthrop for a while, then said, "Any more back talk from you, and I'll tell the boss."

Winthrop looked as if he wanted to pick up Toby and toss him through the side of the tent, but another headshake from Winthrop's partner and Winthrop took a step back.

"Sure. Gotcha," Winthrop growled.

A piano began a hymn, and the two bodyguards and Toby seemed to lose interest in their confrontation. Toby strode toward the front of the tent and took his place alongside the woman sitting to the right of the center stage. From Emily's description Daisy surmised the woman had to be Melissa DeVry, Toby's girlfriend and the daughter of the man who set up the revival event and who was to speak and perhaps heal tonight. She expected the leader of the revival to appear also clad in white robes, but was surprised when the person to step out from behind the curtain on the raised dais was attired in a pair of jeans and a faded, but clean shirt. He wore his thinning brown hair short, and his face was tanned and smooth, almost as if he had spent afternoons in a tanning parlor. His full lips parted, he lifted his strong chin and gazed into the crowd. He held his hands clasped in front of him in a gesture of reverence and humility. Daisy thought he looked as friendly and approachable as a next-door neighbor.

"My friends," he said and smiled a smile so sweet and innocent that for a moment Daisy wanted to come forward and confess every sin she'd ever committed, and she had to admit, there were a lot of them.

He spoke so softly that everyone leaned forward to hear him, and the rustling sounds of people moving around in their seats or talking to others near them ceased. Even the children, whose parents had up to this moment tried unsuccessfully to shush them, quieted and ceased their giggling, pushing and shoving. His speech wasn't exceptional in its content—he simply said to love one another and God—but he said it in such an intimate way that it seemed to Daisy he was speaking directly to her. She was certain others felt the same. After he finished, he encouraged those who wished to confess and be heard to come forward. Many of the people in the reserved seats rose and went to the front, as did a few others, Daisy noticed, who had been singled out by the two guards. Winthrop gave Daisy and Rodney a warning look. Daisy smiled, and she and Rodney remained sitting, but after people returned to their seats, Winthrop approached the reverend and said something to him.

The reverend looked in Daisy and Rodney's direction and nodded.

Winthrop approached Daisy and Rodney and whispered in Daisy's ear, "Our leader would like to speak with you after the end of the worship."

Daisy wasn't certain if her clothes and jewelry made an impression or if the tears shed on Winthrop's mighty shoulder had done the trick. Regardless, they had been noticed.

CHAPTER 12

Emily had tried the doors to most of the travel trailers parked behind the revival tent. Many were not locked, but from her hurried search of them, it was clear they were occupied by people working in the revival event and not by the leader. She wondered if he stayed elsewhere, perhaps with his daughter. The last trailer she came to was no larger than the others, but it was an old airstream, its sides gleaming silver in the moonlight. Emily knew airstreams were considered the crème de la crème of trailers. As she reached out to try the door, a large hand covered hers and held the door shut.

"I've been watching you," said Detective Lewis.

Emily almost couldn't speak for the racing of her heart. "Why do you do that? Sneak up on people like that."

"You mean sneak up on people trespassing on others' property? It's my job. I'm a cop, you know."

"Unless you expect to find a dead body, you're exceeding your job. You're a homicide detective, not a beat cop looking for trespassers. You've been watching me look through all these trailers, haven't you? And you decided to let me do it, so you wouldn't have to break the law or be forced to get a search warrant to do it legally."

Lewis held his finger up to his mouth. "Shhh."

"I will not be quiet," began Emily, but Lewis lifted her off her feet and pulled her behind the trailer.

"Someone's coming," he said.

"Hi there," said a voice from the darkness behind the trailer.

Both Emily and Lewis jumped.

"Who the hell?" said Lewis.

"Clara. What are you doing here?" asked Emily. Another figure appeared out of the shadows behind Clara. "And Hap." The three of them hugged while Lewis stood there shifting from foot to foot.

"Enough with the reunion stuff, be quiet or we'll all be found out," said Lewis.

"And that won't look good for you snooping around in the dark, will it, detective?" asked Emily.

"Not to worry," said Hap. "You've got two good lawyers here. I'm sure we can get you off regardless of the charges."

"Thanks, Hap," said Emily.

"Will everyone just shut up," repeated Lewis.

"Did you hear something?" said a male voice coming from the front of the trailer.

"I'm sure it's just a raccoon," said a voice Emily recognized as Daisy's. By the sound of the wheels on the gravel, Emily could tell Rodney was with her.

Lewis hit himself on the forehead with the palm of his hand.

"Something wrong, detective?" whispered Clara.

"Just a mosquito trying to bite me," said Lewis, but his voice sounded shaky like he was trying to swallow his words.

"My dad always sounded that way when he was furious and trying not to show it," Emily said to Lewis. "Anger makes the throat constrict unless you let it out," she added, unhelpfully.

"Raccoon, huh. Maybe I should shoot the little bugger," said the same male voice as before.

"Oh, no, Winthrop. Don't. Please. I just love them with their little bandit faces." It was Daisy's voice again. *Thank goodness*, thought Emily, *Daisy must have figured out it was me back here. What she doesn't know is that it's me and an officer of the law along with some others not behaving so lawful.*

Emily heard the door open and a smooth, gentle-sounding voice said, "Carry Mr. St. Simonton's chair up the steps, Winthrop." The trailer shook a bit, indicating that several people had entered it. Again, the soft voice said, "You may go now, Winthrop. And I won't be needing you, Toby." The sound of the voices grew muted as Emily heard the door close.

"Don't give me that look. He didn't want you in there either," someone said.

How could Emily forget that voice? It was that of Toby Sands, the creep.

There was silence for a few minutes and then the other man said, "You don't have to babysit me, you know. Go take care of Melissa. I have to stay to help that guy in a wheelchair down the steps."

Emily heard the sound of footsteps recede.

Emily and her small group of interlopers remained in hiding but heard nothing more.

"Stay here," said Lewis.

"Why? asked Emily, but he didn't answer. He walked away from the trailer then turned back. Peeking around the side of the place, she saw him approach the front door as if he was just arriving. A big man emerged from the shadows.

"What do you want?" he asked Lewis.

"Police," Lewis said, and Emily saw him take his identification out of his coat pocket.

The man looked it over then knocked on the door. "Cops. Again."

"I guess the jig's up," said Clara to Emily. "You must have come with Daisy and Rodney. I'll give you a ride home. Unless you want to wait out here and see who spots you first: a gator or that big guy out front."

Her throat closed up on her as the anger flooded through her body. "Well," she said, "if he can do it, then so can we. C'mon." She followed Lewis' circuitous path to the trailer door, encountered the guard there and said, "We're looking for Detective Lewis."

"Why?"

"We're cops too," Emily said.

Winthrop's gaze travelled over tiny Emily, tall, lanky red-headed Clara and then travelled to Hap, wearing his plantation owner's straw hat and dressed in his best white linen suit recently un-packed from storage in a clothes bag filled with mothballs.

"You smell funny," he said to Hap.

"A new designer cologne," Hap replied.

The door to the trailer opened, and Lewis stuck his head out. "What's going on here?"

"These people here claim to be with you," said Winthrop.

Lewis' gaze met Emily's. "Oh, for heaven's sake."

She gave him a tiny smile, just enough that her eyes twinkled in the light from the trailer, but not so much that he'd think she was trying to play innocent.

Lewis let out a deep sigh. "Oh, what the... Let them in."

Everyone filed in. The trailer might have accommodated the three newcomers, but Winthrop also squeezed in his bulky shoulders.

Emily looked up at the huge man. "Could you move a little? Something is poking me in the side."

"Well, this is nice," said the musical voice of the man who was the leader of the revival. "As I was saying to Daisy and Rodney here, I'm the guy in charge around here, well, along with you-know-who," he looked skyward. "You can call me Jim. Coffee, anyone?"

Lewis was polite, but firm. He asked everyone to leave. He was there, he indicated on police business, no help from them needed.

"Of course," said Jim. "Perhaps we can talk an-other time," he said, escorting Daisy to the door while Winthrop carried Rodney out.

Emily, Hap and Clara filed out after them. No introductions had been made, and no one had questioned the presence of them with Detective Lewis. He didn't explain, but whispered in Emily's ear as she left, "We need to talk."

She smiled and said, "Oh, yes we do."

"Not about the murder," he said leaning out to close the door.

"Oh, yes we do," she shot back.

Lewis pulled the door shut.

Emily pressed her ear against the side of the trailer, but she could hear nothing coming from within. *Darn these things were well insulated.*

⚬

Lewis made himself comfortable on the sofa at the rear of the trailer. "There is the matter of a recent murder and your associates," he said with a pleas-ant look on his face as if he were about to take tea with the queen.

Jim raised one eyebrow in a questioning look aimed toward the door of the trailer.

"Yeh, I know them all one way or another," Lew-is said.

"Even the St. Simontons? They're not from around here."

"No, but I used to work in Brunswick, Georgia. I know them from there." Lewis was trying to take the man's measure and gave Jim a penetrating look. "Is that of some concern for you?"

Jim shook his head. "I was curious why they were down here."

"You would know that better than I do. You're a spiritual leader, aren't you? Aren't they the kind of folks you like to attract?"

For the first time since he'd entered the trailer, Lewis heard an edge in Jim's voice. "What do you mean by that?"

"He's confined to a wheelchair. That has to be frustrating for him. Your message might be expected to provide him with some comfort."

"That could be, but I thought they seemed pretty comforted by their money."

"If you think that, then you don't know the St. Simontons."

Jim smiled and spread his hands out as if trying to smooth over the judgment in his words. "They seemed eager to meet me. People in their circumstances often believe that money can be used to win the Lord's favor."

"And you don't?" asked Lewis.

"I assume, detective, that you know something about my background and it has colored your perception of me and what I'm doing."

"That and the fact that you're employing Toby Sands."

"Ah, Mr. Sands. Now he's an interesting case. My daughter took a liking to him. I don't understand why, but she finds it exciting to take on a bad boy," he hesitated a moment, "or she could be punishing me for encouraging her to get rid of her husband. Either way, she is an adult."

"I'm not certain that explains why he's in your employ. You're an ex-con and I must warn you he's not a man you can count on as an associate."

"Are you here to question my employment practices or is there another reason the police are interested in me. Other than the usual harassment I get?"

"Did you know Leonard Parsons?"

Jim turned his back so Lewis could not discern the look on his face when he heard the name.

Lewis was surprised when the Reverend Jim turned to face him and said, "I wondered when the authorities would get around to questioning me. So who told you about Leonard and my association? Was it his wife?"

Lewis gave no reaction to his question about Parsons' wife. "Actually it was Toby who led me to you." *It was Toby who had led Lewis on what he thought might be a dead end. Instead it turned out to be more interesting than he could have imagined.*

"I recommended him to Toby. Mr. Parsons was a very worried man. I thought Toby could help him."

"How?"

"Don't you think that's a question you should ask Toby?" Jim yawned and stretched his shoulders and neck. "I've had a long night, and there are things I need to do before I sleep. I've been accommodating to you considering how you intruded on me and my guests. I'd like you to leave. The next time we talk it should be with my lawyer present." His voice was still smooth, unruffled, but more like polished black obsidian, his true feelings hidden under the impenetrable darkness of opaque glass. Jim the healer and man of God was a complex individual, Lewis thought. And hiding something, as were all the people he had questioned in this case. Jim just seemed better at it than the others did.

⊰⊱

Lewis walked toward the street where he had parked his car beyond the lights surrounding the revival tent. A small figure leaned against the door of his vehicle. It was Emily.

"Give me a ride home?" she asked.

"What are you still doing here? Why haven't you joined your snoopy buddies? Do you think I'm so dense that I haven't figured out you put Daisy and Rodney up to meeting Jim?"

"I know. It was a dumb plan, but I had nothing to do with Clara and Hap being here. I think Clara is concerned because of..." Emily stopped talking.

"Because of what?" asked Lewis.

"Because she's a concerned person maybe?" Emily shrugged her shoulders.

"You can't fool me, Emily. I know Clara is the advisor for the chess club and that Owen Parsons and his pal David Otter belong to the club."

"You know that? Then Owen must have..." Emily stopped talking again.

Lewis walked up close and stood toe-to-toe with her.

Emily looked up at him and gulped.

"I thought you were going to stay out of this case, Emily. Instead I find you snooping around the revival tent, getting your friends involved with a man who I think might be dangerous, and, from what you've almost said, you've been talking with some key witnesses in the case. I don't want to warn you again. Stay out of my case." Lewis punctuated each word with a finger poke to her shoulder.

"Ow. That's police brutality."

"No, that's me warning you not to interfere. Now get in if you want a ride home." He held the door open for her.

"But see, I'm not involved in the case because I haven't told you anything I shouldn't have told you."

Lewis got in the other side of the car, and gave her an exasperated look. "What's that supposed to mean?"

"I can't tell you or I'd be interfering."

Lewis pounded on the steering wheel, then stopped and stared into the night. "What the hell," he said and leaned over and kissed her hard on the mouth. "You are driving me crazy, Emily Rhodes."

There was a knock on the passenger's side window.

"I don't think this is a very good place to park and make out," said Donald Green. Behind him stood Emily's daughter Naomi.

"What are you two doing here?" asked Emily.

Lewis stared at Donald and ground his teeth in anger.

"Did we miss all the fun?" asked Donald.

"How did you know we were here?" asked Emily.

"You told Vicki about Toby's girlfriend and her father, so we thought we'd take a drive down here when you weren't anywhere to be found," said Donald.

"I was worried about you, Mom. You ran out of the house the other night to go see Clara about some chess club thing, and you don't even play chess," said Naomi.

Lewis had been silent the entire time. Now he started up the car. "Say good night to these two," he told Emily.

She barely got a quick wave in when Lewis stepped on the gas and sped off.

⋙

"What was that kiss about?" Emily asked.

"It's about my always wanting to kiss you when I'm around you," Lewis said.

"I really tickle your fancy then?" said Emily. She was pleased. This admission on Lewis' part was as close as he ever got to expressing his feelings for her.

"No, you aggravate the hell out of me, and I don't know what to do about it."

"So do you kiss everyone who aggravates you?" Emily asked.

"No, but if you don't shut up, I'll do it again."

Emily was about to open her mouth to see if he meant it when the radio in his cruiser crackled with a message from the police station. "There's some kid here who says he needs to talk with you. He won't give us his name. He says Clara and Emily sent him."

"That has to be Owen Parsons. Good. I knew he'd come around and talk with you."

"You know what he's going to say then?"

"Sure."

"Good, then you won't ask to come with me to the station to sit in on the conversation."

"You're mean," said Emily, then she said not another word, simply looked out the window the entire hour's drive back to her place. When they arrived at her door, she got out of the car and walked around to the driver's side.

Lewis lowered the window. "What?"

"You must be pretty annoyed at me for talking with Owen before you did. It's not my fault. He came to Clara's house, and she called me."

He nodded his head.

"So don't you want to kiss me?"

"I'm getting used to being aggravated by you. I don't feel like kissing you."

"Liar," she said, turned away and entered her house. She knew she had really aggravated him with that one.

⚬

The officer on duty pointed out the young man seated on the bench outside the office area. Lewis noticed the back of his head when he entered. The hair was short there and an elaborate design was shaved into it. The hair on the top of his head was longer and flopped down over his forehead. He seemed to be hiding his face behind it. The boy was tall and thin, almost to the point of looking emaciated.

"This is Detective Lewis," said the officer.

"You must be Owen Parsons," said Lewis. He held his hand out to the boy, who hesitated a moment and then shook it. Lewis was surprised at the strength in his grip. He'd expected a limp shake. Maybe this lad would surprise him in other ways too, although Lewis thought not. The boy looked too frightened, and Lewis expected getting information out of him although he had voluntarily come in would be difficult. Lewis sighed. As he'd reckoned earlier, this would be a long night.

"I think we'd be more comfortable in my office. There's no one around."

The boy got off the bench and followed Lewis down the hallway.

"Coffee?" asked Lewis.

The boy looked at him for a moment, then laughed. "No thanks. I've heard about coffee brewed in police stations."

Lewis ran his fingers through his hair and grinned. "I don't touch the stuff myself. I didn't have any dinner so if you're hungry we could order out. Get a pizza or something. Some colas."

"Okay. I haven't had much to eat lately."

"I'm sorry about your dad. I guess you and I missed each other when I came to Orlando and to your house." Lewis wasn't about to destroy the kid's trust by reminding him he had run from the cops.

Lewis opened the office door for Owen and showed him in. "A minute," he said holding up a finger. He yelled back at the duty officer. "Order us a pizza and something to drink." Lewis gestured toward the only chair in the room aside from the one behind his desk.

"Wow, you have a really crummy office. It smells bad even," said Owen as he dropped his lanky body into the chair.

"I know."

There was a knock on the door and the duty office stuck his head in. ""We took this off him when the metal detector sounded," he said.

He handed a gun to Lewis.

"I think that's the one used to kill my dad. I'm pretty certain my mom did it," Owen said.

CHAPTER 13

While Lewis was in his office interviewing Owen Parsons, Emily took out her frustrations at him by vacuuming her house and then rearranging the clothes in her bedroom closet, but nothing took her mind off Lewis' kiss. Sweaty from her work, she tossed her clothes on the bed and jumped into the shower. The feel of Lewis' kiss still remained on her lips, and she had to admit she ached to have him in here with her so the two of them could get soapy and slickery together. She and Lewis couldn't seem to come together in any meaningful way. She knew her snoopy nature interfered with Lewis' cases, but she couldn't help it if people liked to tell her things. She also couldn't seem to help herself when it came to concocting ideas for how to get people to talk to her. Or to her friends. She hoped she hadn't put Rodney and Daisy in any danger, but she also believed the two of them were capable of taking care of themselves regardless of what Lewis thought. They were her friends, and Emily's friends had as much resilience and pluck as she did.

"Mom." Naomi stuck her head into the bathroom. "How long have you been in here? There's so much steam built up that it's seeping under the door. I'm afraid the wallpaper will peel off the wall."

"I'll be right out."

"Well, put some clothes on. Donald is with me."

"Why?"

"What?"

"Never mind." Donald wasn't what she needed tonight. She needed to talk to her daughter. Alone.

She slid back the shower curtain. "Hey" she yelled to Naomi. "Could you tell him to go away? I'm dead tired."

"But there's angel food cake with fresh strawberries. Vicki just brought it over."

Well, who could refuse that even if it meant having to tolerate Donald Green?

As she slipped into a pair of jeans and a loose shirt, she heard another car pull into her drive. With Stan the Sedan, Donald's truck and now another vehicle, her driveway was beginning to look like a parking lot. She glanced out the window to see Rodney and Daisy get out of the red Cadillac. *I guess I'm having a party.* She waited several minutes, wondering if Clara and Hap would soon join the group. Nope. Well, some people were smart enough to go home to bed because they had to work in the morning. But Emily was curious. What were Clara and Hap expecting to find at the revival event? And what did they find? She needed to have a chat with Clara as soon as possible.

Everyone stuffed themselves with cake and no one mentioned what had happened in Clewiston. Emily knew Vicki was curious, but she was too polite to ask. Donald continued to stare at Emily while he forked large bites of cake into his mouth. As hungry as she had been—and the cake was delicious—Emily yearned for bed. The last several nights had been taxing. Emily tried to hide a yawn, but Daisy spotted Emily covering her mouth.

"Let's all talk tomorrow," said Daisy.

"What's the hurry?" asked Donald. "There's still a lot of cake left."

"I'll send home a few slices with you. I'm sure you'll want to get right to bed given the fishing forecast for tomorrow," said Vicki, turning her back to Donald and winking at Emily.

"What's that?" asked Donald sitting up in the recliner. "I didn't hear they'd changed it."

"Must have," said Vicki. "Here's your cake, and there's the door. Get a good night's sleep, and good fishing," Vicki said.

Donald grumbled some but left with a bit of a bounce in his step, the to-go cake serving gripped tightly in his hand.

"I thought the fishing was supposed to be awful for the next several days," said Emily.

"It is, but how else do you get Donald Green out of your lounge chair?" asked Vicki.

"Get him in there with the promise of cake. Get him out with the promise of great fishing. It's a formula," said Emily.

"Emily, you look exhausted," said Daisy. "How about we meet you tomorrow for breakfast and we can chat about what's next?"

"You guys were up to something tonight. I know it. Why am I left out of everything? I never have any fun," said Vicki.

"Don't be silly," said Emily, seeing the hurt on Vicki's face. "You're our source."

"Source?" asked Vicki.

"Yeah. You supply us with important information about what's going on around here. You know everything," said Emily. Daisy and Rodney nodded in agreement.

Vicki smiled. "More cake?"

Daisy and Rodney turned down the offer, hugged all around and left, Vicki right behind. When Emily heard the car pull out of her drive, she turned to Naomi.

"Isn't there something you want to tell me?"

Naomi looked puzzled. "No, but maybe there's something you should tell me."

"What do you mean?"

"What were you trying to accomplish sneaking round that revival operation? The guy who runs it, according to Vicki..."

Emily thought back. *Had she told Vicki about him or had Vicki used some of her usual contacts to find out about him? Well, never mind.* Naomi knew what she knew.

"...that guy is an ex-con, and there's suspicion that he's into something unsavory. Like maybe murder."

"I was perfectly safe. I had Rodney and Daisy as backup." Emily was about to explain further when her phone rang. Probably Clara wanting to talk.

It was Detective Lewis wanting to talk. Actually he seemed more interested in yelling at Emily. Again.

To Emily's ear his voice took on that barely controlled, word-swallowing quality, the one that said he was furious with her. Again.

"I had a visit tonight from a young man..."

"Oh, good. We were hoping Owen would go see you. He did then?"

"Yes, he did. What I don't understand is why you didn't tell me what he said to you and Clara the other night."

"Yeah, I'm just your little police informant, aren't I? We encouraged him to step up and be a man. He confided in us, and we weren't about to break that confidence."

"What are you two, priests in disguise?"

Emily had had about enough of this guy. She hung up and turned off her phone.

"A call from your boyfriend?" asked Naomi.

"Don't start. Let's go to bed and deal with this tomorrow."

<hr>

Tomorrow came mighty early. Emily was awakened by the sound of metal rattling and the backfire of an exhaust. She looked out her window to see a beaten-up old truck, one that looked familiar, one she recognized. *What was that ugly troll doing here, in front of her place?* She watched him park the truck in her drive, get out and walk to her door. She threw on a robe and approached her door with a broom in her hand.

"What's going on, Mom?" said Naomi peeking out of her bedroom.

"The creepy cretin is here. Look."

Naomi peered through the side window and grabbed the mop from the broom closet. "It makes me shudder just to see his sneaky fat face."

"Go away, or I'll call the cops," Emily yelled through the door.

"I just want to talk to you," squeaked the rat.

"I didn't know you could do that. I thought you were more into kidnapping women than speaking to them."

"Please," he said.

She examined his image through the safety of a door between them. He looked different from the way she remembered him. Lewis said he was trying to mend his ways with the help of Melissa DeVry. Emily caught sight of Vicki waving at her through the window.

"My daughter and I are both armed, so no funny business. And my next-door neighbor knows you're here. I'll step out of the house and talk with you, but she'll be watching us."

"You're not going out there, are you?" Naomi asked.

"You stay here. He's not going to do anything in broad daylight in such a public place."

"He's dumb. You know that. He's a criminal, but of the stupidest sort. He probably thinks people in a community for residents over fifty-five can't see him well enough to identify him," Naomi said.

"You stay here."

Emily stepped out onto her porch. "You stay where you are, and I'll stand here. What do you want?"

"You've got to get Detective Lewis off my back."

"First, why would I do that? And second, why would you think I could do that?"

"I know he's sweet on you."

Emily thought back on the kiss from last night. *Sweet* wasn't really the word that sprang to mind in describing Lewis' feelings for her, but she wasn't going to tell Toby that. In fact, she'd have had a difficult time explaining just how Lewis felt about her to anyone. She wasn't even certain she understood it.

"See, Lewis came to the revival event last night and started asking questions about me of the Big Guy," Toby said.

"Who is the 'Big Guy'?"

"Jim. He's our leader."

Emily noted with interest the use of the word "our."

She nodded. "What did, uh, Jim tell him that has you so worried?"

"Well, he said he introduced Principal Parsons and me."

"And is that true?"

Toby hesitated for a minute. "Yes."

"So what?"

"I think Lewis thinks I killed the principal."

Emily thought about that. From her perspective Toby's ability to engage in any criminal act other than one that resulted in his botching it seemed unlikely. She knew Lewis felt the same, but Toby's view of himself was of someone who was a misunderstood master criminal. Maybe Emily could get some information out of him. But she'd have to make him feel as if she cared. A shiver ran down her spine. *No way did she have any positive feeling for the toad.* She'd just have to fake it.

"Would you like to come in for a cup of coffee? And a slice of angel food cake? With strawberries." Emily heard a choking sound from behind her.

"Shush," she whispered to her daughter. "The toad knows something important about the murder."

"I'm certain Detective Lewis already knows what he knows."

"But we don't." Emily opened the door and let the troll into her house. *Was she making a mistake?*

Toby sat at a chair by the doorway. He held a coffee cup in one hand and a plate of cake in the other. "Can I pull up to the table? I can't manage my coffee and the cake."

Emily gestured to him to move his chair. "Okay, now let's get to what you know, and how you think I might be of value to you in getting the detective to think more kindly of you."

"I'm just saying that I know he'll keep bugging me until I tell him something."

"And do you have something to tell?"

"Yes, but I know he won't believe me. He thinks I'm scum."

And so do I, Toby, thought Emily.

"You think I'll believe you?"

"Melissa said I should try to get you on my side."

Emily tilted her chair back on two legs and crossed her arms. "Let's hear your story then."

"I was hired by Principal Parsons."

"To do what?"

"To protect him."

"From?"

"Parsons told me he'd had threatening notes left under his office door and someone driving by his house frequently. I was hired to tail Parsons and see if I could determine who was trying to do him in. And I was to protect the principal."

"Does Lewis know all of this?"

"Uh huh."

"Then why do you need me?"

"Detective Lewis doesn't trust me. I thought you could put in a good word for me."

Emily shook her head. If Lewis already knew this, there wasn't much she could say to him to convince him it was true. Not even if she believed Toby.

"It's not going to work, Toby. Now why don't you shuffle back to wherever?"

"There's more."

"This better be good."

"The day of the reenactment?"

Emily nodded.

"I saw a guy following Parsons. I lost him in the crowd."

"What did he look like?"

"I can't really say because it was raining so hard. I thought I saw someone tailing him dressed in blue. It could have been a rain slicker or maybe someone dressed as a soldier. Their uniforms were blue." Toby hesitated. "Or, uh, maybe it was one of the Seminole warriors. A couple of them wore blue shirts."

"So, all in all, you saw the color blue? Lewis knows what you saw??"

"I told him the slicker had yellow flowers on it. It could have been a woman, but I could have been mistaken about the flowers. Something yellow. Maybe. As usual he didn't believe me. Lewis thought my story about being Parsons' bodyguard was exaggerated, so he kind of lost interest in my story."

As usual, Emily didn't believe him either, at least not entirely. Toby loved to exaggerate. Maybe there was someone following Parsons, or it could have as likely been one of the reenactment participants. She was certain he wasn't telling her everything.

"So, will you talk to him? If you don't, he'll plague me day after day."

"If you saw someone following Parsons, Lewis will continue to plague you for more information. You know that."

"Could you kind of serve as a character witness for me then?"

Emily choked and spit out her coffee. "Are you kidding me? You're the guy who tried to kidnap my daughter and sell us both to white slavers."

"I couldn't help it. I was being threatened." Toby spread his hands out in a gesture of helplessness.

Naomi, silent until this point, stepped forward. "I think you should leave now," she said in a voice that was icy.

"But Melissa said people can change and they should be forgiven for the bad things they've done."

"That's only part of becoming a better person, Toby. Did she also tell you the part about punishment?" said Emily, shoving him out the door. "Now get out of here before the garbage collectors come by and think you're curbside trash."

Toby's face darkened, and a look came over it that Emily found familiar, his sneaky, nasty, I'll-get-you-for-this look, one that said that Toby hadn't completely changed from the evil troll he once was.

Emily and Naomi watched from the window as Toby drove off.

"I believe some of what he said," said Emily.

"I wonder what his real reason was for coming here. Toby Sands is never honest. Not completely. I don't care if he's got a girlfriend who's gotten him to pray. There has to be money in this somehow," Naomi said.

Emily believed Naomi was right. Yet there was a part of Toby's story that rang true. Emily and Clara knew Mrs. Parsons had gone to the reenactment. With a gun. After last night talking with Owen Parsons, Lewis would know that too.

"I'm going to have to make peace with Detective Lewis," Emily said to Naomi. "I'll have to tell him what Toby said to see if it was the same story he told Lewis. Oops, look at the time. I've got to meet Rodney and Daisy for breakfast. Do you want to come?"

"No. I've got a dentist appointment." Naomi headed to her bedroom.

"Can we catch up later then?" asked Emily. She didn't hear her daughter reply. She sighed. *We'll work this out sometime soon.* Emily hoped it wouldn't be too late.

⁕

If Donald believed the fishing was going to be good this morning, he wouldn't be at the club to open the bar. And when he found out he'd been lied to, he wouldn't be in a good mood for days. Emily grabbed a quick shower and arrived only a few minutes late for her breakfast with Rodney and Daisy.

"We received a call from the good Reverend Jim early this morning. He'd like to meet with us sometime today," said Daisy.

"What do you think he wants?" asked Emily.

"Money, of course. He thinks we're loaded as well as in search of spiritual guidance."

"When are you meeting with him?"

"This evening before the revival begins, at his trailer. I don't know if we can find out anything important from him with respect to the murder. He's a cagey one, but it's worth talking with him about his operation. Maybe we'll find out something you and Detective Lewis can use."

Emily nodded. She'd gotten the ball rolling with Rodney and Daisy and now she was worried she might have put them in danger.

"You two be careful."

"Oh, we will, honey," Daisy reassured her.

"I had a visitor this morning," Emily said and told them about Toby dropping by.

"He came by to talk with you and wants you to intercede for him with Lewis? He's a nervy little newt," Daisy said.

"I think Parsons did hire him on as protection, and I think Toby knows something, but you never can believe much of what Toby says. I'm concerned Toby met Parsons through Reverend Jim. I believe Parsons went to Jim because he was having a crisis of conscience."

"About what?" asked Rodney.

"I can't say, but if Parsons revealed the specifics of his concerns, then Jim had some very potent ammunition to use against Parsons and a few other people. I'm thinking he could have used it in a way that got Parsons killed. You have even more reason to be circumspect around Reverend Jim."

"I wish you could tell us what you know about Parsons," said Daisy.

"I wish I could, too, but perhaps after Lewis' meeting in Mason City today, he may know what I know. I hope so; otherwise, I think I might have to violate a friendship and put someone in danger of being arrested."

⁂

The night before, Lewis had carefully walked Owen through the day his father was killed, and now knew both Owen and his mother had left Orlando and gone to the reenactment. Owen had not seen his mother there and was certain his father hadn't seen him, but Owen was worried his mother had used the gun to shoot her husband. With very little sleep the night before, Lewis was now on his way to Mason City to meet Martin Rudolf, the principal there and a man Emily had called a friend. It was an interview he wasn't eager for and a man he'd developed dislike for in only one encounter. Still, last night's conversation intruded on his thoughts and he couldn't get rid of the suspicion that he had missed something.

"But why would your mother kill your father?" Lewis had asked Owen.

"She hated him," Owen said.

"Why?"

"He was a creep. He never spent time with us. He came home and locked himself in his study. He wouldn't' talk to my sister and me. He up and moved us from the town where we grew up and here we were. It took me ages to make friends here, and my sister never did. It's better she's in California with our grandparents."

Lewis thought the timing of sending the daughter to California this past weekend was interesting. Was Mrs. Parsons preparing the family for her husband's death and her involvement in it?

Lewis was frustrated by Owen's story. He could find no specific reason for why Parsons' wife should hate him and kill him.

"But you moved here years ago. You mean your mother carried that rage at moving around in her for years and then decided to kill him?"

Owen nodded and repeated, "She really hated him. He betrayed her. He betrayed all of us."

"How?"

Owen shook his head.

"Was there another woman?" asked Lewis.

Owen looked startled for a moment. "Maybe. I don't know."

He knew the boy was finished talking. He had said all that he was capable of saying at this time.

But he was hiding something, something key to this case.

Lewis shook free of his thoughts as he approached the outskirts of Mason City. He parked in the lot by the Mason City School District offices and entered the building, eager to get the meeting over with, but Rudolf's secretary informed him Rudolf was in a meeting. He took a chair to wait. The seat was uncomfortable enough to keep him from nodding off. After half an hour a white-haired man, face red with anger stormed out, and Martin Rudolf beckoned Lewis in.

"Sorry," said Rudolf. "That was Superintendent Riley, my boss."

"I would have liked to have met him," said Lewis. "He seemed very upset."

"He was. It was because of me. I'm willing to talk with you because I have something important to say, but I want a lawyer with me."

CHAPTER 14

While Lewis was in Mason City, Emily was at work. Alone. Donald had called to say he was fishing and wouldn't be coming in for his shift.

"It's your fault I'm not going to work. You let that lie about good fishing stand last night, and I believed it. The lie turned into the truth, and I'm busy here hauling them in."

"I'm so happy for you, Donald, but you're going to have to decide whether you want to fish or bartend."

"I like doing both. I can't help it if the fish bite on an irregular schedule."

Emily sighed. "Fine. I'll take your shift today, and you can work the next two days." Emily could fire him, but she knew he wouldn't care and she'd be left with no backup bartender. Unreliable was turning out to be worse than no bartender at all. *I've got to get that ad in the paper for help,* she said to herself.

Overwhelmed with customers when the rain swept in and thunder and lightning chased everyone off the course and into the bar, Emily cursed Donald for not taking his shift and the fish for biting. The storm soon passed, and the bar emptied.

Emily knew they'd be back in, so she put more beer on ice. After she finished and leaned back on the shelf holding the liquor bottles, her cell rang.

"Hi, it's Martin. I'm in town, at police headquarters. I should be out of here in a few hours. Would you be willing to see me? I did what you said I should. I'll explain later."

She was surprised and pleased. She hadn't misjudged her old friend after all, but she was without anyone to take her place tending bar.

Before she could reply to Martin, the door opened, and Donald came in looking grumpier than usual.

"They stopped biting. I might as well lend you a hand and earn a few bucks."

Well, what luck. She turned her attention back to her cell. "Sure. Let's meet up at the boat launch on the lake. I need a break from bars and people. It's been a long day."

"Emily, I..." he began, but a crowd of golfers entered the bar just then.

"Got to water the herd," said Emily. "See you around six. If I'm going to be late, I'll give you a call."

She hung up, threw Donald his apron and turned to greet the thirsty golfers. "You're on for the rest of the shift, Donald."

He growled his acceptance and began to take bar orders.

She looked across the water as the sun laid down patterns of shimmering coral, purple and turquoise streaks in the western sky. She knew meeting here was the right choice. A passing storm often left towering clouds for the sun to hide behind as it set, leaving a clean smell in the air as well as the panoply of colors, which reflected off the dark and still lake. She stood on the seawall listening to the soft slap-slap of the water below her. It reminded her of the time she had scurried to get away from Donald Green whom she had played a joke on. Back then she hadn't appreciated Donald's sense of humor—none. She'd almost stumbled across an alligator, frightened off by Donald. She chuckled to herself as she remembered how he did that. He'd said, "Shoo," and the gator ambled off.

Emily's reminiscence was interrupted by a hard shove from behind her. Taken by surprise, she couldn't get her balance as she teetered on the edge for a moment and then fell into the water. As she struggled to the surface and looked up, she could only see the silhouette of a person above her, the individual's face hidden by the shadow of a passing cloud and the water in her eyes.

There was no way she could climb out of the water at the seawall. She looked toward the boat ramp at the end of the wall. She'd have to swim there. She wasn't the strongest swimmer, but she knew she could get that far. What worried her was what she was thinking about just as she went in: an alligator out for an evening meal.

As she stroked toward the ramp, a man leaned over toward her. *No, no, no.* It wasn't going to be an alligator that got her, she realized, but the person who pushed her returning to hold her under water. She slapped at the arm extended toward her, and she tried to yell without taking in mouthfuls of water.

"You're scaring all the fish," said the voice from above her. It was Donald Green.

She stopped struggling and let him pull her out. "What is wrong with you? You push me in and now you try to pull me back out. Is this some perverse version of catch and release?" she asked.

She stood dripping water and shivering in the cool air. Donald walked to his boat at the top of the ramp and grabbed a blanket, which he threw around her shoulders.

"This blanket smells like fish," she said.

"Not even a thank you for hauling you out? And I did not push you in."

"Oh, Donald," she said. She fell into his arms, crying with fear and relief. Donald's mouth twitched in what Emily supposed was his version of a smile.

Lewis stared at the far wall in his office and tapped his pen against the desktop after Martin Rudolf left. His lawyer had advised him to cooperate with the authorities because it would look good to a judge and might result in a lighter sentence. Earlier Lewis had been feeling frustrated the case was going nowhere, but after taking a statement from Rudolf, Lewis felt the stirring in his stomach that signaled a breakthrough in an investigation. Now he had to sort out all the paperwork and interviews that were necessary in a situation that went back several years. He'd have to interview Rudolf's superintendent at the time, as well as determine if the details Rudolf provided matched those of others involved, such as the parents and the young woman to whom Parsons had made inappropriate advances.

Rudolf was not the school official who took the original complaint. He only sat in with the superintendent to determine how Parsons would be handled by the school. Rudolf's story included few details. He claimed he didn't know much about the parties involved, only that Parsons had been accused of making advances to a student. Lewis needed names, dates and details. And there was the issue of between-county jurisdiction. He was dealing with not just a murder but also a sexual assault and the failure of school authorities to report it. *What a mess.* Lewis ran his fingers through his hair. Did someone kill Leonard Parsons because he was a sexual predator? Was that why Owen and his mother hated him? But why let all this time pass before anyone took action? Lewis knew this would not be simple.

The officer on duty stuck his head in Lewis' door. "A Mr. Green wants to speak with you. He says someone just tried to kill Ms. Rhodes."

Lewis grabbed the phone. "Donald? Is she okay?"

"She's a little wet and scared to death, but I rescued her. I thought you should know about this. We're at the boat launch."

Lewis threw the phone down and rushed out the door. *Was this somehow related to Parsons' murder? Emily. He promised himself he would make everything up to her, stop making fun of her snoopiness, tell her how he felt about her.... If only she was alright.*

Lewis turned on his flashers and headed toward the boat launch. On the way there he was certain he saw Martin Rudolf's car driving away from the boat launch and toward him. That's odd, he thought. He was certain Rudolf told him he was going right back to Mason City. Lewis stomped on his brakes and turned around to follow Rudolf. Could he have tried to harm Emily? Lewis called in to the station and got his partner Sandy returning from an interview. He told her about Emily, told her he was in pursuit of a suspect and asked her to get out to the boat launch and take Emily's story. Meantime, Lewis wanted to have another talk with Martin Rudolf, a man he was coming to dislike more and more, and trust less and less.

❖

"Where's Lewis?" Emily asked Davis. "Didn't he say he would be right here?"

"He's in pursuit of someone. He asked me to get the details from you."

Emily wanted to cry tears of sadness and fury. She smelled like fish, looked like a piece of limp seaweed and, with all the lake water she'd swallowed, she felt like throwing up. But most of all Emily wanted Lewis' strong arms around her comforting her, not this smelly fishing blanket and not even Donald Green's embrace, lovely as he was to try to comfort her.

"There's not much to tell. Someone came up from behind and pushed me in."

"You're sure it was intentional. You didn't just slip?"

"I think I can tell when someone pushes me. It was hard enough that I'll bet I have bruises on my back." Emily pulled up her soppy shirt to show the detective.

"I can't really see any in this light, but we can take you to the hospital to have you checked out if you like." Sandy held up her phone with a questioning look. "Should I call an ambulance?"

Emily shook her head. "I'm fine." But she wasn't fine. What was not fine about her was the truckload of anger she was building up for Lewis. "Where the hell is Lewis? she yelled. "What good is it having a boyfriend who's a cop if he can't take the time to respond to your call that someone is trying to kill you?"

Emily's harangue got everyone's attention. The "boyfriend" part made Donald's eyes narrow. "He's your boyfriend?" Donald asked.

"Well, kind of. He kisses me."

"I could kiss you," offered Donald.

"It's not the same. You're not mad at me."

"Did she hit her head when she went in?" asked Sandy. "Maybe I should call an ambulance."

"Never mind. She's always screwy like that," said Donald.

Emily paced around the boat launch area dragging the wet blanket and muttering. Spectators gathered to see what was happening, and Davis asked if anyone had seen Emily fall into the water. No one had.

"I'm calling for help to search the area, and they should arrive soon," said Detective Davis. "Is there someone I can call for you? You should get home and rest."

"My daughter," said Emily.

"I could give you a ride home," said Donald.

"What are you doing here anyway? You're supposed to be working the bar. I should fire you."

"That's the thanks I get for saving your life?" said Donald.

"I'm sorry, Donald. I'm a little put out right now."

"She's probably not herself, the shock and all," said Davis.

"No, she's herself. The apology is a little unusual, that's all."

Emily went over to Donald and put her arms around him. "Thank you for saving my life. You always come through when it's important, don't you?" She stood on tiptoes in her squishy shoes and gave him a kiss on the cheek. "And here's your blanket."

Donald reddened and looked embarrassed. "Uh, they closed the course. Too wet. So I thought I'd come back and try some more fishing. I should have told you sooner."

Donald almost sounded contrite.

Vicki pulled up in her Crown Victoria with Naomi in the passenger's seat. "Are you okay?" said Vicki, jumping out of the car. "You leave your car here, and I'll drive us home."

Naomi rushed over to her mother and threw her arms around her. Emily looked into her daughter's eyes and said, "Did anyone bring something to eat? I'm starved."

"Well, I guess you'll be fine if you've got an appetite. We could go for ribs if you'd like," Naomi said.

Emily looked down at her wet clothes. "Take out, maybe?"

❖

Lewis called Davis to check on what was happening at the boat launch.

"Ms. Rhodes is fine. Donald Green fished her out of the water and had wrapped her in a blanket when I arrived. Someone did push her, she's certain of that, but she can't identify the person. I think she knows more than she's saying. She might have gotten a look at the person. Donald Green says he didn't see who did it, so I'm corralling others at the scene and trying to find out if anyone saw her being pushed. It appears folks around here are more interested in how many fish got away today than in any attempted murder. Emily went home with her daughter."

"Donald Green saved her?" he asked Davis.

"Yep, and he seemed more than a little pleased to be the hero of the day."

I'll just bet, thought Lewis. "Let me know if you get a good description of the person who shoved Emi.., uh, Ms. Rhodes into the water."

Lewis closed in on the car he was pursuing and got close enough to get a good look at the driver. As he suspected, it was Rudolf. Lewis turned on his lights and pulled the vehicle over.

"I thought you were on your way back to Mason City," Lewis said to the driver.

"Uh, I was, but, uh, I thought I'd stop at the boat launch for a few minutes. The view at sunset is spectacular there."

"I'll bet the view of Emily Rhodes plunging into the water was pretty interesting too. Did you push her?"

"Me! No, I, uh... I'd never do that to Emily. The truth is that Emily and I arranged to meet at the boat launch. Ask her. She'll tell you. I had just pulled in and spotted Emily's car near the launch when I saw someone looking down at the water at the seawall. I was pretty sure it was Emily. Then suddenly she disappeared."

As usual Rudolf was light on the details. "So you left to let her drown. You know, Mr. Rudolf, you seem to have a way of failing to come forward when it's most important."

"No! I saw a guy pull her out of the water, so I knew she was safe. I thought maybe she fell in. Someone pushed her in? That's awful. Is she okay? Whatever happened wasn't my doing."

"I guess you thought the near drowning of a former girlfriend wasn't your business?"

"No, I, I didn't want to get involved because of what was already happening with the Parsons case." A bead of sweat ran down the side of Rudolf's face.

"So you did see something?"

"I couldn't really tell. I was too far away."

"Did you see who pushed her into the water?"

"No. Like I said, I was too far away to identify the person."

"Was it a man or woman?"

"A man, I think. Or maybe a tall woman. I can't be sure. The person was wearing jeans and a tee shirt. That's all I saw."

"What kind of car?"

"I didn't see it. Maybe it was a truck."

Getting information out of Martin Rudolf was like getting bubble gum off the bottom of your shoe.

"Leave your car here. I think we need to go visit Emily to get the whole story."

When Rudolf reached to take his keys out of the ignition, Lewis could see his hand was shaking. The guy was scared as hell. Was it because he'd fled an attempted homicide or was he the one who attempted to kill Emily? Lewis ground his teeth together in anger. If this dude pushed her, Lewis would have his butt behind bars in a heartbeat. Lewis grabbed him by the shoulder and pushed him toward his cruiser.

"Ouch. That's kind of rough. I could file charges against you," said Rudolf, but his voice was shaky, not threatening.

"Try it," said Lewis. He considered taking Rudolf to Emily's house, but thought better of that move. He hated to impose upon Emily, but he needed her help with Rudolf.

"Where are we going?" asked Rudolf.

"Back to my office. I may decide to arrest you. Until I make up my mind, I want to keep an eye on you."

Once at the station, Lewis shoved Rudolf into an interview room—the one with the AC that worked half the time.

In his office, he called Emily. Her daughter answered.

"I'm not certain Mom wants to talk with anyone right now, and I know for sure she doesn't want to talk to you," Naomi said. There was a noise on her end of the line.

"Give me that phone." It was Emily.

"I thought you didn't want to talk to me."

"I don't. You kissed me the other night and now, when you're called to save my life, you run off chasing someone and leave your partner to do all the work. Worse yet, I made a fool of myself in front of her and Donald Green. I called you my boyfriend. How humiliating is that?"

"I don't see what kissing had to do with this."

"You wouldn't, would you? Well, it will never happen again."

There was silence on the line, and Lewis knew Emily was angry, but he had to take a chance. "I need your help."

"Repeat that."

"Emily, I need you to help me with Martin Rudolf. Could you come to my office?"

"Now, you mean?"

"Yes. Now."

"I'll have to bathe first. I smell like the swamp."

"Okay, but I need to know. Are you bathing for me or Martin?"

"Detective, you are an idiot." She disconnected.

CHAPTER 15

Naomi insisted she drive her mother to police headquarters. Emily tried to talk her into stopping by the boat launch for her car, but Naomi said she could pick it up tomorrow. "I don't want you driving right now."

Emily entered Lewis' office intending to remain cool toward him, but the concerned look on his face and the way he held out his hands to her made her melt, as did the fact that, as usual, the AC in police headquarters was working at half capacity.

"You're sure you're fine?" he asked.

She nodded. Not trusting herself to say anything else for fear she'd just blubber at his solicitous demeanor, she decided she was safest with a businesslike approach.

"Now what's this about Martin?" she asked.

"Was he supposed to meet you at the boat launch today?" asked Lewis.

"Yes, but he never showed."

"Oh, he showed, but he claims he got there after you were pushed in and rescued by Donald. I'm wondering if he was the pusher. I was on my way to the boat launch when I saw him driving the other way out of town. I gave chase and pulled him over."

"That's what you were doing when I needed you?" She couldn't keep the snappish tone out of her voice.

"Emily, I sent Detective Davis. I had the opportunity to grab the person who might have been responsible for trying to kill you. Would you want me to ignore my duty?"

"Yes," Emily said, her voice firm.

Lewis threw his head back and looked up at the ceiling in frustration. "You don't mean that."

"Okay."

They stared at one another, each trying not to blink or break eye contact before the other. Lewis blinked, which Emily took as her win.

"Rudolph and his lawyer visited me earlier today and made a statement about Parsons. It was light on detail. He said he didn't know much, but I'm guessing he does. He's in an interview room, waiting for his lawyer to put in another appearance, although I haven't charged him with anything yet. I know the bare bones of the situation from what he told me this morning in Mason City, but I have no names, no details. Rudolf seems always to have a story to tell, but he doesn't like to elaborate much. My next move is to talk with the superintendent, Rudolf's boss then and his boss now. The guy came roaring out of Rudolf's office earlier today when I was in Mason City. He looked furious. I think Rudolf told him he was going to speak to the police. I guess the super knew the jig was up and that he'd have to confess his part in covering up Parsons' behavior and not reporting it to the authorities."

Emily thought about the jeopardy Rudolf, his boss and Parsons had put innocent children in. "How can I help?" she asked.

Lewis' body visibly relaxed. "Thanks, Emily."

"You're certain that Parsons' past led to his murder?"

"At this point, it's my best lead. Can you talk to him?"

"You mean, act like we're friends, like maybe he didn't try to kill me? Sure. I can do that," Emily said.

"Just say if it's too much," said Lewis.

She shook her head. "I want to help."

"I heard from my partner while you were on your way here. She can't find anyone at the launch who saw you being pushed, but Rudolph told me he did. Maybe he'll tell you more."

"He saw what happened to me and he did nothing?" Emily tightened her hands into fists and looked around Lewis' office as if she was searching for a weapon she could use on Rudolph. "Well, I know you won't do anything illegal to get him to open up, but I'm not bound by that consideration."

"I could kiss you," said Lewis.

"No, you couldn't. You only do that when you're mad at me."

"I can change."

"Why do I not believe you?"

"Okay, look. Here's what I have in mind." Lewis laid out his plan to Emily. "What do you think?" he asked.

"I like it fine."

Lewis entered the interview room with Emily right behind him. The air was stale, hot and humid, but he and Emily pretended not to notice the sweat running down Martin Rudolph's face.

Rudolph jumped out of his chair. "Thank God, Emily. Your detective friend here thinks I tried to kill you. Tell him he's wrong."

He didn't seem concerned Emily's life was in danger. Why hadn't she noticed how selfish Martin was before. "Thanks for asking, Martin. I'm feeling refreshed after my dunk in the lake."

"Oh, Emily. I was so worried about you. You look like you've recovered just fine."

She decided not to tell him the obvious: it took longer than a few hours to recover from someone trying to kill you.

"Is there anything that says I can't talk with Martin alone, detective?"

"You mean you want to talk with the man who tried to kill you?" asked Lewis.

"I've known Martin for many years. I just want to find out what happened before you arrest him for his attempt on my life." Emily kept her tone neutral, hoping Rudolph would be so focused on his own problems that he wouldn't notice Emily's lack of friendliness.

"It's your call, Ms. Rhodes, but I'll station an officer outside the door."

Rudolph turned pale and staggered back into his chair. "You think I tried to kill her? But I told you I didn't. Are you going to arrest me?" He looked so crushed by the thought of being arrested that he didn't mention getting his lawyer back.

Lewis left, and Emily took the chair across from Rudolph. She would have liked to have asked Lewis to turn the AC on, but she decided making Martin sweat more and her a little was worth what he might say without anyone other than her in the room.

"Tell me you didn't try to kill me, Martin."

"I didn't. Honest."

"Okay, but someone did. Do you think the attempt was related in any way to Parsons' murder?"

"How do you mean?"

"I'm not certain but I think he was killed in relation to being a sexual predator. So think back. Tell me everything you remember about the deal that was made for him to get off being arrested for what he did to that girl. Don't leave out anything."

"I told all that to you before. And earlier today to the detective."

"Really, Martin? How about some names?"

"Okay, you know my super Mr. Riley was the one who took the complaint."

"Given to him by a parent, right?"

"Yes."

"Parent's name?"

"Oh, God. I shouldn't tell you that."

"Fine. Bye now, Martin." Emily got out of the chair and prepared to leave the room.

"Okay. Okay. Clarence Goodman. He's good friends with the super. And was on the school board then. His daughter's name is Cindy. She graduated college last year and now works down here."

"Where?"

"At the Biscuit. I wondered if I would run into her when you and I had lunch there the other day, but I think she bartends at night."

"She's a bartender? But she's got a college degree."

"Yep. She's only working there until she finds something more in line with her degree."

"Did Cindy ever talk to any school officials, your boss or you?"

"No, that was part of the deal. The super promised Goodman that Cindy would never have to talk to anyone about what happened."

"Is there anything else you can think of?"

"No. Is that cop really going to arrest me? Can you put in a good word?"

"I can try, Martin. I can only try."

Emily left Martin sweating in the room and reported back to Lewis the details of her conversation with Rudolph.

"I really hate all this. I suppose now that everything is in the hands of the authorities that Cindy will be interviewed. That's going to be horrible for her."

Lewis listened to Emily's information and was silent when she mentioned the names she had gotten from Rudolph, but began flipping pages in his note book.

"Did you hear me?" she asked.

"I took down the names of all of the school authorities when Parsons was principal at Mason City and also the ones now there. The man who replaced Parsons as principal was someone named Richard Goodman." Lewis entered something into his computer and focused on the screen for a few moments, then said to Emily. "Guess who Richard Goodman is."

"Related to Riley's good pal somehow. Right?"

Lewis nodded. "He's Clarence Goodman's brother. And now he's principal at Mason City. Riley used Parsons' sexual victimization of that young girl to put her uncle in as principal. Richard Goodman took over the position when Parsons left. That can't be a coincidence. Talk about a horribly sleazy deal."

"I wonder how Cindy Goodman feels about being used as a pawn in getting her uncle that job. Do you think she knows what happened and the part she unwittingly played in it? Did anyone think to get the kid some counseling?" said Emily.

Lewis looked at Emily. "You need to keep those names under your belt, you know. That's not information that should go public now or maybe never, but it's necessary for the cover-up case. Right now I have to file a report and follow up on the information, but sooner or later, someone will talk to Cindy Goodman."

"How awful. She thinks this is all behind her."

"There is nothing I can do. It's now in the hands of the court. My job is to take a closer look at the superintendent, his buddy and the buddy's brother as possible murder suspects in Parsons' death."

Lewis tapped his pencil in frustration against his desktop. "All of this is somehow related to the attempt on your life, but I can't for the life of me figure out how."

"Me either."

Lewis stopped his frenetic tapping and looked up at Emily. "You say Cindy Goodman is working as a bartender at the Biscuit, here in town?"

Emily nodded.

"You could drop by the Biscuit and try to wheedle information out of her."

"Stanton Lewis! I am not an insensitive woman. I would never put the victim of sexual predation into that position. She thinks her story is safely buried. I respect that and I won't be the one to dig it up again."

"Good. I knew you understood."

"But just so you know. I need a backup bartender. I may offer her a job."

Lewis gave her a level stare. "That's all."

"That's all."

Unless she mentions something about her past.

"I do have to tell her I know Martin Rudolph."

"Maybe it would be better if you tried to hire someone else."

"Don't be silly. She's qualified. That's all I need to know. Besides another woman behind the bar would be just what I need to keep Donald in line."

"Just make certain you keep yourself in line with respect to this case, Emily."

"I will if you promise to find out who decided I was so snoopy that I needed a dunking in the lake."

"That's my top priority as well as my duty," Lewis said.

—❖—

After Emily left, Lewis pondered both his cases. Superintendent Riley might have wanted to get Emily out of the way. Maybe Rudolph had told Riley he confessed to Emily about why Parsons left Mason City. But the motive didn't make sense, especially when Rudolph had told Riley he was going to talk about his part in it to the police. Who might know Rudolph had talked to Emily but didn't know Rudolph had spoken to the authorities? Rudolph might have told someone else, but who? Lewis shook his head. Rudolph wasn't to be trusted. He told the truth but only part of it. Well, thought Lewis, the guy was still sweating up a storm in the interview room. Now was the time to pry more of the story out of him.

Lewis gave it an hour longer and got no more from Rudolph. He called the county district attorney and let him know about the deal that had been made years ago in Mason City, a case that would now come back again to revictimize a young woman. Sometimes Lewis wondered if the job was worth it.

⬩

David Otter had lied to Detective Lewis the day of Mr. Parsons' murder. He woke up each morning wondering if this was the day the detective would seek him out and ask him questions he didn't want to answer, questions that might lead to his best friend being arrested for the murder of his father. David had told the detective that the members of Parsons' family were not at the reenactment, but that wasn't true. David had seen his friend Owen following Principal Parsons to the edge of the battle site as David prepared to take his position with the Seminole warriors. He was about to yell a greeting and wave to Owen when he heard father and son exchange angry words.

"Get the hell out of here. I expect you to take care of your mother and sister, not try to spy on me. And don't accuse me of something I never did and wouldn't ever do. I've told you again and again, but you don't believe me. Your mother doesn't believe me either," said Parsons.

"Listen to me. I'm trying to save your life, but maybe it would be better if you were dead." Owen's words were choked with anger, and he had grabbed his father's sleeve to prevent him from pulling away. Parsons slapped his son's hand off and strode off to the end of the field. Owen ran after him.

The downpour of rain increased so that David found it hard to follow Owen and his father, but there was a break in the curtain of water for a moment and in that moment David saw the older Parsons drop to the field. At the same time, the cannon roared signaling the beginning of the battle. David couldn't see where Parsons had fallen or if he had managed to get up to lead his troops into the battle, but only a few shots had been fired when the battle was halted. A tall man dressed as a soldier bent over an object on the battlefield, and a few minutes later the scene was swarming with emergency personnel and police officers. That was when the rumor went around the soldiers and Indians in the reenactment that the man playing Zachary Taylor was dead, apparently shot. David knew Mr. Parsons had Taylor's role, and it looked to David as if Parsons' son was responsible for his death. There had to be some reason for Owen to kill his father. David knew he should have tried to talk to Owen, but he didn't know what to say, so he had avoided him all week.

Each night David tossed back and forth in his bed, sleep refusing to come. He had skipped school for the past several days and had ignored the ring of his cell phone knowing it was Owen trying over and over again to get in touch with him. Owen had never visited David at his house, but he knew Owen would seek him out soon. Would that be before or after he was forced to talk with the detective?

After a day of wrestling with his nagging conscience, he knew it was time he faced his demons. He had to talk with Owen. He hit connect on his phone.

"Owen? Hi. It's David."

"David! Where have you been? I've been frantic. Didn't you get my messages?"

"I've been, uh, I've been kind of tied up." He didn't say he'd been tied up by his conscience telling him not to be a coward, to face his best friend. "We need to talk."

"What's this about?" Owen asked.

"I know who killed your dad."

"What do you mean you know who killed my dad?"

"We need to meet. How about at the lock, out by the highway intersections?"

"We'd better hurry then. The sun is going down and the cops park in that area looking for drug deals going down. I sure don't want to get picked up by the police," said Owen.

Owen had no idea he and David shared a similar concern about meeting up with cops, especially one tough homicide detective who seemed especially fond of making teenage boys shake in their Nikes.

David had his own pickup, a battered model he'd bought with money he saved working a relative's cattle ranch in the summer. He told his mother he'd be back later, that he was meeting Owen at the library in town to study for an exam.

"How's the boy doing after his father's death?" asked David's mother.

"He's good, I guess. We haven't talked about it."

"Well, tell him how sorry we are." She finished washing up the dishes at the sink, then reached for a dishtowel. "Hey, aren't you supposed to dry tonight?"

"I'll do it tomorrow and the next day. This exam is really important."

She cuffed him on the ear then grabbed him and gave him a kiss. "Don't stay too late," she cautioned.

David jumped into the truck and urged the old pickup to "please start" when he turned the key. It did not. He tried it again. It turned over, but wouldn't catch. He hammered on the steering wheel in frustration.

His father walked out of the barn and up to the driver's side of the truck. "I don't think beating it will make it start. Did you put gas in it recently?" he asked. "They run better with gas in them." Laugh lines creased his face.

"Ha, ha," said David. "Of course I put gas in it. I think it's the fuel line clogged."

"Here," said his father, handing him a set of keys. "You can take my truck. I'll see what I can do about yours."

"Thanks, Dad."

David slid behind the wheel of his father's truck, marveling at how luxurious it was compared to his. It had power windows and air conditioning. Before he could start it up, he heard his own truck roar to life.

"I got it to turn over. I'll take it down the road to see how it runs. Your mother wanted me to hop down to the minimart and pick up some coffee anyway."

He waved as his father turned out of the drive onto the road. The guy was a real whiz with engines, and David was grateful to have him look at the old truck.

"David," yelled his mother from the door. "You're not going to do much studying tonight if you don't take your books and backpack."

She gave him a skeptical look as she handed him his backpack. "Studying, are you? Or are you meeting a girl?"

"Aw, Mom. I'm meeting Owen."

"Take care, son," she said.

He knew she didn't believe his story. He turned off the engine. Maybe he should talk this over with his mother. She'd always been a good listener and she'd know what to do.

"Mom...?"

She turned.

"Never mind. I am meeting with Owen, not a girl. I promise you."

She smiled and nodded.

-❖-

Owen watched in horror as the other pickup rammed into his friend David's truck, then backed up and pulled out of the parking area.

Owen ran to the truck and tried to open the driver side door, but it would not budge. Smoke billowed from under the hood and a small flame flickered from the hood air vent.

"David, David!" yelled Owen, pounding on the door and window, but the crumpled figure fallen halfway under the dash made no movement or sound.

CHAPTER 16

Daisy and Rodney could guess why Reverend Jim had wanted to meet with them—money. They both figured it was another chance to see how he might be connected with the death of Principal Parsons. According to what Emily had learned, he admitted to knowing the principal and to connecting him with Toby Sands when the principal said he needed a bodyguard.

"I'm with Emily on this one," said Daisy as she nosed the car up to the reverend's trailer. "Our reverend must be short on smarts if he thought Toby Sands could handle the job of protecting anyone. I'd be more inclined to feel *less* safe with him around."

Daisy unlocked the trunk and extracted Rodney's wheelchair. She was about to help him into it as the door to the trailer opened and Reverend Jim stood in the light from inside, dressed as before in jeans and worn cotton shirt. Winthrop stood at his side.

"I'll give you a lift up," said Winthrop and lifted Rodney into the trailer as if he was moving a bag of feathers. He settled Rodney on the couch.

Jim offered coffee but Daisy and Rodney refused.

"So I guess you're wondering why I asked you to come here?" asked Jim.

"I assume it's related to the revival cause. I think we misled you into thinking we were interested in becoming big donors," said Rodney.

"It is related to revival, and you didn't mislead me. I always knew you were here because you were more curious than committed to our good cause. I don't want to mislead you."

"Us?" asked Daisy.

"Yes. I'm sure you think my cause is such that I lure people in and then ask for money. Nothing could be farther from the truth. I try to save people."

Daisy rolled her eyes, figuring now they would get the usual spiel about souls and coming to God and...other spiritual things.

"Mrs. St. Simonton, please let me explain."

"Go ahead," said Rodney. "I'm in no hurry to move."

Jim smiled. "Take Toby Sands for example. Little did I know that when he came to us, my daughter would fall for him." The reverend tried to hide the look of disappointment that briefly crossed his features, but Daisy and Rodney caught the look. "No matter. Melissa's never had good sense when it comes to men. Her husband is a no good...but that's another story. I decided this time I'd have a hand in her choice. I decided that if anyone needed saving, Toby Sands was the one. He wasn't perfect material, but it was what God sent me."

"Amen," muttered Winthrop under his breath.

"Winthrop was Toby's probation officer, so he knows him well, so well that he worried he might go bad."

"From what we know he was bad to begin with. How could he get worse?" asked Daisy.

"There's always a worse unless you're at the very bottom. Toby wasn't."

"Most people we know thought he was," said Rodney.

"They were wrong. Melissa saw good in Toby, as did I." Jim turned to Winthrop. "Winthrop took some convincing."

Winthrop curled up the corner of his mouth in a look that said he still wasn't convinced of Toby's inherent, but misguided goodness.

"So when Principal Parsons came to me for both spiritual guidance and other help, I decided to bring these two lost souls together. Toby's job was to follow the principal, watching him like a guardian angel, and then report back to me. Unless he saw Parsons directly threatened, he was not to intervene. I believed Toby could handle that."

"Well, it looks like he didn't. Parsons was killed while Toby was 'watching over' him," said Daisy.

"And you have no idea how sorry he is about that slipup."

"Look, I can appreciate your good intentions, but I wouldn't call Parsons' death while Toby was playing guardian angel a 'slipup,'" Daisy replied.

"Yes, I know, but Toby is trying to make amends by talking cooperatively with the police and telling them all he knows. I'm sure the police will solve this case with Toby's useful information."

Somehow both Daisy and Rodney suspected Toby's cooperative attitude was more like a "how do I save my butt on this one" stance. One glance at Winthrop confirmed he felt the same.

"So, I wanted you to know what kind of service I bring to people here. And, if you feel it is worthwhile, I'm happy to accept any donation you'd like to make."

There it was, thought Daisy. He was making a pitch for their money based upon the sad story of the reforming of Toby Sands.

"We'll surely give it some thought," said Daisy.

The reverend ushered them out with Winthrop's help.

When Daisy turned the car around and looked into the rearview mirror, she saw a broad smile on the reverend's face, while Winthrop screwed up his large, broad-nosed face in continued disbelief.

"Winthrop's not convinced, but won't say so" said Daisy.

"No, well, he's not going to utter a word against the reverend, his beliefs or how he saves his folks. The reverend's the one who signs his paycheck," said Rodney. "I like Winthrop. I'll bet if you got him in the right mood like in a bar with a few beers in him, he'd have plenty to say. I know he's a drinking man because I was close enough to him to smell whiskey."

Daisy turned to look at her husband. "That's something to think about." She focused her eyes on the driveway for a minute, then shifted into drive. They proceeded slowly toward the street.

"What's the real motivation behind the reverend asking us to visit him? I didn't believe his story of wanting to use Toby's reformation as a way of convincing us we should part with some money," said Rodney.

"Maybe he wants us to share Toby's good story with Detective Lewis, take the heat off Toby, and by extension, the reverend's operation."

"Is the reverend telling us the truth or simply blowing smoke up our, er, in our faces? Does he believe he's helping others? He's a very charming guy." Rodney adjusted his seat belt.

"I don't know what he believes. I think you're right. We should try to get Winthrop chatting. From what I saw, he thinks Toby is a fat bumpkin. We need to find out where Winthrop hangs out."

"Okay, then. Let's get out of here, then circle back to see if Winthrop feels like taking the night off. I'd need a stiff drink if I'd been party to the reverend's Toby-the-New-Man story. I know I can use a whiskey and soda and maybe a game of pool about now."

Daisy patted her husband's shoulder. "It's been a while since you had the opportunity to run a pool table. Let's see if Winthrop will show us the way to a bar with cold beer and a hot pool table."

"Hot zigiddy!" said Rodney slapping his knee.

⁂

Owen called 9-1-1, then tried to open the door to remove his friend, but it had been jammed from the impact. He reached through the open window and tried to feel for a pulse, but he couldn't reach far enough to touch David's neck.

"Can you hear me? Help is coming, but for now you shouldn't' move."

He heard a groan escape David's mouth. *Good. He is still alive.*

Owen turned when he heard another truck approach.

"What's happened?" said the driver, jumping from the truck's cab.

What's going on, thought Owen. "David! It's you, but who's in your truck?" asked Owen, surprised, but relieved to see his friend wasn't the victim of the accident.

"It's my dad. We traded rides for the evening. Is he...?"

"He's alive, but he's jammed under the dash, and the door won't open. C'mon. Let's try the other door."

Both young men pulled on the passenger's side door, but it was locked and the window closed.

"I'll see if I can reach the keys in the ignition and unlock it," said Owen, rushing back around the cab and reaching in for the keys. "Got 'em."

They both heard sirens in the distance and saw the flashing light of an ambulance make the turn and approach.

David unlocked the door and crawled across the seat of the truck to his father.

"Dad? You're going to be okay. Don't move. We'll get you out of there in a minute."

An EMT approached and cautioned David about trying to move his father. "I can't tell the extent of his injuries. Trying to drag him out of there might aggravate a possible neck or spinal injury. We'll wait for the jaws of life. Step back so I can monitor his vitals."

David and Owen walked over to Owen's vehicle. "Did you see what happened?" asked David, glancing anxiously over at the EMT with his father.

Owen nodded.

"Tell me."

"There's not much to tell. Your truck turned in here. I thought you were driving it, then suddenly before it came to a stop another larger truck rammed it from the side. I think the guy had just pulled in here following you. It was intentional. I know he meant to crash into you."

An unmarked police car pulled into the lot and stopped a few feet from the EMTs. Detective Lewis got out and talked for a few minutes with the EMTs still awaiting the jaws of life.

"Here comes trouble," said David.

The two boys watched the detective approach.

With no greeting other than a nod of his head, Detective Lewis said, "Let's hear what happened."

Owen repeated the story of what he witnessed.

"The guy who rammed the truck, can you give me a description?

"The windows were black," said Owen.

"Description of the truck? Or which direction it headed when it left?"

"Big, black, you know, about like all the trucks around here. Everything happened so fast I didn't notice where it headed," said Owen. David's face had gone gray in the flashing lights.

"I think you'd better sit down for a minute," said Lewis. He helped David into the back seat of his car, then signaled to one of the paramedics. "I think he's going into shock. The guy in the truck is his father."

David groaned. Were it not for Lewis' quick re-flexes, he would have pitched forward through the open door and onto the ground.

Sandy Davis, Lewis' partner, pulled up in her car. She gestured toward David who the paramedic had laid out on the ground. "Another victim?"

Lewis shook his head. "The victim's son. He arrived right after it happened."

The color came back to David's face, and the EMT helped him sit up.

"I heard the alert and your APB on the truck, but seventy-five percent of the trucks around here fit that description," Sandy said.

"There should be damage on the right front fender of that truck," said Lewis, "But he's probably long gone now. If he knows this area he can use all the back roads."

The jaws of life arrived several minutes later and worked for a half hour until the driver's side door was removed, and David's father was finally stabilized and lifted out of the cab.

"He wants to know if his son is okay," yelled one of the EMTs.

Lewis helped David to the ambulance. "Let him ride with his dad to the hospital. He's not in such good shape himself, so you can keep an eye on him. Don't worry about the trucks. I'll take care of them. We'll need to process the evidence from your truck."

"Evidence?" asked Owen as they watched the ambulance pull away.

"The truck that hit him left paint and other evidence," Lewis said.

"So you'll be able to find the guy who did this?"

"Eventually." Lewis took Owen's arm and directed him toward Lewis' car. "Let's sit a while. I have some questions. Coffee?" asked Lewis, taking out his thermos.

Owen shook his head.

"The two of you were meeting here. Why? You know this place is notorious for drug deals. Was that what you were doing?"

"No way. Neither of us are into that. David called me and told me we needed to meet because he knew who killed my father."

"Did he say who that was?"

"No."

"Would he have shared his suspicions with anyone else?" Lewis asked.

"Neither of us have many friends, and I don't think that would be something he'd share with his family."

"I'll drop you at home on my way to the hospital. It's important I talk with David," said Lewis.

❖

The detective walked Owen to the front door of his house and rang the bell. Mrs. Parsons answered the door, took one look at her son with the homicide detective and said, "You got yourself in trouble with the law? Don't I have enough to handle?"

"He's pretty shook up. He just saw someone plow into what he thought was his best friend's truck."

"Whose truck would that be?" she asked.

"David Otter's. You do know the two of them are pretty tight, don't you?"

"Sure," she replied, but there was no conviction in her tone of voice.

Lewis looked around the living room and saw two martini glasses on the coffee table. "Is someone else here?" he asked.

"No. What business is it of yours?"

"Tell him, Mom. He'll find out anyway," Owen said.

"It was Harold Bundy, the Assistant Principal. He was checking with me on the arrangements for our father's funeral service tomorrow. Apparently, many teachers wanted to speak about your father. Mr. Bundy and his wife were kind enough to help me with the funeral arrangements."

"Right, Mom. Funeral stuff. Whatever."

Lewis didn't think Owen cared anything about the funeral details. His mother sank down onto the couch, exhaustion written all over her face. That martini couldn't have helped her fatigue.

"You could use some rest, Mrs. Parsons," he said. "We can talk later. Right now, I need to get to the hospital to speak with the Otters.

"Tell David I'll talk to him soon and that I hope his dad is okay," said Owen.

By the expression on Owen's face, Lewis could tell he genuinely cared about his friend, which was more than the boy seemed to feel toward his mother or had expressed about his father.

Emily really did need another bartender, so what better a possibility than one around here, a gal at the Biscuit, a person who knew the sexual harassment case against Leonard Parsons well? While

Daisy and Rodney were off pumping the Reverend Jim for information—or being conned by him— Emily decided she would take her daughter out for drinks so they could talk. And Emily could watch the bartender. There was a lot a person could find out observing a prospective hire at work, information that was not found on a résumé.

There were few cars in the lot at the Biscuit. Emily and Naomi had missed the dinner crowds, and the dedicated drinkers and those who came to hear karaoke tonight wouldn't start showing up until after nine. The bar area located to the rear of the dining room was quiet. One couple sat at the far end of the bar, and they were too involved in their conversation to pay much attention to Emily and Naomi.

"Hi," Emily said, taking a stool at the bar. Naomi pulled out the one next to her. *I'm in luck. There's only one bartender, a woman. That has to be Cindy Goodman,* thought Emily. "Are you Cindy?"

"Yes."

Emily introduced herself and her daughter, then said, "I've heard you're a great bartender."

"That's nice to hear."

"I need a great bartender. I'm the bar manager at the country club. How good are you at cutting off drunk cowboys?"

"Stick around for a while. You can watch me in action."

Emily liked the sound of that.

"Well, lookee here," said a voice from behind her. Emily recognized it, and a shudder of revulsion ran through her.

"Toby Sands. Go away."

"Aw, that's not nice," said Toby. Behind him stood the woman Emily had seen him picking up at the casino. "Melissa and I were just finishing up our dinner when I saw you come in. I thought I'd stop by to say hello."

"That's what friends do, Toby, but you're not my friend."

"But he'd like to be," said Melissa, stepping in front of Toby.

"I don't mean to be rude, but could you take your troll home?"

"You're a mean woman," said Melissa.

"And you're a deluded one if you think I would ever be friends with someone who tried to arrange to kill my daughter and me."

"Let's be clear here. I wasn't trying to kill you. I was trying to sell you," Toby said.

"Oh, that's so much better. But I still don't like you. I don't care how well this woman has cleaned you up. You're still a toad to me."

"There's no forgiveness in your heart, is there?" Melissa said, shoving herself forward.

"Toby should be in jail, but he was given a chance to reform by the judge. I don't think he needs any breaks in his nasty life, at least not from me.

"Evil! You're evil!" shouted Melissa, exploding in a rage. She cocked her arm and let fly with her fist. She missed because Emily saw the blow coming and ducked, but the momentum of Melissa's punch threw her into Emily's bar stool and the two of them went down onto the floor. What followed was a lot of hair pulling, slapping and kicking.

"Okay, you two," said Cindy, emerging from behind the bar and carrying a can of something which she sprayed into Emily's and Melissa's faces.

Emily felt the burn in her eyes and stopped trying to grab Melissa's ear. Melissa turned her face away from the spray and crawled away from Emily.

"What was that?" asked Emily, coughing and wiping her eyes with her hands.

"Hairspray," Cindy replied. "Does that answer your question about whether I can handle drunk folks?"

"I'm not drunk," said Emily, grabbing the edge of the bar to pull herself to her feet.

Toby stood frozen, his mouth agape.

"You could have come to my aid," said Melissa. "Give me your hand and help me up."

Toby didn't move for a moment then held out his hand.

"Now the two of you either mind your manners in here or I'll call the cops," Cindy said.

"We were just leaving," Toby said and tried to steer Melissa toward the door.

"We were not," Melissa said. "We have a right to be here and not to be insulted by this little tart."

"Tart?" Emily was about to leap on Melissa, but Naomi grabbed her around the waist.

"You either make up or get out," repeated Cindy.

Melissa swept her hands over her beehive hair-do, which Emily had deconstructed during their encounter. "Let's get out of this place. The food is as lousy as the service and the company." Melissa grabbed Toby by his shirt front and pulled him out the door.

"Okay," said Emily to Cindy. "I've seen enough. Melissa is right in a way. This isn't the place for you. I can offer you a job in a much tonier place, Cindy. What do you say? It'll be better pay, too."

"How do you know that?" Cindy asked.

"I worked here a couple of years back. Drunk cowboys are always a problem."

"Yeah, I guess. But now it looks as if cat fights are, too," Cindy said, but her words were accompanied by a smile, and she held out her hand.

They shook. Now Emily had all the ammunition she needed to keep Donald Green in line. And who knows what she might find out about Principal Parsons.

CHAPTER 17

Cindy was unwilling to leave the Biscuit without giving them two weeks' notice—she was an honorable person, and Emily liked that—so Emily promised she'd arrange Cindy's schedule at the country club around her hours at the Biscuit. Cindy's work at the country club would fit well into Emily's day. Emily could schedule Donald at whatever times she found convenient and not be held hostage to his fishing needs. If he didn't like it, too bad. He could come in early and do setup. Donald hated to set up. She smiled to herself.

Emily shifted around in her seat as she and Naomi drove home from the Biscuit. Her butt felt sore where she had landed on it when Melissa took her down, but otherwise she was unhurt. Despite the altercation resulting in a few bruises and pulled muscles, the night had a satisfying outcome. Emily chuckled, thinking about how Donald was going to take working with another woman.

"You laugh now, but you're going to be sorer tomorrow," Naomi said, noticing Emily's squirming.

"You're probably right," Emily said. "My back is already feeling the effects of that fall."

"Get into bed and get a good night's sleep. Tomorrow you'll have to get up early to be at the bar for Donald's arrival and your announcement you hired Cindy. I wish I could be there to hear that."

Once back home, Naomi threw her purse on the couch and gave her mother a hug and kiss. "I'm beat." She headed toward her room.

"Hey. We never got a chance to talk tonight," said Emily. She patted the couch next to her. "Sit down. This is important."

"You're scaring me. Are you dying or something? Getting married? Moving?"

"It's not about me, honey. It's about you."

Emily's cell rang. She muttered a hello into the phone.

"Is this a bad time?" asked Daisy.

"Daisy. Are you okay?"

Naomi gave her a tiny finger wave. "Later."

"What's all that noise in the background?" asked Emily.

"We're at some bar called the Catfish Corral. Rodney is trying not to beat the pants off Winthrop in pool. I thought you'd like to know. The guy is getting drunk. We'll drive him to his place and see what we can get out of him."

"Be careful. I don't trust any of the Reverend Jim's people. His daughter just tried to beat me to a pulp earlier tonight."

"I'd love to hear that tale. We can exchange stories tomorrow. Breakfast?"

"Okay, but I need to be at the country club around nine when Donald comes in. I hired a third bartender."

"Donald might like that. More opportunity for him to ask for time off to fish."

"The bartender is a woman."

"He won't like that."

—✦—

David Otter's father was a lucky man. Aside from some contusions, bruises and a dislocated shoulder blade, there were no other injuries. Lewis entered his emergency room cubicle where he had returned from X-ray. The attending physician was just leaving.

"I don't want to stay here overnight. You said I was just fine," said Mr. Otter.

"No, I said your injuries weren't serious, but you suffered quite a blow when the other vehicle hit you. I'd like to keep an eye on you until tomorrow," the doctor replied.

"C'mon, Dad. Listen to the man. It's for tonight and then you can come home early tomorrow." David Otter stood at his father's bedside. His appearance was improved over that of the green-hued young man who fainted out at the lake, but Lewis could tell from the quaver in his voice that he was still shaken up about the incident. Not only had someone harmed his father, but the circumstances seemed to indicate it was because the hit-and-run driver wanted to target David and had mistaken his father for him. *So who,* thought Lewis, *was following David Otter? And why?*

Lewis introduced himself to David's father. "I'm sorry to bother you, Mr. Otter, but I need to know if you saw someone following you when you pulled out of the driveway of your place?"

Mr. Otter shook his head. "I wasn't paying attention. I was tuned in to the truck. I'd made some adjustments, and I wanted to see if she was running smoothly."

"How about you, David? Did you see anyone near your house during the day, someone parked at the side of the road, maybe watching the house or you?"

"No."

"I just talked with your mother. She told me you and Owen set up this study time tonight and that the two of you hadn't spent much time together since Mr. Parsons' death. Why was that?"

"He wanted time alone. He was pretty upset up about his father you know."

"But then you called him tonight."

"I wanted to touch bases and see how he was. We had a math test coming up, so we decided to study together."

"Your mother said you were meeting him at the library." Lewis left the question that followed unasked and let the silence descend.

David swallowed and dropped eye contact with Lewis. "We changed our minds."

"The lake is a pretty odd place for a study session."

"He wanted to talk, so we decided to forget the studying."

David's story made sense, yet Lewis knew from the nervous twisting of his hands and the way his glance jumped around the room never really landing on any one object or person that he was lying. He was hiding something, but what?

Lewis decided to back off for now and come at him another time. "Well, I guess that's enough for tonight. You both need to get some sleep. Ah, here's your mother."

Mrs. Otter rushed into the room, hugged her husband and son and turned to the detective. "You don't think this is a hit-and-run, do you Detective Lewis?"

Mr. Otter's gaze moved from his wife to his son. "Not an accident? Who would want to kill me?"

"Perhaps not you, Mr. Otter. I think the target was your son. I'm going to find out why and who's responsible. Right now I need to have a long talk with your son's friend, Owen. I think he knows more than he's telling, don't you?"

"He doesn't know anything. I'm the one who knows." David slumped into the chair by the bed and dropped his head into his hands.

"Know what?" asked Lewis.

"I know who killed his father, I do. I've known from the first, from when your girlfriend stumbled over the body."

Lewis wanted to say, "She's not my girlfriend," but instead said, "Who killed Mr. Parsons?"

"Don't. Please don't make me tell." David's eyes filled with tears.

"Better tell what you know, son," said Mr. Otter.

"He's my best friend," David answered in little more than a whisper.

—❖—

Lewis' partner Sandy had remained at the crime scene to help finish up the collection of evidence. He called her once he left the hospital and told her they needed to visit the Parsons' residence.

"I thought you interviewed Owen's mother already tonight," said Sandy, talking on her phone from the scene.

"I did but something else has come up." Lewis shared with her David's story that Owen was responsible for his father's murder. "The interesting thing is that he also believes the murderer was wearing a blue slicker with yellow flowers on it. That's the same story Toby Sands gave me. I never believe what Toby says, but maybe this time he knows something. I'll pick you up in about five minutes. We can plan our strategy in the car on the way to talk with Mrs. Parsons and her son."

—❖—

"We have no end of suspects and clues in this case," said Sandy as she slid into the passenger's seat of Lewis' car.

"Ballistics says the weapon Owen gave me was not the one responsible for Parsons' death. He believes his mother was responsible for his father's death. Toby thinks he saw someone wearing a blue slicker with yellow flowers on it tailing Mr. Parsons the day of the reenactment, and David Otter believes Owen killed his father. They all have motives of a sort, but everyone's possible motive has to do with Parsons' sexual assault of a teenaged girl years ago. If Owen did kill his father, why did he try to blame his mother? It doesn't track. I think he sincerely thinks she did it."

"Maybe the murder of Principal Parsons has nothing to do with what he did to that girl years back."

Lewis considered this possibility. It had merit. "What then?" asked Lewis.

"Maybe something more recent. Parsons could have taken up where he left off years ago. He could have assaulted another girl. You know these pedophile offenders often repeat if they're not stopped."

"Leaving his wife and son with the same motive, just updated."

"And fanning the flames of an already hot fire of hatred and resentment on the part of his wife and son."

"Let's see what they have to say now," said Lewis, pulling up to the Parsons' house. The place was dark, not even a night-light shone through the windows. When Lewis rang the bell no one came to the door, and there were no sounds form inside.

"Did they decide to do a runner?" asked Sandy.

Lewis turned away from the house and stomped back down the sidewalk. "It makes someone in that family look guilty."

━━❖━━

The next morning Emily awoke early, grabbed a cup of coffee and left to have breakfast with Rodney and Daisy. She was eager to hear what they had found out last night from the Reverend Jim's drunken bodyguard, Winthrop.

She waved to Rodney and Daisy seated in a booth toward the back of the Glades diner. The place was filled with snowbirds, ranchers, farm-workers and local businesspeople, all of whom adored the "world famous Glades sausage gravy and grits," known for its salty flavor and ability to produce twenty-four-hour indigestion. Yet people stood in line for the breakfasts, perhaps because they were so memorable—all day long.

As she worked her way through the crowd toward the booth, Emily could see someone was seated with them, his back to her. There was something familiar about the shape of his head. *Oh glory,* said Emily to herself. *It's Detective Lewis.*

He patted the seat next to him, and she slid in. He draped his arm across the back of the bench and smiled at her. "What's new?" he asked.

"What do you mean? I didn't do anything. Nothing. I'm staying out of your case," she said, a defensive tone in her voice.

"Sure thing, but you do know how to get your friends working for you, don't you?"

Emily's glance shot accusatory arrows at Daisy. "You told him what you were up to."

"Yes, but no. He lied to us. He said you'd be a bit late and to go ahead and tell him how the snooping went. I assumed you'd let him know we were visiting the reverend last night, so I told him about it," Daisy said.

"Now he knows what happened and I don't?" asked Emily.

"I'll get the pot and pour us another cup of coffee. Daisy will fill you in." Lewis signaled to the waitress to let her know he was getting more coffee. She gave him a smile about ten degrees warmer than a steamy August in central Florida.

"Hi, honey," the waitress said as he picked up the coffee pot. "I didn't see you come in. I missed you. You haven't been here for a while. Lost your appetite?" She gave him a one-armed hug and planted a kiss on his cheek. Emily thought that was better service than she'd be likely to get. It was surprising what being a big, handsome cop could do to women. Emily couldn't help but wonder if there had ever been anything between them. *But that's not my business, and I don't really care*, she reminded herself. Lewis and the waitress exchanged a few words, then she gave him another kiss on the cheek, this one much longer in duration and accompanied with a friendly caress of Lewis' arm. Emily felt her blood pressure rise. *It's not your concern*, said a voice in her head, but the flame of jealousy churning inside threatened to obliterate any rational thought.

"Are you listening to what I said?" asked Daisy, tapping Emily's hand to get her attention.

"Yes, sure. So what did Winthrop tell you?"

Lewis came back to the booth with the coffee pot and refilled everyone's cup, as well as placed an empty cup in front of Emily.

"Pay for detectives must be bad if you have to moonlight as a waitperson here," said Emily.

Lewis laughed. "Coffee?" he asked, holding up the pot and giving Emily one of his smiles meant to convey innocence. It was Emily's opinion that Lewis was never innocent of anything and hadn't been since he was nine years old.

"Grateful that we were willing to give him a ride home from the bar, Winthrop blabbed about Reverend Jim's interest in the Parsons' case, but it wasn't because the reverend knew anything about the murder. Winthrop thinks part of it was because he was concerned the cops might look at him as a suspect and, even if they didn't arrest him or bring him in for questioning, Winthrop said his revival business wasn't pulling in enough money to pay its bills. Word gets around in these rural areas, you know. Suspicion directed toward a spiritual leader could sink his reputation. Winthrop said he hadn't seen a paycheck for over a month. The reverend is having trouble making saving of souls pay."

"Well, that's a dead end with respect to the Parsons murder then," said Emily.

"Maybe, but we discovered the good reverend found a way to make even more money," said Daisy.

Emily leaned across the table, her eyes alight with eagerness. "Tell." In her excitement over what her friends might have found, she gripped Lewis' arm. He gave her a look of surprise accompanied by a sexy, lopsided grin. Emily hated when he got cute like that. It made her head spin in confusion and her breathing quicken.

"You tell the rest of the story, honey," said Daisy. "My eggs are getting cold, and you've already downed all of your biscuits and gravy."

"I haven't heard this part yet," Lewis said.

"Our spiritual leader has moved on to blackmail, and Parsons was easy picking. According to Winthrop, Parsons went to the reverend for comfort and forgiveness, telling the reverend about resigning his position over a sexual harassment issue. If Parsons expected spiritual enlightenment, he didn't get it."

"Instead he paid for revealing that secret to the reverend," said Lewis, and was about to say something else when Emily jumped in.

"But why would the reverend bump off Parson or have someone do it for him? Isn't that like killing the goose that laid the golden egg?"

"That's what I was about to say," said Lewis.

"Well, I got there first," said Emily, lifting her chin and giving him a haughty look.

"Could you two just get over it for now?" said Daisy.

"Sure," said Lewis, and he captured Emily's hand in his and wouldn't let it go. She struggled for a moment then gave up and relaxed her hand. *Might as well enjoy the truce*, thought Emily.

"Well, Winthrop said the reverend continued to receive blackmail payments even after Parsons was killed. Apparently, a payment appeared at a drop site every Monday. Winthrop collected it. It was there the Monday after Parsons' death."

"Maybe he paid early," said Emily.

"There's no early pay-off program for blackmail," said Lewis. "Something isn't quite right here. I wonder if the payment will appear this coming Monday. Where's the drop-off location?"

"Winthrop was sobering up and wouldn't say. We both got the sense that he didn't like the reverend's new line of work. Winthrop seemed to think Reverend Jim was about to work on us to find out if there was any information he might use to put us on his blackmail list." Rodney gave them a conspiratorial grin. "I led him to believe I had a few run-ins with the law before I became wheelchair bound."

"It's a story Rodney likes to tell strangers," said Daisy.

"It's true," Rodney insisted.

"I don't think several speeding tickets quite constitute a 'run-in' with the law." Daisy leaned over and gave her husband a kiss. "You old reprobate, you."

"I'm sorry I got the two of you into this. On the off chance the reverend takes a few payments off his victims and then kills them, I've put you in danger," Emily said.

"That's why amateurs should let the cops do their work and keep out of it," Lewis said.

"Then you wouldn't have known about the blackmail scheme," Emily pointed out to him with a self-satisfied tone in her voice.

Lewis ignored her. "Do you think the two of you can find out from Winthrop where the drop site is? We can keep it under surveillance this coming Monday. I want to know who's making those payments," Lewis said.

"Winthrop is a funny fella," said Daisy. "He has an odd sense of loyalty. Once he told us about the blackmail and began to sober up, he seemed regretful he'd said anything. I think Winthrop will be extra careful what he says from now on."

"I guess we'll have to use another approach then," Lewis said.

"What would that be?" asked Emily.

"Threats," Lewis replied. He then signaled Emily to slide out of the booth. "I've got to get to work."

"Oh, me too," said Emily. "I've got a new bartender coming in later this morning, a woman, and I need to be in the bar before Donald gets there to prepare him."

"Oh, ho," said Lewis. "That should be interesting. Just how do you 'prepare' Donald Green for the appearance of a woman hired to work side-by-side with him? If I didn't have this case I'd love to be there when you tried telling him about his new mate in the bar."

Daisy and Rodney also expressed interest in watching Donald Green's reaction to Emily's new hire. "We might as well leave for the country club now. We've got a tee time at ten. We'll hang out in the bar for a half hour. This should be fun, huh, honey?" said Daisy, helping Rodney into his chair.

Emily grabbed a final sip of her coffee and all four of them left together. Emily noted the waitress blew someone in their group a kiss. She guessed it wasn't her.

"So who's the new hire?" asked Lewis.

"Is that police business or are you being nosy?" asked Emily.

"You're hiding something, aren't you?" Lewis asked.

"Me?" Emily batted her eyelashes at him and turned away before he could see how relieved she was not to tell him who she had hired. *I'm gonna catch hell for this when he finds out,* she told herself.

CHAPTER 18

Emily was not looking forward to telling Donald about the new hire. She considered using the presence of Rodney and Daisy in the bar as an excuse for not confronting him. Maybe she'd just let Cindy show up and let Donald figure it out for himself. That was cowardly, she told herself, and a mean thing to do to Cindy her first day of work. She worried Donald might outright quit at the news, and although he was a pain in the rear, he was a reasonably good bartender who handled the drunks well. The only time Emily ever saw him smile was when he was talking fishing with the guys who came in after a round of golf. As for the women players, Donald could be friendly, even flirtatious.

When she told him about Cindy he was silent, other than his usual "humph,"

Emily held her breath when Cindy entered the bar a few minutes later.

"Sorry, but children are not allowed in here unless accompanied by a parent," Donald said in a sneering tone.

Cindy smiled and held out her hand, "I've heard all about you, Donald. It'll be unique working with you. I'm Cindy."

"Yeah, so I gathered. I gotta get some fresh air." Donald stalked out the door.

Emily let Donald stew on the back steps to the bar, then decided she should try to talk with him. "That was very rude, Donald, and not very professional. I expected more of you."

"Did you? I thought I was pretty restrained given that I'm going to have a mere child work next to me. Are you certain you're not breaking some child labor laws? What can she know about bartending?"

"She went to the same mixology classes I did, so I know she's got the skills. You can tell by her attitude just now that she's also got the chops for working with someone with few social graces and absolutely no sense of humor. I think the two of you will make a good pair."

"Is that what you think of me?" he asked.

"Naw, Donald. You're a real pussycat. Now lose the attitude and get back to work."

<hr />

Lewis had assigned someone to sit on the Parsons house. Owen and his mother reappeared home the next day.

"We needed to get out of town for a while. There's so much coming down on us, and now this: my son's best friend appears to have been the target of a hit-and-run. It doesn't look to me as if the police are able to handle any of this, not my husband's murder or the attack on my son." Mrs. Parsons paced nervously around the room as she talked.

"The person who was hit was Mr. Otter, you know," Lewis said. He didn't mind concern for her son, but he wanted to remind her who had actually gotten hurt. "But he wasn't who was targeted. We think it was his son. He's in danger from someone, maybe the person who killed Owen's father."

Owen sat in a chair next to the couch, his hands fidgeting, his eyes fixed on his mother.

"Did you get a look at the person driving the other truck, the one that hit Mr. Otter?" Lewis asked.

Owen shook his head.

"Tell me again why the two of you decided to meet there and not in the library to study? Who arranged when and where to meet?" Lewis asked.

"I did. I called him as I told you. I hadn't seen him for a while. I told you all this before. Why are you harassing me?"

"Exactly what did you say on the phone?"

"I don't remember," said Owen.

Lewis looked toward the hallway where several coats hung on hooks near the door. He got up and moved toward them, taking one off the hook.

"Is this your raincoat, Mrs. Parsons?"

He held up a blue one with yellow sunflowers on it.

"She gave a derisive laugh. "Well, it surely isn't my son's."

"Someone was seen the day of the reenactment wearing a rain slicker identical to this one. Can either of you imagine who that could have been?"

Owen said nothing, staring at the carpet as if he wished it could come up and swallow him. Finally, he gulped and, raising his gaze said, "It was me. I wore it, but I didn't kill Dad."

"Don't be silly, Owen. You didn't wear that coat. I wore it. I went to the reenactment. I killed my husband, then came back here and took the kids to Orlando to their grandparents."

"Mom, don't," said Owen.

"How did you kill him, Mrs. Parsons?"

"He was shot, wasn't he? I shot him." She threw herself down on the couch and crossed her arms over her chest.

"What weapon did you use?" Lewis' look locked with Owen's as he asked this question.

"My husband kept a gun in the house here."

"And you used that?"

She nodded and glanced over at her son.

Lewis got out of his chair. "I know about the gun, and so does your son. He brought it to me. Ballistics determined it wasn't the weapon responsible for your husband's death. Now, I'd like to go back to the beginning and find out why both of you are lying to me."

Mrs. Parsons looked over at her son, her jaw dropping in disbelief. "You went to the police and told them I killed your father? Why would you do that?"

"I followed you to the reenactment and saw you tailing Dad. The next I knew he was dead and you ran off toward the parking area. What was I to think?" Tears rolled down Owen's cheeks.

"David called you last night and told you he knew who killed your father, didn't he? That's why the two of you were going to meet," said Lewis.

"Yes," Owen admitted. "I knew what he was going to say. He thought you were responsible, Mom."

"I guess this means both Owen and his mother are off the hook for the murder," said Sandy Davis as she and Lewis got into the car.

"I don't know if it does. Could they both be confessing to confuse the situation, protecting the other? I don't get it, but I know I'm missing something here. I need to go back to the beginning and reinterview people, both those in the Mason City schools and those in the school system here. I still like Emily's friend Rudolph for a bad guy. He's a coward, has no backbone and kind of goes along to get along with the wrong people, including his boss in Mason City."

"You don't like him because he's getting too cozy with your friend Emily," said Sandy.

"That's only part of it. Someone threatened her and pushed her into the lake. I'm certain that is somehow related to the murder. Emily must know something someone doesn't want known. The same with David Otter. What do they know? What?" Lewis beat his hands on the steering wheel in frustration.

"Okay, then. Let me take a run at the people Parsons worked with here. Maybe I'll see something you didn't. Meantime you can talk with the people in Mason City. I know you'd love to have another chat with Martin what's his name."

"He'll call in his lawyer when he sees me coming. They all will. And why do you get to stay here, and I have to drive all the way to Mason City? You don't want to drive that far?"

"No, I don't fancy chatting with all those men who were responsible for covering up a sexual assault. They make my skin crawl."

"You assume they don't do the same for me?"

"I assume they do make you want to take a shower every time you talk to them, but you're better at worrying them than I am."

"I won't be able to talk with either Martin or his boss. Their lawyers will prevent me from getting close. Once the DA looks at what Martin told me, we may get some action on the assault case, but it won't help us." Lewis gave the steering wheel another good pounding.

"Stop that," Sandy said, placing her hand on his. "You could be charged with destruction of government property if you damage this car."

Lewis let his rigid shoulders relax and gave a deep sigh. "Okay. You're right. I'll see if there's anyone associated with the Mason City school system who's not hiding behind a lawyer. Someone there must know something about Parsons' leaving.

There are always rumors. So what's your game plan for the folks in the school system here?"

"I'll be friendly. You know. I'm the cop that looks just like your kid sister or the girl next door, the cop to whom you want to confess all your crimes."

"Does that really work?" asked Lewis.

"I don't know. I've never had the opportunity to try it. You're always one step in front of me, threatening enough to scare the scales off an alligator."

"Okay. Give it a whirl. Maybe if we keep up the pressure on everyone associated with Parsons something will break."

⁂

The funeral for Principal Parsons was held on the next day, the Friday following his murder. Lewis and Davis attended and ran into Emily and Clara. Lewis decided to take the empty seat next to Emily, but before he could claim it, a young woman rushed in and sat in it. Lewis and Davis slid into the seats immediately behind them.

Emily turned and whispered to Lewis, "This is Cindy Goodman, my new bartender. Cindy, these are Detectives Lewis and Davis. Davis is good at what she does and is a good, kind human being. Lewis? Well, that's another story." But she said it with a twinkle in her eye. If Lewis was surprised at being told about Emily's new hire, he hid it well.

Cindy twisted around in her chair and offered her hand to each of them in turn.

"Don't worry, Detective Lewis. I know all about you. I'm not worried," Cindy said with a grin.

Emily continued to glance around the room. Mrs. Parsons was seated in the front row, her son Owen at her left. A man Emily didn't recognize sat on the other side of Mrs. Parsons.

"Who's the guy seated next to the widow?" asked Emily.

"That's Harold Bundy, the Assistant Principal," said Lewis.

"Bundy's wife is next to him," said Clara. "I recognize most of these folks from town, administrators and teachers from the school and a few of the kids from the chess club and their parents, but no one I'd guess to have been a personal friend of his."

Emily leaned back in her seat and said to the two detectives, "Didn't the guy have any guy pals, someone he went fishing with or bowled with?"

"Everyone we talked with told us he was a total loner," said Lewis. "Was there anyone from the reenactment he seemed to talk with?"

"Nope," replied Emily. The background music stopped and a minister appeared. He was joined by Reverend Jim.

"Whose idea was that?" asked Emily, too stunned to whisper. She was heard throughout the room.

From the front row, Mrs. Parsons arose from her seat and turned around to face Emily. "It was my idea. The reverend was the only real friend Leonard said he had in this town."

Or so she thinks, thought Emily. *His good friend, the guy who was blackmailing him.*

"She doesn't know about the blackmail," said Emily, careful this time to lower her voice.

Lewis leaned forward until his mouth was almost touching her cheek. His breath smelled minty and tickled her ear, making her give a small shudder of desire. "We need to talk, Emily," he said.

"Would you two lovebirds carry on your conversation after this is over? This is a funeral, not a social club or the squad room," said Clara.

Emily's face reddened. Lewis dropped his gaze into his lap.

"Look at that, would you?" said Clara. The casket was carried up the aisle by six men including Toby Sands and Reverend Jim's right-hand man, Winthrop. Emily choked back her words of disgust at seeing Toby.

Lewis settled back in his chair and shook his head.

The service began with short, polite speeches about Parsons given by several colleagues. Just before Reverend Jim was about to speak, several men entered the back of the room, and found seats in the last row of chairs.

"Now I've seen everything," muttered Lewis.

"What?" asked Emily, twisting her head around to look at the newcomers. She gasped as she recognized one of the men, Martin Rudolph. She assumed the others were former Mason City colleagues of Parsons.

Clara tapped Emily on the hand to silence her.

Reverend Jim stepped to the microphone and talked at length about what he knew of Leonard Parsons. The man he described was probably unrecognizable to any of the folks attending the funeral. The reverend described him as "a man who fought his demons and won," and as "a man who reached out for help and found it." Hearing this, Toby Sands bowed his head and nodded in agreement.

The reverend continued his speech. "He admitted his transgressions to me and we talked of them together. It's not only important to confess to someone, but it's more important to publically admit your sins and ask for forgiveness. I know Leonard would want to do that if he lived."

No he wouldn't, thought Emily. Was Reverend Jim about to confess for him?

At this point, Emily leaned forward to get a glimpse of Mrs. Parsons and her son. Both of their faces looked frozen.

"Leonard suffered and so has his family. Perhaps now is the time for the family to come forward to talk about Leonard's sin, to ask on his behalf for forgiveness and for our support in their grief."

The reverend held out his hand to the family. No one moved for a moment, then Mrs. Parsons pitched forward in a faint. Harold Bundy caught her as she slumped forward.

"Make room. Let her breathe," said Mrs. Bundy.

Mrs. Parsons' eyelids fluttered, and she began to regain consciousness. She grabbed Bundy's arm and said, "Kiss me."

Bundy jerked back, and his wife's jaw dropped in shock.

"Oh," said Mrs. Parsons, reddening in embarrassment. "I thought you were my husband, come back to life. I'm so sorry," she stammered.

Bundy patted her hand. The funeral director rushed to her with a glass of water, and everyone seemed to gather themselves together.

"Now wasn't that weird," said Emily. When she looked around the room again, she noticed the seats occupied by Martin Rudolph and his Mason City colleagues had emptied so quickly it was as if the men had never been there.

After the service, Lewis pulled Emily to one side away from the crowd outside the funeral home.

"That was quite a show," Emily said. Lewis knew she was hoping to deflect his attention away from the reason he wanted to talk to her. "What was the reverend trying to pull?"

Lewis thought about the reverend's speech. He had to know no one was going to step up and confess about the sexual assault. *What was he trying to accomplish?* Lewis was puzzled, then Emily as if reading his confusion, said, "I think the reverend was warning someone that he would tell all unless..."

"Unless what?" asked Lewis and then he knew. It was a reminder to the person continuing to pay the blackmail. The reverend knew who it was, but Lewis could only guess.

"I have some pretty good guesses, too," said Emily.

"Are you reading my mind?" Lewis asked.

"No, but I know you don't know the drop site unless you get Winthrop to cooperate. Can you do that?" asked Emily. Maybe he could. Everyone had secrets they wanted kept, even Winthrop.

"Sorry, but I have to run. There's something I have to do back at the office."

"I thought you wanted to talk."

"Uh, I can't right now. I really just wanted to tell you not to bring up the topic of Leonard Parsons with Cindy."

"Before you rush off, I've got a question for you. Don't you find it odd that the victim of sexual assault shows up at her victimizer's funeral?"

"Maybe it was a way of saying good riddance," Lewis said.

"I don't think so. Unless Cindy is a great actress, she said something today that doesn't fit with the my-assaulter-got-what-he-deserved scenario."

"Tell me," he said.

"She said she came to the funeral because she really liked Mr. Parsons. She was unhappy when he left Mason City, but she was able to stay in touch with him when he took the job here."

"She met him? Here?"

"Yup," said Emily. "She said they would some-times meet for a cup of coffee at the diner halfway between here and Clewiston."

Lewis couldn't imagine what Cindy had in mind, unless she killed Parsons after cultivating his friendship for years, setting him up to be killed for ruining her life. *She certainly took her time leading up to the murder*, thought Lewis. He shared his thoughts with Emily who couldn't believe Cindy capable of murder.

"You've only known her for a few days." Lewis pointed out.

"I'm a good judge of character. Preschoolers taught me not to simply listen to what is said, but also to look at body posture and facial expression. You can't rely solely on words. Sometimes it's what the person doesn't say. You know all this, too. If you spent some time with Cindy you'd see what I mean."

Emily was right. He should spend some time with her.

"I don't mean time in an interview room, you know," she said to him as he prepared to drive off. "Quality time. Like in the bar."

Lewis waved and chuckled. Emily was quite the gal. He should spend some quality time with her al-so. Maybe after this case was over he would do that.

Back at the office Lewis ran a check on Winthrop and found a record as clean as Monday's laundry. *Darn.* He knew the guy liked to drink a little too much and that usually meant at least a DUI somewhere, but there was nothing. *Maybe too clean,* thought Lewis. He made a call to a guy he worked with before he moved back to Georgia for a few years. Jerry Garcia was sheriff in an adjacent county, the one where Winthrop worked for most of his career as a parole officer.

"Hi, Jerry. It's Stanton Lewis."

They took a few minutes to catch up, then Jerry, knowing Stanton for many years, said, "I know you didn't call me because you might owe me a phone call after all this time, so what can I do for you?"

"I've got a guy here with a record so clean I think it's made up. He worked in your county for years. There's nothing official on him, so I'm looking for anything you heard."

Lewis gave him Winthrop's name.

"I don't know the guy and nothing comes to mind, but I know what you mean. It's as if the record is incomplete or it's been scrubbed. I'll ask around and get back to you."

"I need something by Monday."

"It's Friday now. You're the same old Lewis I knew back when. You just don't know how to take it easy, do you? What you need is some gal to give you something other than cop work to live for."

"I tried that once, you know." Lewis remembered how unsuccessful his marriage had been.

"I hear she was a handful."

Lewis thought about Emily. She was a handful too, but in a different way. Emily was a caring, loving woman, maybe a bit too snoopy for her own good, but she was a gem compared to his ex-wife.

"I'll look forward to your call."

Lewis disconnected and leaned back in his office chair. It was all he could do for now. He'd have to wait, and waiting was not something he did well.

It was late Sunday night when Jerry returned his call.

"You're going to love this one," said Jerry. Lewis could almost hear him smiling into the phone.

CHAPTER 19

Emily and Cindy both worked the bar together on Friday night because the country club held a dinner for one of the leagues. That meant folks coming off the course looking to wet their whistles, as well as the diners ordering drinks. It would be a hectic night, but Emily was certain Cindy, new as she was to the bar, would handle the action well. One of the golfers in the league was Donald, who grabbed an empty bar stool early in the evening.

"Aren't you worried you won't get a seat in the dining room if you don't get in there now?" asked Emily. She felt as if Donald were spying on Cindy, waiting for her to make a mistake.

"I got someone saving me a seat for dinner," said Donald, giving her a look that might be considered Donald's version of a smile—his bottom lip moved toward his eyebrow a fraction of an inch.

"You can drink in the dining room, too," said Emily. "One of the waitresses will take your order in there."

"Naw. I like the atmosphere out here."

"The atmosphere would improve out here if you moved in there," said Emily. Emily could never tell if her barbs got to him because the look on his face never wavered.

Cindy came up behind her. "He's not bothering me if you're worried about that. I'm used to having his sour old face staring back at me." Cindy smiled and grabbed a shaker for the drink she was making. "You need a refill on your drink, Donald?" she said.

Donald growled something under his breath, slid off his barstool and left.

"You remind me of me," said Emily.

Cindy smiled and said, "Thanks. There's nothing I like better than giving sass to men who think they can get the better of me."

"You don't appear to have any problems dealing with any of the guys around here."

"No. Should I? You're not going to tell me Donald is a problem, other than the obvious one. You wouldn't have hired him if there was anything odd about him. Is there someone else I should know about?" asked Cindy, twisting the cap off a bottle of beer for a customer.

"You said the other night that you were friends with Mr. Parsons."

Cindy looked down at her feet then raised her gaze to Emily. "His death was awful" she said, a quaver of sadness in her voice.

"Wasn't he the principal in Mason City when you were in school there?" Emily grabbed five beers from the ice and ran them down to the end of the bar.

There was a lull in the orders coming in from the dining room wait staff and the bar patrons. Cindy leaned back on the shelves holding the liquor bottles.

"I guess you're surprised I would be friends with my old principal, huh?"

"Not really, except that I got the feeling he didn't have many friends around here."

"Yeah. I know. He was a really quiet guy, but he was a great principal. When I was in high school some guys said suggestive things to me on my way home after school. I told my parents but they told me to just ignore it. The boys kept it up. One day I was sitting in the hallway after school hours dreading my walk home, knowing they would be waiting for me. Mr. Parsons came out of his office and asked me what was wrong. I told him, so he went outside with me and confronted the boys. He told them he'd expel them and let their parents know what they were doing. One of them was Superintendent Riley's son. That guy was such a creep. Anyway, Principal Parsons let them have it. They never bothered me again. He left soon after that. I was sad to see him go. When I moved here, he and I ran into each other in the supermarket. He looked kind of down in the mouth, so I invited him to have coffee with me. We met maybe two times. Totally innocent. Why are you so curious about him?"

Emily caught sight of a patron at the other end of the bar who held up his glass to signal her he needed a refill. "Back in a jiff," she said to Cindy.

There were a whole lot of questions that went through Emily's mind as she took his order, made the drink and took his money. *Parsons stepped in with Cindy's bullies and he felt she owed him sexual favors? Then she told her father about Parsons' advances because she had second thoughts about the sexual encounter? Now she has guilt over Parsons' losing his job, so she invited him for coffee to make it up to him? Did they talk about what happened over coffee?*

When she returned, she said. "As to your question, I'm curious because I was the one who kind of "discovered" his body in all that mud. And I'm good friends with the detective who's lead on the case." Emily wanted to kick herself for continuing to encourage their discussion of Parsons. She was doing just what Lewis told her not to do.

"I hear you and the detective are more than just friends," said Cindy with a grin.

"I help him out on some of his cases," Emily said.

"That's not what I meant," replied Cindy, "but it's really none of my business, is it?"

"No more or less than your friendship with Mr. Parsons is mine." Emily hesitated for a moment. "Do your parents know the two of you were friends?"

"No. It's really funny. When I told them about how he handled the bullies, Dad said he overstepped his position, and told me to stay away from him. I don't think my parents would like my having been friends with him."

Emily could almost not believe what Cindy was telling her. *Was this a case of a woman identifying with her abuser? That couldn't be true.* Emily knew Lewis would hate what she did next, but she couldn't help herself.

"I did hear some rumors about Mr. Parsons, uh..." said Emily.

"Rumors? What about?"

"I heard the reason he left Mason City was because he was accused of inappropriate behavior with a student."

"You mean sexually inappropriate?"

Emily nodded.

Cindy shook her head. "I can't believe that. He never said a thing. Except..."

"What?"

"He told me to keep our coffee meetings to myself, that it wouldn't look right for a principal to be socializing with a former student."

Emily decided to plunge in with both feet. "He was asked to leave his position at Mason City because of the accusation. Nothing would go on his record if he left."

Cindy's mouth dropped open in shock. "He didn't try to fight it? I don't get it. Why would he just cave in?"

"Maybe because it was true. Would you know anything about that?" asked Emily.

"Of course it wasn't true. Who would say such a thing about him?" Cindy stopped wiping down the bar and looked up at Emily, squinting her eyes in suspicion. "Why do you think I would know about this?"

Emily shrugged. "I thought perhaps you'd heard gossip at school."

Cindy sighed, slipped around the end of the bar and sat on the bar stool. "I did hear something at the time," she said.

Finally, thought Emily, *we're getting somewhere. I broke through the shell she's built around herself to ward off the trauma of betrayal by someone she admired for helping her.*

"My best friend at that time, Diane Ross, said Mr. Parsons left because he had an affair with the home economics teacher. I don't remember her name, but she was single and left very suddenly. It was rumored she was pregnant. Diane said the baby was his. We argued. I defended him saying he'd never do anything like that. She accused me of being sweet on him. She and I were never very close after that."

Denial, denial, denial, thought Emily. *The hold he had on this young woman continued from beyond the grave.*

From what Emily knew, such behavior wasn't unusual in victims of sexual assault, especially if the assault occurred when they were young. Because their victimizer was someone they had learned to rely on, they didn't give up their trust easily. In Cindy's case, she continued her relationship with her abuser years after the abuse. She seemed like such a normal young woman with no hint of what had happened to her, as if the abuse was tightly locked in the past or was interpreted by Cindy as something other than assault.

"Did you and Mr. Parsons ever talk about those rumors and why he left?"

"Emily, there was nothing to talk about. He's gone now, and that makes me very sad, but there's nothing I can do to bring him back. He seemed like such an unhappy person and I felt sorry for him." Cindy held out her hand to Emily and gave her a pat on the wrist. "Okay?"

Emily felt as if Cindy was deliberately putting an end to the conversation. Cindy gave Emily the sweetest and most innocent smile, her eyes wide, lips pursed in a Kewpie doll smile.

One of the waitstaff approached the order station and waited for Cindy to come take the drink order.

"I think we're going to get slammed in a few minutes. There's a league that got off late and they'll he heading our way," said Emily.

"That means trouble then because they won't have eaten anything yet for their evening meal, so the booze will go right to their heads. I've seen that before."

"We'll keep the peanut dishes full and hope for the best," said Emily.

For the rest of the evening they were swamped with orders, but Emily couldn't forget her conversation with Cindy. She kept glancing over at her new hire as they worked. Donald came back into the bar and claimed the first empty bar stool despite a golfer ahead of him, but one icy look from Donald was enough to encourage the other party to find a seat on the other side of the room.

"You're back so soon," said Emily, slapping a bar napkin down in front of him. "What will it be this time?"

"The usual," he replied.

"The usual beer or the usual Crown and Seven?"

"Both. Golf banquets drive me to drink. How many times can a guy replay a hole?"

"How many times can you recatch a fish?" She slid the beer down the bar to him and followed with his mixed drink. She skated the drinks with a practiced hand while Donald caught them with equal ease. It was a ritual they practiced often. Neither ever missed.

Instead of savoring his drinks as he usually did, Donald downed his drinks quickly and held up his fingers for two more.

"You're doing a double shift tomorrow, Donald. Afternoon and evening. Cindy won't be in until after five. Better go slow on the booze or you'll be working with a hangover."

"I've never had a hangover," Donald said.

"That's encouraging," said Emily.

"But I've been drunk plenty of times," he said.

Overhearing the conversation, Cindy came over. "Maybe you were too drunk to know if you were hung over," she said.

"I guess we'll find out tomorrow," he said.

"What's the problem, Donald?" said Emily after another hour watching him down drinks. Donald had ordered two more drinks and was leaning on the bar with his elbow. Emily thought he certainly looked well on his way to drunk.

"I'm feeling old," he said.

"It's about time," said Emily.

"I guess I'm doing some reassessment of my life," Donald said after a sip of his whiskey.

"You aren't going to quit fishing are you?" asked Emily.

"Don't mock me, woman, when it's you I choose to confide in," he said.

"I'm sorry, Donald. Sometimes I can't tell when you're serious or when you aren't."

"I'm always serious."

"I should know that. So what is it other than feeling old?"

"I'm lonely." He looked at Emily with eyes that had lost their icy hue. Instead she saw they were soft robin's egg blue.

Oh, no. Donald was about to make a move on her.

"Emily, would you do something for me?" He wiggled his finger at her to come closer. She did, worried she was making a big mistake. She wanted to be supportive because this was the first time he had opened up to her, probably to anyone. *But what if the dude tried to kiss me?* He did that once before. It was kind of nice, but then there was Lewis and her. Whatever that was.

"Donald Green, are you putting the moves on my girl?" asked a voice from behind Donald. Detective Lewis had entered the bar without Emily's notice.

Donald didn't twitch a muscle. "Nope. I was just asking her to call a taxi for me."

"He's a little drunk," said Cindy. "If my boss lets me go early tonight, I can drive you home, Donald.

"Or you could, detective," said Emily.

"I'm here on business," said Lewis.

"I don't like you interrogating folks in my bar," said Emily.

"It won't take long. No one will know."

"You're known by folks all over the county as a member of the local police, and for those who don't know you, your presence just screams 'cop.' Everyone will know exactly what you're doing. No one will want to come in here if they think a cop is hanging out here."

"If a person isn't up to no good what should it matter if there's a police officer in a bar."

"You said it once yourself, detective, everyone has something to hide." Emily finished washing glasses and stacking them. She looked around and noticed the crowd had thinned in the bar and the dinner had let out. "Isn't there a little room down at headquarters where you prefer to take suspects?"

"So is it okay if I take off?" asked Cindy.

"Go ahead," said Emily.

"C'mon, Donald," said Cindy, taking his arm and steering him off the stool and toward the door.

Lewis and Emily watched them go. "Do you think that's a good idea?" asked Lewis. "Donald and a girl?"

"She's a young woman, not a girl. Besides, I'm not worried. I don't think Donald knows what to do with females other than to growl at them and insult their intelligence. She'll be fine."

"You've been talking to her, haven't you? I told you to stay out of this."

"She's one of my employees. Of course, I talked with her. What am I supposed to do? Send her notes about the job?"

"What did you find out?" he asked.

"You don't want me to talk to her, but you want me to tell you what I found out doing what you don't think I should do? Go find the person you came in here to ask questions of. Do your job and then leave."

"Answer my question."

Emily crossed her arms over her chest and tried to look defiant, which was difficult for someone short, blond and cute.

"Look, Emily. It would be a big help if you have any insight into this woman. She may be responsible for killing Parsons. She certainly had motive. He assaulted her."

"Something isn't right about this story. I get the feeling she really liked the guy, so she's either in a state of deep denial or…"

"Or what?"

"I don't know. I just don't. Talking with her I get the feeling she's not hiding a dark past."

Emily and Lewis stared at each other for several minutes until the last customer left the bar.

Lewis offered to stay until Emily closed up, worried that whoever pushed her into the lake might try to harm her again, but Emily insisted she was just fine because the wait and kitchen staff were still working. But he insisted so Lewis walked her to her car. The illumination from the streetlight cast shadows from the waving palm fronds of the tree near the dumpster.

"Do you remember the night we met?" asked Lewis.

"I do. You accused me of murder."

"I did. I know you better now." Lewis moved closer to her, reached out and pulled her to him.

"Why detective, I thought you were working tonight," she said, a flirtatious note in her voice.

"I am. I'm working on getting you and me a lot closer than we have been." Lewis kissed her, a soft kiss to begin with, but it soon became more insistent on both their parts. Lewis pressed Emily up against her car. She returned the pressure. "Emily," he began.

"Stanton, you've got to let me go."

"Why? We were just getting started."

"Yes, I know that, but there's something unromantic about a passionate kiss delivered to the smell of rotting garbage." She pointed to the dumpster near the palm.

"Oh, right."

"And something else," she said, disentangling herself from his arms.

"What?"

"There's some guy behind us. He's big and from where I'm standing he looks mean."

"Oh." Lewis turned to look at the interloper. "It's just my contact, the guy I was supposed to meet here. He's got some information for me."

"Honestly, detective. You're as clueless about women as your friend Donald is." Emily could tell from the look on his face that her remark hit and hurt. She twisted around and opened the door to her car, got in and stepped on the gas, then abruptly slammed on the brakes. Emily rolled down her car window and yelled back at Lewis. "Why do I bother with you? And what is there about you that I find so irresistible and so, so, so annoying that I just want to throw you on the ground and ravage you most of the time?"

"You're kind of tiny to be ravaging someone my size, but I can't tell you how much your impulse means to me," Lewis said.

Emily gritted her teeth and let forth a howl that got a baying response from the band of coyotes that roamed the fields near the country club. She tromped on the accelerator and spun gravel.

"That your gal?" asked Winthrop.

"I really can't say," said Lewis. "So what do you have for me? Have you decided to cooperate?"

"I don't think I have any choice, now do I?"

CHAPTER 20

"Let's talk in my car," said Lewis, gesturing toward his SUV.

"Good idea. No one seems to be around, but I'd just as soon keep this conversation private." Winthrop plopped his massive body into the passenger's seat. Lewis could smell the alcohol fumes coming off him.

"Need courage to talk with me, did you?"

Winthrop said nothing for a minute, then, "Booze is what got me into trouble at my job, although no one except the reverend and I knew it. Until now. How did you find out I had fudged my records, making it look as if I met with my parolees when they didn't show?"

"Your record looked too clean to me and to the sheriff in the county where you worked, so I encouraged him to do some poking around. You covered for parolees that didn't show up for their appointments. Instead of reporting them, you took money from them and changed their records. Now that's what I call petty, petty theft, Winthrop. How much money can you get off an ex-con whose job probably pays minimum wage if he can get a job."

"I know. I know. The drinking and what I was doing finally got to me. I had to get out."

"I don't think that's the real story, is it? You went to Reverend Jim as a spiritual advisor, confessed what you were doing, thinking he could ease your conscience, but instead he pulled the same con on you. He told you he'd report you if you didn't come work for him. The money was far less than your job as parole officer, but what choice did you have? He would have gone to the authorities, told them what you were pulling and you would have lost your job, gone to jail and probably lost your pension. You certainly never would have worked for the state again. And Reverend Jim wouldn't have hired you then either, would he? I mean, how would it look if he had a felon working for him?"

Winthrop pushed his hand through his hair. "Okay. What do you want from me?"

"I want you to go to the drop site for the blackmail money from Leonard Parsons. I think it will still show up tomorrow as it did last week, even though he's dead. Somebody is paying. I want to know who and I want to know why."

"I don't know. I just pick up the money."

"I believe you, but I need to find out where the site is and the time for the drop-off. I want to be there when the person leaves the money."

"What do I get in return?" asked Winthrop.

Lewis gave a short laugh. "I don't think you're in a position to be making a deal, do you? I'll see what I can do after I arrest the reverend."

"I gotta tell you I don't think he killed Parsons. I know killers and he's just a slimy little crook who likes to get people to reveal their shady pasts, then takes advantage of their trust in him."

"You could be right about the reverend. Listen, Winthrop, you'd be doing yourself a favor if you dried out and went to a few meetings. It would look good when you got to court also," said Lewis.

"I'd be more than happy to start attending meetings, but not one where Toby Sands is present. He may have turned his life around/ I'd rather do hard time than listen to that guy whine about his life."

Lewis understood his sentiments oh so well.

❖

Emily could see someone moving around in her living room as she pulled into the drive. Naomi was home. Good. As she opened the door to her house, Vicki yelled out the window next door. "Coffee, or is it too late? Maybe lemonade?"

Emily wanted alone time with her daughter, but she hadn't seen Vicki for several days and felt guilty about ignoring her, especially when she was so generous with her food and hospitality. Vicki seemed to be the only one Emily knew who could deal with Donald's irascibility. Everyone else found him annoying. Vicki just fed him pie, cake and casseroles and ignored any grouchy remarks he made.

"Sure, but give me ten minutes to jump in the shower. I smell like the bar."

"Hi, Mom. Hard night?" Naomi asked.

"The usual. Cindy is working out well. She was even kind enough to drive Donald home after he drank too much. Now that's going way beyond what anyone can expect. She's a gem."

"Maybe she can make Donald into something like a human being."

"She's a sweet gal, not a miracle worker."

Naomi let forth a laugh of agreement.

"Listen, Vicki will be over soon with some kind of treat, but first..."

"First, you need a shower. I heard you tell her."

"No, first we need to talk."

"About?"

"About what I found in the waste in the bathroom the other day. You know what it was. I don't' mean to pry, but it was in plain sight, so when are you due?" Emily asked, trying for a joking tone.

Naomi went white for a moment, then recovered herself. "Oh, I almost forgot about that."

"How could you forget?" Emily's voice changed to one of anger and confusion.

"Don't get your panties in a tangle. It's not mine. My friend Sharon came over the other morning and showed me the results on the stick. She wanted confirmation of what she saw. So I told her. 'Yep. You're pregnant.'"

Emily gave a deep sigh, then tried to cover her relief, saying, "I don't know her, do I?"

"No. She came down here for a few weeks' vacation with her grandparents. She's married, and she and her husband have been trying for a baby for over a year. I guess it's finally happened."

Emily flopped backward onto the couch. "Oh, my."

"You thought it was me? I think I'm insulted that you thought I'd get myself pregnant"

"I was more worried someone else got you pregnant."

"Very funny, Mom."

Vicki threw open the door and yelled, "It's cake. Lemon Bundt cake. This is the first time I've baked it. It could be awful."

It wasn't.

Emily was still in bed, dreaming she was eating another slice of Vicki's lemon cake while Winthrop and Lewis waited outside an abandoned citrus processing plant near Indiantown. As the sun rose over the lip of the lake, the conical towers looming over the single-story buildings cast long, eerie shadows onto the area. Lewis always thought the place looked as if it belonged on the moon, an outpost for aliens to spy on earth and perform scientific experiments on captured humans.

"Despite not being in operation for six months, the place still smells like orange juice cooking. I love Florida citrus, but if I worked here, I might never drink another glass of it," said Lewis.

"That sweet smell gets to you when you're up close," agreed Winthrop.

The two men had hidden Lewis' car behind a railroad car parked on the spur that ran from the main rail line into the plant. From their vantage point behind a rusting bucket loader, they watched a car bump across the weeds growing through cracks in the concrete parking area. The vehicle nosed into a space near a building marked by a sign that read, "Administration." No one got out for a few minutes, then the driver's side door opened, and a figure clad in black sweatpants and a hoodie emerged. Lewis couldn't see the person's face, but he recognized the car, and somehow he wasn't surprised.

The individual carried a plastic bag and dropped it into an overgrown planter at the foot of the sign. Lewis and Winthrop watched the hooded figure visually scan the area, then turn and get back into the car. Lewis jumped from behind the bucket loader and raced over to the car. He pulled open the door and yanked the driver out of the seat.

"Mrs. Parsons. Out for an early morning drive?" he asked.

"Let go of me. It's no business of yours why I'm here." The hood slid back on her head. Her eyes snapped with anger, but Lewis could also see fear there.

Lewis walked her back to the planter, stooped and picked the plastic bag out of the tangle of weeds. "What do we have here? Bread crumbs for the birds? Winthrop, come out here and take a look at this. Is this the correct sum of money the reverend asked you to pick up?"

Winthrop emerged from behind the machine, his head down, his tread heavy with the knowledge that his future looked grim.

"Did you know the reverend was blackmailing Mrs. Parsons, not her husband?" asked Lewis.

Winthrop shook his head. "No. I thought it was Mr. Parsons until the money continued to appear after his murder. I thought it odd the reverend insisted I still come for the money. He instructed me to continue to appear for the drop-off and not show myself. I was always here ahead of time, but I never saw the person's face because it was hidden by the hood, and the morning light came in at such a low angle."

"You must be one of Reverend Jim's crew," she said to Winthrop.

"Probably not any longer," said Winthrop with a sad smile. Lewis handed the bag to him. He counted the money in it and handed it back to Lewis. "Two hundred dollars. Just like in the past."

"Okay. Winthrop. I'm going to trust you to follow me back to the station in Mrs. Parsons' car. No trying to get away."

"I know." Winthrop got into the Parsons' car and waited while Lewis walked Mrs. Parsons to the police car, then followed it out of the lot onto the road.

"Was the reverend blackmailing you all along, not your husband?" Lewis asked as they drove north.

She nodded.

Lewis smiled at how duplicitous the reverend was in all his relationships. even those people closest to him like Winthrop, led to believe Mr. Parsons was the blackmail victim and too worried about his own hide to question why he was instructed to continue to wait for the money.

"I was so ashamed of him. I wanted to make certain no one ever learned of what he had done, so I continued to pay after his death."

"Did he know you were paying the reverend?"

"I don't know. Maybe. We weren't very close after we left Mason City," she said, then surprised Lewis by chuckling. "I thought everything was up when the reverend talked about going public with Leonard's sins at the funeral. For a moment I felt kind of relief along with my initial sense of horror at letting everyone know what Leonard did in Mason City. It was almost like a black huge cloud had finally passed overhead and disappeared, but then I realized he wasn't asking me to tell on Leonard. It was an implied threat of what could happen if I didn't continue to pay."

"So I don't quite understand why you wouldn't have grabbed for that relief, if not at that moment then later. It would have ended all of the lies and secrets."

She shrugged. "I couldn't. I needed to protect..."

Lewis waited for her to finish.

"I needed to protect his past for the kids' sake. Besides," she said, staring at him, "you already seem to know about Leonard's past. I won't have to say a thing." Her mouth was set in a tight, defiant line for a moment, then it began to quiver. "I don't want to talk about this anymore." She turned her head and looked out the window.

Raindrops hit the windshield and soon became a sheet of water, reminding Lewis of the torrential downpour the day of the reenactment. He turned the wipers to their fastest speed and looked over at Mrs. Parsons. He wondered if she was reminded of the day also. He thought he saw a tear on her cheek, but it could have been the windshield reflecting rain drops onto her face.

Vicki had left the lemon cake, so Emily and Naomi finished it off for breakfast.

"It's always great visiting you and seeing some of my friends here, but I've got to get back to my little apartment on the coast," said Naomi, taking a sip of coffee to wash down the cake. "I heard yesterday. I've got a part-time position in a daycare center. I begin next week."

"Oh, honey," said Emily. She came around the table to where Naomi sat and embraced her. "You're going to follow in my footsteps and go into child care."

"Well, only for now. It will give me time to take some night and online courses so I can complete my four-year degree."

"In psychology, right?" asked Emily, eagerness in her voice.

"Uh, no. It's in political science."

"You're going to be teaching preschoolers poli sci?" Emily thought kids were pretty smart, but what four-year-old was interested in political science?

"No. Don't be silly. Political science makes the perfect major for applying to law school."

Emily's mouth dropped open. "You mean you'd rather be like Clara than like me?"

"Oh, Mom." Naomi reached out and patted Emily's hand. "No. I'd rather be like myself. I want to be a lawyer and deal with family law, especially spousal and sexual abuse cases."

"That's much better." Emily felt a sense of joy that her daughter wanted to help others.

"A few years doing that, then I'll change to corporate law, maybe sign with a prestigious law firm in NYC." The side of Naomi's mouth lifted in a half smile, but Emily didn't see it.

"What!" Emily said, choking on the sip of coffee she'd just taken.

"Kidding. Just kidding," Naomi said.

"Well, of course, you should do what you want to do," Emily said dabbing coffee off her shirt front.

"Don't worry yourself. I intend to devote myself to helping others." Naomi smiled at her mother.

Emily's cell trilled. Cindy was at the other end of the call.

"Hiya. I thought I'd get in touch and let you know Donald was in no shape to come to work this morning, so I'm at the course setting up the bar. It should be a slow day. All this rain and no special events are scheduled this evening."

"Thanks so much, Cindy. But wait. How do you know Donald is in no shape to bartend his morning's shift?"

"I gave him a ride home last night. Remember?"

"And then you did what?"

"Held his head over the toilet bowl while he let go of his dinner and drinks, threw him in a cold shower, then shoved him into bed. I slept on the couch. He could barely get one eyelid open this morning."

"Listen, I appreciate you going out of your way for Donald and for me, but I'm coming into the bar in an hour or so to help you out." Emily mulled over in her mind whether she should ask Cindy if she removed Donald's clothes before she turned on the cold water in the shower. She decided against it. For now.

"It's your decision to come in or not, of course, but I could just call you on your cell if I run into anything I can't handle."

"I'm sure you'll have everything under control when I get there, and if you really don't need me I can play a round. I'm sure someone will let me fill in a threesome...if it stops raining."

On the way into the bar, Emily had second thoughts. Maybe she wasn't showing enough confidence in her new hire by rushing to the country club to "help her out." That could be perceived as "check up on her." *Oh, well,* thought Emily. *I'm almost there now, and there are errands I can run. Maybe I should look in on Donald. Better yet, I could track down Lewis and see if he'd like to have lunch.* Emily mentally shook her head. Who was she kidding? It wasn't lunch she was after. She wanted to be updated on the Parsons case. Although that case was none of her business, the investigation into who pushed her into the water was, so she had a reason to see the detective. *Surely trying to make contact with him wasn't personal,* she told herself. She squared her shoulders as she walked into the bar at the country club.

"Well, you look very determined. What's up?" asked Cindy.

Emily looked around the bar. No one was there, and, although the rain had stopped, the pro was keeping everyone off the greens until things dried up. It was going to be a slow day.

"This is silly, I know. I shouldn't have bothered stopping by," said Emily.

"I understand perfectly. I'm new to the bar, and this is the first shift I'm doing on my own. I'd be worried, too."

Emily laughed. "I'm not worried. Really. If you can handle a drunk Donald Green, you can deal with anything." She slid onto one of the barstools.

"Coffee?" asked Cindy.

Emily nodded. "If my daughter and I hadn't been such pigs last night and this morning I could have brought you some lemon cake. I'm sure Donald's cupboards afforded you little for breakfast."

"I was surprised. He had an unopened box of cereal and milk in the fridge. Of course, the cereal was two years old, and the milk looked like cottage cheese. Don't worry. I stopped at Dewey's Drive Thru and got myself a breakfast burrito."

Cindy poured two cups of coffee. The two women smiled at each other over the rims of their cups.

Emily turned in her seat and looked out at the tee box for the first hole and the green beyond. "I'll bet the pro will keep the course closed for the rest of the day. It looks pretty soggy out there."

Cindy nodded. "You know, Donald can be a real pain, but I kind of like him. Under that unpleasant exterior he's a pretty kind guy."

"Don't tell him you figured that out. He'll break into tears knowing you saw through him."

"Right," said Cindy. Another long silence ensued. There was more smiling, more blowing on hot coffee, more sipping.

"Donald's a little old for you," Emily said, knowing she wanted to use the topic of Donald as a way to discuss Parsons. It was a subject she shouldn't broach. Lewis would be so mad at her if it went from Donald to older men to Parsons.

"I like older men. They're so much more interesting than guys my own age."

"You liked Principal Parsons, too." *Just drop this, Emily,* said a tiny voice in her head.

"I did. He not only rescued me from those bullies, but I admired him. He was quiet, but when he spoke, he said things I needed to hear."

"Like?" *Emily, Emily, Emily,* said the voice. Now it sounded more like Lewis' voice than that of her conscience.

"We only saw each other on rare occasions, but we talked about books, books we both read. He recommended other books to me. When we had coffee recently, he remembered the books he had recommended years ago, so we talked about those. He was a good, good man, but so sad after he left Mason City. I think something happened to him."

"You didn't know why he was sad?"

Cindy shook her head. "Not really, but I think it had something to do with his family. I think he and his wife didn't get along."

Oh, how awful, thought Emily. *Did Cindy think she could fill that void?*

Cindy seemed to realize what Emily was thinking. "You think I would come on to him? He would have been horrified."

Emily realized how delusional Cindy was about what happened in high school with Parsons. It was something she knew a professional should handle, yet the story about the cover-up would soon break publically either in a news story or from the police themselves. Neither was any way for Cindy to hear what happened to her in high school was now public knowledge. Maybe a bar was no place to break the news but it was better than the other alternatives.

"What happened between you and Principal Parsons will soon be out there," said Emily, searching Cindy's face for her reaction.

"What?"

"Everyone will know that what happened in high school was the cause of Parsons leaving Mason City."

"You mean he was fired because of what he did for me with the bullies? It was because of Superintendent Riley, wasn't it, because his son was one of those guys who bothered me? He decided to take it out on Principal Parsons because he stepped in when Riley didn't do anything. I never meant for that to happen. I should have kept my mouth shut about it when Principal Parsons asked me that day what was wrong."

Emily took a deep breath. This was going to be harder than she thought, and she didn't have the skills to get beyond Cindy's denial.

CHAPTER 21

As difficult as it was going to be to tell Cindy the reason for Principal Parsons' leaving Mason City, Emily knew she couldn't retreat at this point. Could she get through Cindy's denial to the truth? Was it something she should do? *Of course she should tell her,* thought Emily. The shock of discovering the truth from Emily was far less than from the police or the newspapers.

"He wasn't let go because of the bullying incident. It was something else. But it involved you."

Cindy eagerly searched Emily's face. "What then?"

"It was because of the sexual advances Principal Parsons made to you."

Cindy's face turned white. "What?"

"Your father went to Superintendent Riley and told him he had learned from you that Principal Parsons had made inappropriate comments to you. And maybe there were other things, too. I don't know the details."

"Details? What details? It never happened."

"I know it's difficult to acknowledge what someone you liked and trusted did to you. It always is with sexual abuse."

Cindy threw her arms out in a gesture of disbelief. She spun around as if she didn't want to face Emily and what she was saying, then she turned back to look Emily in the eye. "It never happened. Where did you hear such a thing? Did you make this up? Why would you do that? Or someone made it up to hurt me or Principal Parsons' memory. I don't understand." Cindy looked as if she were about to break into tears.

"No one made it up, Cindy," said a voice from the doorway

Emily turned to find Lewis standing there.

"What are you doing here?" Emily asked, her tone indicating that she thought he was eavesdropping on a sensitive conversation, and she wanted him to go away.

Cindy's gaze travelled to Lewis. She seemed to collect herself by scrubbing at her cheeks to remove any tears that might have escaped her eyes. "What do you know about this ridiculous story?"

"I'm sorry I came in on you two like this, but it's better you know that what happened to you will be made public. The adults who covered up the assault, Riley, your father and Assistant Superintendent Rudolph will have to pay."

"My father told the Superintendent that I said Principal Parsons assaulted me?" Cindy shook her head, then her gaze locked with Emily's. "How did you find out about this? How did either of you find this out?" The look on her face wasn't one of a woman who had been assaulted but rather of a woman who had been lied to by people she trusted.

"Martin Rudolph is a friend of mine. I guess the burden of guilt he carried for all these years finally got to him when Parsons was killed. He told me about it, and finally told his story to Detective Lewis," Emily said.

"You both believed him? Have you talked to my father?" Cindy asked. Her tone was devoid of the earlier note of disbelief, and it carried no suggestion that she might break down in tears. In fact, thought Emily, the expression on Cindy's face seemed to indicate she has just put together something important.

"Not yet," said Lewis. "Why?"

"Ask him how his brother got Principal Parsons' job in the Mason City schools so quickly after Mr. Parsons left. Better yet," she said, "let me do it."

Before either Lewis or Emily could stop her, Cindy took out her cell and made a call. "Dad? Right. We haven't been in touch much lately, but then you've never been much of a father to me, have you? No, no. You listen. You used me. No. You know how. Years ago with Mr. Parsons. How could you. Does Mom know? I didn't think so. No. Don't bother coming down here to see me. Go to the authorities who think you and your pals covered up my assault by Parsons. Explain how you lied. And why. No, Dad. Don't try to explain anything away. I know why you did it. Your brother, my uncle Tommy has been a lousy principal since he stepped into

Mr. Parsons' position." Cindy's face got redder and redder as she talked. When she abruptly ended the call, she threw the phone across the room. It hit the far wall and fell to the floor in several pieces. She shrugged. "I guess I need to get a new phone. That's just fine with me, since my father knows this number. I'm not sure I can talk to that man again. Ever." She slumped onto a bar stool.

Emily poured her a shot of bourbon.

"Aren't I still on duty?" Cindy asked. Her face had returned to its normal color and her eyes were the clear blue of a woman who has confronted a nightmare but worked through it. *Dang powerful woman,* thought Emily.

"The bar is officially closed. I think we all could use a nip," Emily said. She held up the bottle and looked at Lewis.

"What the heck." He removed his cowboy hat, smoothing his hair back, and then mounted one of the barstools s as if it was his steed.

Cindy downed the shot and eyed both Emily and Lewis. "Don't feel bad that ya'll were taken for a ride on this story. My dad usually gets what he wants. I remember him saying he thought his brother deserved the principal's position at Mason City, but Mr. Parsons got it instead. Uncle Tommy doesn't deserve the janitor's job much less principal, but Dad had a lot of pull in that community. Still does."

Cindy looked at Emily and Lewis. "I hope the two of you believe me."

Lewis was about to open his mouth in reply when Emily said, "Of course we do." She turned to Lewis. "Where do we go from here? There was no report filed, no cover-up, because there was no assault. If Parsons was still alive, he could sue for the loss of his job, but I doubt he would have done that. He knew he'd been framed."

"He also knew I wasn't the kind of person to lie about him, but he would never come out and tell the truth without dragging the situation out into the open and making my life miserable. He was a good man. I can't believe that happened to him. He kept it from me, from everyone," said Cindy, grabbing the bottle for another shot.

"I'm sure he kept it from his family also. He probably denied the phony charges, hoping his family would believe his side of the story."

"Did they?" asked Cindy.

Emily shook her head.

"I should make a call," said Cindy, looking across the room at the pieces of her phone on the floor.

"Here. Borrow mine." Emily handed Cindy her cell.

"Mom?" Cindy said. She glanced at Emily and Lewis, then walked out of the door into the restaurant to complete the rest of her call.

"Here we thought sexual harassment had destroyed a family, but it was a false allegation that has destroyed another family," said Emily, thinking of the Parsons family.

"It gets worse," said Lewis, telling her of how he thought the reverend had blackmailed Parsons, but instead found Mrs. Parsons had been the target. "Well, I guess I'd better get back to work." He clapped his hat back on his head and looked out the windows. The rain had started again. Emily could read fatigue as well as disappointment in the lines on his face. She knew he was relieved to know that Cindy hadn't been molested, but that information didn't help him solve Parsons' murder nor identify who made attempts on Emily's life and that of Mr. Otter.

She reached out her hand and touched him as he hesitated at the door. He put his arm around her and the two of them looked out at the rain.

"This day reminds me of the day of the reenactment when Parsons was murdered. It would have been poetic justice if this was the day you uncovered his murderer."

"The legal system doesn't provide poetic justice, Emily. You know that. Sometimes there's no justice, not even legal justice." He opened the door, ducked his head into the blowing downpour and headed out the door for his car.

Cindy returned Emily's phone. "Well, if the bar is closing I'd better get on home, too."

"No you don't. You've had too much to drink and now is not the time for you to be alone. You're coming home with me. You can meet my other house-guest—my daughter, Naomi."

Cindy began to argue, but both of them were interrupted by the sound of the wind and a wall of rain as the outside door opened. A man appeared in the doorway. He stood there with the wind and rain at his back, the streetlight from the parking lot framing him in a dancing flurry of raindrops.

"We're closed. And could you shut the damn door and get out of the rain, Donald?" said Emily.

Donald replied with his usual greeting, a simple one syllable utterance that sounded more like a growl than any human language.

"How's the hangover?" asked Cindy.

"Dpn't have no hangover. It must be a touch of the flu."

"Well, I don't know how you managed to get yourself over here, but I assume you're here to pick up your truck," said Emily.

Donald walked across the room toward the bar like someone stepping on thin ice, as if he feared it wouldn't hold him. He stopped next to Cindy who looked up at him with a weary expression. "You drunk?" he asked.

"Yes," she replied.

"I could give you a ride to your place," he offered.

"She's coming home with me as soon as I turn off the lights here and secure the place."

"I'll join you then. Maybe your next-door neighbor has baked something she'd like to share."

"You're not coming home with me. You said you had the flu, and I haven't had my flu shot yet."

Emily tossed Donald his truck keys, which he almost missed catching, grabbed him by his belt and then shoved him out the door.

"Drive carefully, Donald," Emily said, watching him dash through the downpour to his truck.

She checked the doors from the bar to the kitchen and restaurant to make certain they were secure, then took Cindy by the arm. They hesitated for a moment at the door hoping the rain would let up, but it continued to come down in sheets. Emily nodded an "Okay" at Cindy, and the two of them plunged into the storm and headed for Emily's car. Donald's truck still remained in the parking lot. When she started the car and began to pull out of the lot, she looked in her rearview mirror and could see Donald had gotten out of his truck and was shaking his fist in the air.

What is going on with Donald now, she wondered and then thought, *I don't want to know.* She gave a tiny beep on her horn as she pulled past him, but he signaled her to stop. She rolled down her window an inch.

"Truck won't start," he said.

"Do you know what's wrong with it?"

"No, and I'm not interested in getting any more soaked finding out." Donald opened the back door of Emily's car and got in. "You can drop me at my place, or better yet, I could accompany you home and you would make me tea."

Tea? Donald must be sick. Well, it was clear she wasn't going to get rid of him soon.

"If I take you home with me, then how will you get to your place?" asked Emily.

Cindy turned in her seat. "Take my car, Donald."

"Great." Donald grabbed the keys, jumped out and ran to Cindy's car.

As Emily pulled onto to the main highway, she could see the headlights from Cindy's car behind her.

"No wonder he thought it was great you gave him your car. He's going to follow us to my place. I think Donald's lonely." She grabbed her cell and connected to Vicki. "You got anything in the oven? Donald's on his way."

Cindy laughed, then slid down in her seat. "I think I could use a nap."

It was obvious Cindy wasn't a big drinker, and the three shots she'd consumed were getting to her.

"I'll wake you when we get there," said Emily, directing her attention to the rainy road ahead.

The roads were empty except for Emily's car and Donald in Cindy's car behind her. Neither of them paid any attention to the other vehicle, which had pulled onto the road and followed them south toward town.

Donald maintained several car lengths behind Emily until they neared the city limits when he suddenly pulled forward, his headlights filling Emily's rear window. *What the...?* thought Emily. He continued to close the gap between his front bumper and her rear one. *He's going to hit me.*

She took out her cell and connected to him. "What are you doing? If I put on my brakes, you'll be sitting in my trunk."

"The guy behind me is almost sitting in mine. He must be drunk."

Donald had no sooner gotten the words out of his mouth when the truck pulled around Donald and began to pass Emily. "The guy is nuts. It's not safe to be going as fast as he..."

The other vehicle was even with Emily's front end when it swerved back into Emily's lane, just missing Emily's front fender. To avoid a collision, Emily jerked the wheel to the right, hitting the soft shoulder. Her car lost traction and headed into the swampy ditch at the side of the road.

Emily tried to get control of the car, but only managed to slow its descent into the canal. The car came to rest with its front end slowly sliding into the water.

"Let's get out of here," Emily said, trying to open her door, but it was stuck in the mud at the edge of the canal and wouldn't budge.

"Try your window," shouted Cindy, freeing herself from the car through the passenger's door. She ran around the back of the car and tried to open Emily's door from the outside, but the door was now up to the window in the sucking mud. Emily slid over to the passenger's side and exited the car. The two women struggled out of the water and fell onto the embankment as the car continued its slide into the canal. Donald appeared at the road above them and rushed down the slippery slope to them.

"Are you both okay?" he asked.

"Just wet," said Emily, taking the hand he offered to help her to her feet. Cindy stood up and pointed toward the car, now almost totally underwater.

"Did the jerk who tried to pass me stop?" asked Emily. "He must have seen me go off the road."

"Nope," said Donald. "He's long gone."

"Do you think he did that on purpose?" asked Cindy.

All of them stood paralyzed with the thought that Emily might have been the target of yet another attack.

Emily shivered as she felt the cold and wet penetrating her clothes. "Let's get out of this rain and into your car, Cindy. I'll call a tow truck and let them take care of the car."

"I think you should also call your detective boyfriend," said Donald. "Just in case this wasn't an accident."

"I am not waiting out here until he shows up. I'm freezing, and all of us need warm, dry clothes and something hot to drink. This feels just like the day I stumbled onto Mr. Parsons at the reenactment. Too much mud and rain in my life lately. Why is it nothing bad ever happens on a sunny day? I should probably move to the desert. Let's at least talk in the comfort of a dry car." Emily started up the embankment toward Cindy's car.

"I'd reconsider that move if I were you," said Donald, holding out his arm to prevent her from moving.

"What is wrong with you, Donald? Let's go before we all die of hypothermia," Emily said.

"That might be a lot better than dying in the jaws of a gator." Donald pointed toward a heavy, dark object which lay between them and Cindy's car.

"Don't be silly, Donald. It's just a downed tree. See. It's not moving." Cindy said.

The object moved.

Cindy and Emily jumped behind Donald.

"Make it go away, Donald," said Emily, remembering an occasion on which Donald did chase off an alligator.

"I don't think that will work this time," he said.

"Lost your touch, have you?" Emily said, the mocking tone doing little to cover up the quaver of fear in her voice.

"No, but we've unwittingly placed ourselves between her and her nest. Listen," Donald said.

Through the pounding rain, Emily could hear the sounds of high-pitched squeaks, baby alligators calling for their mama.

The alligator moved toward them, then stopped and gave a loud hiss.

"Yikes," said Emily.

CHAPTER 22

"Now would you call Detective Lewis? We're going to need help to get out of this one," Donald said. All three of them stood unmoving as the rain poured down. The alligator eyed them with what Emily believed to be a look of culinary speculation—lunch, dinner, a midnight snack?

"I guess alligators don't mind getting wet," said Emily. She felt around in her pockets for her cell. She came up empty-handed. "Damn. My phone must be in the car. Do you have a gun, Donald? You could shoot, and we would run like crazy to Cindy's car."

Donald reached into his pocket, and Emily gave a sigh of relief. Donald probably was a pretty good shot. He'd take care of the big gal, not kill her but scare her off with a warning shot or whatever.

"Let's not make any sudden moves, and keep quiet," Donald said, turning his back on the alligator.

"What are you doing, Donald? Your target is the other way." Emily tried to keep her voice low as Donald suggested, but her fear made it sound high and squeaky. The alligator made a movement forward and delivered another hiss.

Emily heard Donald speaking in a whisper, and thought he was praying before he took a shot at the gator. Instead she heard Donald talking to the only other person who could make this situation more difficult to bear—Lewis.

When he finished his brief call, he said Lewis would be there as soon as possible. "He's at the station."

"Will he shoot her then? Because I think it's cruel to kill her. What will her babies do without her?" asked Emily.

Donald leaned close in to Emily's ear. "First, it's against the law to shoot alligators. Second, maternal instinct in gators is nothing like that in humans. Now, I suggest we move slowly and quietly to our right, out of the direct route between her and the family. On three. One, two, three. Let's slide right."

They did. So did the alligator.

"That's funny," said Donald.

Emily looked up at him and then at the alligator. She saw nothing funny about their dilemma.

"Again. Let's move to the right."

They moved. The alligator moved.

"Hmm," said Donald.

"What now?" asked Cindy.

Emily began to think that Donald didn't know as much about wildlife as she had once thought. Maybe he knew only about fish.

Another hiss. This one came from the direction of the nest.

"What is going on?" asked Emily.

The rain let up enough that Emily could see the nest of little ones hadn't been abandoned at all. An alligator sat at its edge. The gator near Emily, Cindy and Donald opened its mouth and then clapped it shut. Maybe that was a yawn of boredom and it would go away, thought Emily.

"That's what I thought," Donald said. "Mama's on the nest protecting her young."

"And that's Daddy protecting his wife and kids from us then," Emily said.

"No, that's Daddy or some other male trying to get to the nest to have a midnight snack," Donald said.

"Oh, yuck," said Cindy. The earlier trauma with her father, three shots of booze, rain, cold and the accident finally caught up with her. She leaned to one side and threw up. Unfortunately, she chose the side where Donald was located.

"If you want to throw up on a gator, over there, not on these fine alligator skin boots." He pointed toward the male gator.

"You realize we're now stuck between two gators, one who thinks we're threatening her kids and the other who wants us out of the way of his food, or who considers us food." Emily put her arm around Cindy.

The lights of a vehicle from the direction of town moved through the misty rain toward them.

"That must be Lewis," said Donald.

"I can't see how another human added to the already yummy count of three is going to help," said Emily.

The vehicle slowed and then maneuvered between the potential diner alligator and his about-to-be-consumed dinner. Lewis opened the window of his cruiser and yelled for them to get in the back door. Everyone piled in, he backed out, made a U-turn and started back toward town.

"Now can I get the details?" he asked.

"You tell him," said Emily, cradling Cindy in her arms.

Donald began to relay the evening's events, beginning with his truck's failing to start.

Lewis interrupted him. "Uh, I don't mean to be insensitive, but did someone just throw up? I can pull over if you like."

"It's my boots," said Donald.

"You threw up on your boots? I didn't think you were so scared of alligators, Donald," said Lewis.

"He's not. Cindy was sick back there. In fact, I think our first stop should be the emergency room at the hospital. She passed out." Emily continued to hold the young woman, trying to transfer her body heat to Cindy. Lewis turned on his flashers and stepped on the accelerator. He radioed his destination to headquarters. The blue lights of the hospital emergency room flickered up ahead. "Hurry," said Emily, checking Cindy's pulse in her wrist. "Her breathing is shallow, and her heartbeat is weak."

Lewis jerked the wheel to the left and slid into the hospital's emergency room parking area. He and Donald took Cindy out of Emily's arms and carried her into the hospital. Medical personnel transferred her to a gurney, and she disappeared behind a curtained petition.

Lewis provided registration with information on Cindy and what had happened to her. Emily came up from behind and interrupted. "I think it's probably dehydration from the booze and hypothermia from being out in the rain so long."

"You are Dr. who?" asked the woman behind the desk.

"Oh, I'm not a doctor," Emily said.

"She thinks she is. She also thinks she's a private detective. There's no end of professions Emily doesn't dabble in," said Lewis. Lewis glanced down at Emily and his look softened. "Are you okay? You look, uh, you look not so good. Maybe the docs here could take a gander at you. To make sure you're okay."

She leaned into him. "I'm fine. Thank you for rescuing us."

"You need dry clothes, maybe a hot toddy," Lewis said. "I've got some cognac at my place."

"Sounds great, ole buddy," said Donald, slapping Lewis on the back. "We're about the same size. I could borrow some of your clothes until I get home to my place. But what's she going to wear?" Donald crooked his thumb at the bedraggled and wet Emily.

Emily ignored Donald and pushed Lewis to one side. She spoke to the registration clerk who allowed Emily to use her phone. Emily called Cindy's mother to tell her where her daughter was, then contacted Clara who would know all the legal ins and outs of what was sure to come after the authorities sorted through the fraudulent case of sexual abuse in Mason City. Besides, Clara had a car that worked. Emily would be damned if she'd go home with Lewis if Donald was going to be a roomie also.

"This feels like the time we spent wet and cold in your condo on Jekyll Island during that tornado. Except we didn't have Donald with us," said Emily.

"We won't have now either," said Lewis. "Donald, old man, come with me and I'll drive you home. I know you'll be more comfortable in your own clothes in your own place."

"But what about her?" asked Donald, sliding his glance toward Emily.

"She's staying to wait for Clara," said Lewis.

"So Clara will take her home, not to your place?" asked Donald. Emily could hear the sense of having put one over on Lewis in Donald's voice.

Lewis started toward the door with Donald, but turned for a moment and mouthed "I'll be back to pick you up." Emily grinned in anticipation, but until Lewis returned for her, she had work to do.

Emily hadn't spent the entire evening being terrified. Beneath all that fear generated by her "old brain," the primitive brain matter like that governing the gator's flee and fight responses, her cortex had been humming along with some interesting thoughts.

❖

Clara arrived in half an hour, and Emily filled her in on what was happening. Cindy's mother driving in from Mason City took longer. Emily introduced the two women to each other.

"We can talk later. I'm just here in case you have some questions about what might happen legally. I can give you my take on the situation once your daughter is settled in," Clara said.

"Are the police involved tonight?" Cindy's mother asked, concern making her voice quaver.

"Yes. There was a police detective here who knows the whole story of the cover-up, but I don't think he's interested in taking any action such as questioning your daughter at this time. Given the time lapse between what your husband said that led to Principal Parsons leaving Mason City, we may be beyond the time allotted for filing a case against them, but there may be other actions that could be taken. We can talk about that later," Clara said.

"My husband won't be arrested then?" asked Mrs. Goodman. Emily couldn't tell from her tone of voice if she was relieved or upset to hear the police wouldn't be pressing charges at this time.

Cindy's condition had improved so that when her mother entered the cubicle where she was being examined, she was breathing without the benefit of oxygen and had been bundled in heated blankets to bring her core temperature back to normal. Cindy and her mother hugged for almost an entire five minutes.

"Your father told me what he did to you. He wanted to come along with me, but I told him to stay home. You need time to heal from this evening. We can deal with the other later," her mother said. It was clear to Emily where Cindy had gotten her tall, blond good looks and her can-do attitude. Cindy's mother wasn't about to let anyone, not even her husband, compromise her daughter's health. She was also realistic.

"You'll have to talk to your father soon, you know, and eventually you'll have to forgive him. I will too."

Cindy shook her head. "Dad's a jerk."

"Yes, he is, but you know you love him, and so do I. He's not as strong as you or me, especially when it comes to his brother. Your uncle could talk your father into anything, but I think this may have taught your father that brotherly love should only go so far. Whether it taught his brother anything is anyone's guess." She pushed her shiny blond locks back from her face and pressed her lips to her daughter's forehead. "For now, you don't need to think about anything except getting better. The hospital said they're keeping you overnight, and they've set up a cot for me in your room." She arose and hugged Emily. "Thanks for being there for her. I'll be talking with you later."

"Please tell her not to worry about her job. She should take all the time she needs. Her job will be there waiting for her."

As they wheeled Cindy out of the cubicle, she reached up to grab her mother and spoke into her ear. Mrs. Goodman turned and said, "Cindy wants you to get a message to someone called 'Donald.' Does she have a boyfriend I don't know about?"

Emily shook her head. "A friend. The other bartender."

"She said he should take care of his cold or flu or whatever it is."

Emily smiled to herself. Maybe there was more between Cindy and Donald than she thought. Ah, well. She could worry about the age difference between the two, but Cindy was one heck of a gal. If Donald needed handling, Cindy was the only woman Emily knew who could do the job.

There was a tap on Emily's shoulder. She turned to look into Lewis' eyes. "Let's go to my place and get you into some warm clothes, unless you'd prefer your home and something that will fit you a lot better than my old sweats."

"Nope. Naomi will be there. We need to talk, and other stuff, and we don't need company. Besides I look terrific in oversized sweats."

"Do you want to call her on my cell?"

"I did that already when Clara came."

"Did I hear my name?" asked Clara from the seat she had taken in the waiting area. "I wasn't sure if you might need a ride, Emily."

"I've got one, but thanks." Emily let Lewis take her arm and direct her toward the door. She shivered again, but this time it wasn't from her damp clothes. It was from anticipation, and not merely anticipation at talking over the case with Lewis. It was more like...desire. Finally she and Lewis could be honest with each other. All obstacles including their pig-headed mistrust of their relationship had been swept away, thought Emily.

How wrong she was.

❦

Emily leaned closer to Lewis on the way to his place.

"Are you certain this is what you want? I can take you home where you have your own clothes."

"Are you saying you're not interested in seeing how I look in your sweats?"

"No, Emily. I'm saying this can wait. You've had quite a night what with supporting Cindy through learning the truth about her father, someone driving so recklessly that you were forced off the road, and finally the gator showdown."

"What can wait? Us or talking about the case?"

Lewis glanced over at her. "Uh, both?"

"Good." She snuggled even closer to him.

Once she had used his shower and changed into the clothes he provided—a long-sleeved shirt and a pair of jeans, rolling up the legs and cinching in the waist using the tie to his dressing robe, she felt warm and ready for whatever might come.

Lewis brewed coffee, and they took their cups to the living room and got comfy on the couch.

Emily saw the look of defeat in Lewis' eyes and realized talk of the case had to come before anything else.

"No sexual assault, but that doesn't mean Parsons wasn't killed because somebody thought there was an assault," said Emily.

"Only a few people thought an assault had occurred: The Parsons family, the reverend and Winthrop, Superintendent Riley, and your boyfriend, Martin."

"First, he's not my boyfriend. Second, someone else might have known about the so-called assault," said Emily.

"Who?"

Emily thought back to what she knew about Owen Parsons and his mother. "I don't think Owen told anyone, not even his good friend, David Otter. The boy was just too ashamed of his father's behavior and too anxious to keep the secret within the family to tell anyone else."

"Winthrop is right about the reverend. He's a petty crook, involved in blackmail, not murder."

"The Parsons' daughter is out of the picture as well. She's too young." Emily pictured the day of the funeral when she had the opportunity to see all the parties together. There was something else, but Emily was too exhausted to think it out.

Lewis looked at her. "You look beat. You need to go to bed, not mull over this murder."

"Go to bed as…"

"Sleep, my darling. You should sleep."

She knew he was right, but they never had a chance to be alone unless it was to argue. Tonight they were getting along fine, quite fine.

"So, kiss me even though you're not aggravated," Emily said, reaching up to embrace him.

Lewis pulled her off the couch and she slid easily into his arms. Maybe she wasn't so tired after all.

Lewis caught the electricity in her body and responded with his own jolt of heat. "The only problem is I can't tell where you begin and all these clothes end."

"You poor thing. Let me help you." Emily slipped the shirt over her head and stepped out of the oversized jeans. "Now it's your turn." She began to unbutton his shirt. They both stopped for a moment, waiting for someone to knock on the door or a cell to ring, but this time, there were no interruptions.

Lewis carried her into his bedroom and laid her gently on the bed. As soon as her body felt the embrace of the mattress and before Lewis could drop down beside her, she knew this was a bad idea.

He wrapped his arms around her.

"The rain's letting up some," he whispered in her ear.

Her only response was a soft snore.

Emily was aware of two things that night: the rain had increased, and Lewis lay next to her cradling her body close to his. She slept more soundly than she had in weeks, and when she awoke, she wondered why she and Lewis didn't do this more often, a thought she shared with him when he brought her a cup of coffee.

"We don't do this every night because you either have to be mad at me before I get to kiss you or there has to be some life-threatening event to scare you into my arms."

He'd said it with humor, but it still rankled that there was some truth to it. She decided not to break the mood that remained from a night's sleep in the arms of someone you, uh, liked a lot.

"The rain is never going to stop. But that's good for me. I won't have to open the bar. I'll bet the course will be closed all day and maybe tomorrow." She stretched, and the sheet slipped off her. She realized she had no clothes on, blushed and pulled the sheet back up.

Lewis almost dropped his coffee cup. He swallowed and set the cup down on night table. She wanted to laugh out loud but knew he wouldn't understand. He was more embarrassed than she was at her nudity. She watched him recover his strong guy demeanor before he replied. "You can stay here if you like, but I've got a murder to solve and cops don't operate only on sunny days."

"Drop me home. I can spend the day with my daughter—girls catchup time. We can also check on Cindy."

When he let her out in front of her house, he grabbed her hand to stop her from getting out of the car.

"I've been thinking about what you said."

"What? When?"

"You wondered why we weren't together more often."

Emily smiled at him. "Oh, we know what that's all about. We don't get along well. We argue almost every time we're together. You don't respect my ability to think through murder investigations. You find me too emotional. I find you condescending. I could go on and on."

"You usually do. But I've got an idea."

He was serious, and she could see he wanted her to be also.

"Okay. What's your idea?"

"We could get married."

His words took her breath away, but only for a moment.

"If that's a proposal of marriage, the answer is yes, but only if there are no 'obey' promises in the vows."

He hesitated for only a minute. "You mean I don't have to obey you?"

"You know damn well what I mean."

"It's a deal then?"

"You are so romantic, you know that? But yes, it's a deal."

"Do we shake on it?" he asked.

"Should I reconsider my response to your proposal?" She kissed him on the cheek, and they parted without another word. When she entered the living room to find her daughter seated on the couch sipping a cup of coffee, what had happened between her and Lewis finally hit home.

"Are you okay, Mom? You look kind of funny. I'll bet you didn't get a moment's sleep last night." Naomi winked at her mother, a twinkle in her eye.

"It was quite a night, that's true. But the morning was even more amazing."

"All night long and again this morning. Maybe this isn't something a mother should discuss with her daughter."

"You're right. Any word about how Cindy is doing?"

"Donald called and said she had been released from the hospital. Her mother took her back to Cindy's apartment. He said he was going over there to be with her."

Emily stared out the window into the small back patio and yard onto the canal beyond.

"Mom? Did you hear me? Mom?" When she got no response from her mother, Naomi got up from the couch, went to her mother and touched her shoulder. "What's with you? You seem to be in another world."

"Would you be my matron of honor?"

CHAPTER 23

Despite the great night's sleep, Emily felt exhausted, probably as much from the shock of Lewis' proposal and her acceptance as from everything that happened earlier last night.

She crawled under the covers and began to drift into sleep, the image of Lewis' face before her, his strong arms cradling her. Ah, there was nothing like a guy to share your difficulties in life. Suddenly, she sat up. A guy there by your side when things got really bad. It was the missing piece and the key to Parsons' murder.

She grabbed her cell to call Lewis, but he didn't answer. Instead it went to police headquarters.

"I'm sorry, but Detective Lewis has directed his calls back here. Can I take a message?" said the desk sergeant who answered.

"Tell him Ms. Rhodes called and have him call me. It's important. And tell him it's not about marriage. It's about murder."

She didn't want to wait until Lewis returned her call. Who knew how long that would be. He could be on the road, and Emily needed her suspicion confirmed now. She jumped into a pair of jeans and a tee shirt and joined her daughter in the living room.

"How about taking a ride with me? I've got a lead on who killed Leonard Parsons." Emily reached for her keys on the hook by the door, then remembered. Her car was in the repair shop after being pulled out of the canal.

"What are you up to now, Mom? I thought you had decided to let Lewis run his own cases. Besides it's still pouring down rain out there."

"He doesn't know what I know."

"Tell him."

"He's out chasing some other criminals. I can't reach him. Grab your rain slicker. I'll borrow Vicki's car."

Emily phoned her next-door neighbor who sounded excited at Emily's request.

"I'll bet you're running down some bad guy, aren't you? And here I am whipping up some cakes for the church bake sale. The car is all yours. If I need a ride, I can take hubby's SUV. He's at the course playing a round with his golf league. Darn, I wish I could come with you when you go after these criminals. Maybe I should just leave the baking."

"No, no. You do enough for all of us crime fighters—local gossip that provides us with leads in the cases—and don't forget we depend upon your culinary skills to keep us in food. Otherwise both our brains and our bodies would starve and no one would get arrested."

"Well, as long as you think I'm doing my part."

"You are. Trust me."

"Good. I'll make you a snack for the road."

⁂

Lewis had gotten a lead and was anxious to check on it. He drove out to the boat launch and almost missed the entrance because his wipers couldn't keep up with the downpour of rain that came in sheets blown by a strong wind off the lake. He pulled into the empty parking area. Even the most dedicated angler knew the fish wouldn't be biting today. One of the workers at the site had called the station earlier with news Lewis needed to pursue. He pulled up alongside the covered pavilion where a man dressed in the gray uniform of the park personnel waited.

"Sorry to bring you out in this weather, detective, but I thought you'd like to see this. I didn't notice it until today because I haven't been emptying the trash barrels lately. All this rain means no one's using the place, so there's not much in the receptacles."

"Glad you called. Where is it?"

"Right over here behind the bathrooms. It looks as if someone parked here several days back. It got me to thinking about the incident the other day when that woman was pushed into the river. Maybe it's related." The man pulled his raincoat hood over his head and signaled Lewis to follow him.

The man led him to the back of the building where the ground sloped down into an area filled with tangled brush. The guy pointed toward something metallic and rusty lying partly obscured in the weeds.

"I left it there and called you fellows. This is on the other side of the seawall where the woman went in, not an area you'd think to search. Besides it's almost hidden in the brush. I didn't notice it until one of the trash cans was blown by the wind down here."

Lewis headed down the slope toward the object. It was a piece of a truck, an old battered truck. Lewis smiled despite the cold rain, which hit the back of his collar and slid down his neck. It was a piece of Toby Sands' truck.

"Now who would want to park their car down here when there's a huge paved parking area over there?" The man pointed back up to the lot.

"No one would unless the person was trying to hide their vehicle."

Lewis called his office to get a truck out to the river to pick up the truck part and a crew to check for other evidence, although he was certain any tire tracks would have been washed out by the rain. His partner had the day off, but he called her to let her know what he'd found.

"You want me to come in to talk with Toby with you?" Davis made the offer knowing Lewis preferred confronting Toby on his own.

"Nope. I want to do this one, up close and personal. I'll keep you posted."

"Don't you want to wait for forensics to confirm it's part of Toby's truck?"

"I haven't any doubt it is. Besides, I only want to scare him today. We'll arrest him tomorrow." With a chuckle he ended the call.

He knew Toby had to be involved in this case somehow. Lewis was certain the truck part would connect Toby to shoving Emily off the seawall. How it related to the attempt on Mr. Otter's life and Parsons' murder, he didn't know. Sneaking up behind someone and pushing them into the water was the kind of cowardly act Toby would pull. Lewis knew Toby wasn't responsible for the hit-and-run with Mr. Otter's truck because Toby's truck didn't match the vehicle that hit Otter. Shooting someone also didn't seem to be part of Toby's criminal nature. The toad was a sneak, but Lewis found it difficult to imagine him trying to kill someone, or actually doing it, even for a lot of money. Getting Toby to confess he pushed Emily and to spill information about the other crimes would take all of Lewis' skill as an interrogator. He looked forward to the challenge.

Toby's swamp shack was only a few miles away. Lewis hoped he was home and not spending time with the reverend, but Lewis didn't mind if he had to drive all the way to Clewiston. Lewis would drive to Mars and back just to see Toby squirm.

When he pulled up to the house, he saw Toby's truck in the driveway. He got out and inspected it, and, as he suspected, most of the back bumper was missing.

He knocked once and threw open the door, not caring if Toby was sleeping or wooing his lady love.

The pile of clothes on the bed moved, revealing Toby alone. Lewis sniffed and looked around the room. The old Toby and his chewing tobacco smell was back, as was the smell of unwashed body and bedding. Dishes sat in the sink, flies buzzing around the food, which had dried on the plates.

Toby struggled to sit up on the edge of the bed. He looked up and blinked as Lewis approached. The closer Lewis got to Toby, the more he smelled alcohol. Toby was no longer on the wagon. A brown, tobacco juice stain ran from the corner of Toby's mouth to his chin. His beard was beginning to grow in, and if Toby thought it would give him that European playboy look he was wrong. The bristly growth accented his fat chin and made it a likely catchall for food falling out of his mouth.

Much as Lewis didn't want to do this, he knew he'd have to sober up Toby before he could ask him any questions. Lewis found the coffee pot and stoked the fire in the wood stove.

"Go away. I need my rest. I've been through the wringer." Toby curled up on the bed.

"No more sleep. I need some answers from you. Your little gal friend won't be coming in to disturb us, will she?"

"She left me. Broke my heart. And the reverend fired me. How am I to pay the mortgage on this place? I'll have to live out of my truck."

"I can help you with that, Toby. How does a charge of attempted murder and housing in a prison cell sound to you?"

Toby groaned and reached into his pocket for a chaw. "Now where's my spit bucket?"

"You don't seem surprised at the charge."

"Melissa said God would get me if I strayed. I guess God sent you as his messenger. There's no reason for me to stay sober and clean if Melissa's not in my life."

"Except for self-respect." Lewis poured Toby a cup of coffee. "Drink that. We have a lot of talking to do."

⸺◆⸺

Lewis told his partner he would only be talking with Toby, but Toby was so forthcoming with his story that Lewis decided to make the arrest today, although he was darned if he'd let the smelly wart in his car. He called for one of the police cruisers, figuring it could be easily fumigated after Toby was dropped at the jail.

Toby admitted to pushing Emily off the seawall and into the lake. His cowardly act had nothing to do with Parsons' murder. No one paid him to shove her into the water. It was Toby's idea, brought on when he pulled into the boat launch area on the way back from Clewiston and saw Emily standing there looking at the lake. He said it seemed like a great opportunity to make her pay for all the trouble Toby said she had caused him. Of course, Toby didn't see his troubles as being brought on by his own not-so-cunning version of hiring himself out to dump bodies or engage in kidnapping. He'd lost his job with the department for those crimes but had managed to slither around jail time in exchange for working undercover for the department as a snitch, a job he also botched.

"No more pardons for you. You're going to be doing hard time this time, Toby," said Lewis as he walked Toby out of the house to the waiting police car.

At that moment, Melissa pulled into the drive and jumped out of her car. "Toby. What's going on?" When she got close enough, she sniffed and scowled. "What have you done?"

"You left me. I'm a weak man. I need you." Tears ran down Toby's dirty cheeks.

Lewis kind of felt sorry for the man. Toby clearly did love Melissa and he'd lost her.

Melissa swooped down on Toby and threw her arms around him enveloping him in a hug. "Don't worry, my love. I can bring you back into the fold. I can save you."

The grateful look on Toby's face almost made Lewis a believer in forgiveness, but as Toby and Melissa were separated and he turned to get into the car, he gave Lewis a look filled with scorn and mouthed the words, "Watch your back."

—◈—

Emily pulled up in front of the Parsons' house and found a silver Audi convertible parked in the drive.

"That can't be Mrs. Parsons' car, do you think?" Naomi began walking up to the front door.

Emily followed, stopping for a quick peak at the convertible. She heard a shot come from the house and grabbed Naomi before she could take another step.

"Stay here with the car. I'll take a look through the front window. Call the police." Emily stooped low, then poked her head above the bottom of the large window into the living room. She saw Mrs. Parsons lying on the floor, blood flowing from a wound in her shoulder. Standing above her was a man holding a gun. As Emily moved away from the window, the front door slammed open and the armed man signaled with his weapon.

"Get in here. Now!"

Emily turned back to look at the car, hoping that Naomi would drive off, but the car didn't move, and she couldn't see Naomi. Emily hoped her daughter was hiding.

"Where is she? I heard you call to her."

"I don't know, but I do know she's calling the police. Give it up." Emily moved into the house and kneeled next to Mrs. Parsons, who was conscious but appeared to be in a lot of pain. "She needs medical attention. She could bleed to death."

"It's no less than she deserved. She told me her husband lost his job at Mason City because he was a sexual predator, so I did what needed to be done. I got rid of him for her sake and for the sake of all the kids at the school. She lied about him. I loved her, and she betrayed me. She made me into a killer."

Emily thought the man had lost his mind. His face was red, and he paced around the room, muttering to himself, sometimes waving the gun in the air, then leveling it at her.

"That's your lover, Mr. Bundy. Right?" Emily applied pressure to the wound. Mrs. Parsons nodded in answer.

"I don't know how you found out the truth about those sexual allegations from years ago, but Mrs. Parsons wasn't lying to you. She thought her husband was guilty although he insisted he was not." Emily thought telling him how blameless Mrs. Parsons was would change his mind about helping her. It did not.

"I killed for her, and now I gotta make certain no one ever knows the truth. Leave her here to die. It's what she deserves. You come with me. You're my ticket out of here."

He pulled Emily to her feet and shoved her toward the door. When she opened it, Naomi stood on the other side.

"Run!" Emily yelled, but Naomi stubbornly refused to budge. "I'm not leaving you with that maniac."

Bundy pointed the gun away from Emily and toward her daughter.

"Leave her here. I won't give you any trouble," Emily said.

"She knows. She comes along. Two hostages are better than one anyway." He herded them toward his car. "You drive. Your daughter can take the passenger's seat and I'll be in the back with this gun pointed at both of you. Head north out of town."

Emily did as he ordered, hoping some ingenious plan would miraculously materialize in her snoopy brain. Nope. Nothing came to mind. She gripped the wheel and headed north toward the country club.

"Isn't this the place where we were run off the road the other night?" asked Naomi.

Thank you, thank you, clever daughter of mine, said Emily to herself. She shifted her gaze and caught her daughter's look of agreement.

"Shut up you two. And keep your eyes on the road. All this rain is making the pavement slippery, and I have no intention of dying in a car accident."

Neither did Emily, so she slowed up and focused on the road. Bundy seemed to be reassured by her caution. She then yelled, "Gator!" and twisted the wheel to the left at the same time stomping on the brake. She'd seen this maneuver on internet videos. *How hard could it be?* The tail end of the car slid to the left, and the car slipped sideways toward the canal. That was kind of what she had planned. *So far, so good.* Emily intended for the maneuver to stop the car and head in it in the direction from which it had come, but she hadn't counted on the slippery road. Instead of stopping, the car continued to slide sideways down the embankment and into the black water of the canal. *And here we go yet again,* she thought. Bundy might not know what lurked in those waters, but Emily and Naomi did.

CHAPTER 24

As the car slowly slipped driver's side first into the water, Naomi pushed open her door and reached in and pulled her mother out with her. The car continued its downward descent and soon the canal water rushed into the passenger compartment. Stuck in the rear of the convertible with its small back seat, Bundy struggled to extract himself by thrashing about feeling for the lever to push the seat forward. There was little Emily and Naomi could do to help him out of the water without joining him in the inundated car. With a final swoosh the car tipped on its side, then upended and continued its descent to the bottom of the deep canal. It soon disappeared. Emily and Naomi stood at the canal's edge scanning the water for sight of Bundy.

"If I could see him or the car, I might have a chance of helping him by diving in." Emily heard the splash of something large enter the canal nearby.

"Too late," said Naomi.

Suddenly a hand arose from the water's edge and grabbed for Naomi's ankle. She kicked at it, but the fingers dug into her leg and wouldn't let go.

"Help me," Bundy said.

The head of a large alligator appeared in the water several feet away. It began a glide toward them.

Emily and Naomi reached out and grabbed Bundy by the arm to pull him out of the water to safety. The alligator continued its glide in their direction. Bundy began to struggle up the embankment on his hands and knees.

"He can save himself now," said Emily, grabbing Naomi's hand and pulling her toward the road.

"He'll never make it," said Naomi. They turned to help him up, but his eyes were so filled with fear that he didn't register they were trying to rescue him. He shoved them away from him, got to his feet and began a feeble run along the canal into a group of palmetto and cypress trees not far from them. They lost sight of him in the tangle of vegetation. When Emily looked back to where they spotted the alligator, she saw two eyes and a snout disappear under the water's surface.

"That didn't quite turn out the way I'd planned," said Emily, brushing tendrils of wet hair out of her face.

"What do you mean? When I reminded you that we were near where the alligator threatened us the other night, I assumed you were going to ditch the car in the canal and let nature take its course with Bundy. I knew he'd have difficulty getting out of the back seat. That wasn't what you intended?"

"Yeah, sure. Whatever."

"Do you think someone will be by here to flag down?"

"You called the police back at Parsons' house, so someone should be on the lookout for us."

"Well, I meant to tell you."

"Tell me what?"

"I didn't bring my cell phone. I couldn't call them."

"What? Bundy might still be a threat." Emily looked around, trying to spot him, worried he might come back and threaten them.

"Sorry."

They heard a siren approaching and saw the lights of a police car.

"This can't be coincidence, so who called them?" Emily asked.

A police cruiser pulled up followed by Lewis.

"I was at the station when the call came in from the Parsons' house. Owen had come home from school and found his mother who told us what happened. A police car spotted Bundy's car heading north out of town. I headed here as quickly as I could. Are both of you okay?"

They nodded.

"Bundy may be hiding out in those trees." Emily pointed. "And I think the alligator claimed the car."

Lewis scanned the area and spotted something in the nearby field. "I think he's over there." Lewis pointed to a large live oak tree in a pasture adjacent to the canal. "He used that driveway bridge back there to get over the canal."

Emily looked to where Lewis pointed. She could make out the figure of a man, back to the tree, cowering as three large Brahman bulls with horn expanses of five feet or more moved toward him.

"He's a goner," said Emily. "They'll tear him apart, not that he doesn't deserve to die, but not that way."

Lewis laughed. "Don't worry. They're just curious. Those bulls are sweet as pussycats."

They watched Bundy drop to his knees and raise his hands as if he was praying.

"I guess we don't have to worry about him getting away then. He won't want to chance running into the gator. He's trapped," said Emily.

"I'll call it in and get a car out here to pick him up. He'll be very grateful." Lewis glanced over his shoulder as he walked Naomi and Emily to his car. One of the bulls had approached Bundy closer and seemed to be licking his face. Salt from Bundy's tears, thought Lewis. Like a human salt lick.

───※───

Lewis said nothing as he drove them back to Emily's place. She could hear him thinking lots of things, but he remained quiet and seemed composed. That couldn't be a good sign, she thought. He waited until both Emily and Naomi had taken hot showers and changed into dry clothes.

"You suspected Bundy, and you just had to go looking for him, didn't you?" he finally said in a cold judgmental tone.

"Actually, I wasn't looking for him. I wanted to talk with Mrs. Parsons about what I suspected. He was there. He thought she had lied to him about her husband's sexual misconduct."

"She told me when I talked to her at the hospital. She'll be fine, by the way. What made you suddenly suspect Bundy?"

"It was what Mrs. Parsons said to him when she fainted at the funeral. We all heard her and accepted her excuse of mistaking Bundy for her dead husband coming back to life, but that wasn't true. Mrs. Parsons and her husband were emotionally estranged for many years. She hated him. Why would she ask him to kiss her? It took a little cuddle fest of my own to figure it out. It's what I said to you, what lovers would say to each other. She and Bundy were having an affair."

"Cuddle fest," snorted Naomi. "I'm going to bed to get some sleep. I'm bushed." She turned back before she got to the hallway. "Speaking of that. Detective, if you're serious about marrying my mother you could at least give her a good hug and tell her you're happy she's still alive."

"I'm happy you're alive, too." Lewis smiled.

"Good. Mom likes all her men to like me, you know." Naomi winked at her mom.

"All what men?" asked Lewis.

"Well, there's Donald, of course..."

Lewis grabbed Emily in his arms and then kissed her, hard, on the lips. When they parted, it took Lewis several minutes to gather together his interrupted thoughts. Emily pushed him onto the couch and sat on his lap.

"You're not helping, Emily."

"I know. Continue"

"Maybe I should have figured out about the affair also. I knew Bundy was having cocktails at the Parsons' house when I stopped by to talk with her. She said they were doing funeral planning. I should have known better. At the hospital today, I also went back over the conversation Owen and David had the night Mr. Otter's truck was hit. When Owen and David were talking on the phone about where to meet, Owen repeated what David said to him. 'You know who killed my father?' was what he repeated back to David. Bundy was at the Parsons' house to overhear that. He decided to take action by ramming who he thought to be David Otter, but instead it was David's father."

"And Mrs. Parsons never suspected?"

"I think she was too busy hating her husband and what she thought he had done to think about who killed him."

"Why did Bundy push me into the lake? I don't get that one," asked Emily.

"He didn't. Toby did, just for spite."

"I could have figured that out if Toby hadn't reformed and quit being such a pig. I would have smelled him." Emily wrinkled up her nose in disgust.

"I arrested him this morning. Unless Melissa reforms him again—and she might—Toby is back to his old stinky ways. That woman has questionable taste in boyfriends."

"Did they pick up Bundy?" asked Emily.

"He's in a cell as we speak. The officers who arrested him told me he hasn't done anything but babble nonsense. When we searched his house, we discovered he had quite a gun collection. I'm sure we'll find he used one of his rifles to kill Parsons."

Emily shuddered, suddenly cold thinking back to her recent alligator encounters. Two run-ins with the denizens of the swamp in a few days was more than she needed. Lewis felt her tremble and decided the best remedy for the cold was another hot shower. She didn't argue, so he took her back to his place and they ran his house out of hot water several times that night.

❖

Lewis and Emily decided to wed on Jekyll Island where they had experienced their first soapy shower together. Damp and cold followed by warm and sudsy seemed to be the story of their relationship. Not a bad way to end what began as wet and chilly events.

Naomi was maid of honor, Clara and Daisy bridesmaids, Donald best man and Rodney and Hap groomsmen. Emily had worried Donald might put a damper on the happy day by appearing gloomy, but he was in good humor, Emily suspected, because Cindy accepted his invitation to attend the festivities with him. Cindy confirmed the two of them were just friends, and she and Donald left the postnuptial party early because Donald was eager to get back for the annual bass tournament. Fish still seemed to come first in Donald's book.

Vicki served as caterer for the affair. Instead of a wedding cake, she served up Key lime pies. In traditional fashion, Emily smashed a slice of the pie in Lewis' face. He quickly wiped it off with his fingers and popped it into his mouth so as not to waste a bit of it.

"I hope I won't stumble onto any more dead bodies," Emily confided to Lewis as later that night they strolled arm in arm along the beach.

"Good. Leave the bodies to me," he replied.

"But, if there is a body, whether I find it or not, I'm more than willing to help you identify the killer." She glanced at him out of the side of her eyes to see if she had aggravated him.

She felt his body stiffen.

"Emily," he said in a warning voice, then pulled her into him and kissed her.

She hadn't lost her touch. He still found her aggravating.

THE END

Fresh Veggie Dip

1 C. sour cream
½ t. onion salt
1 C. Mayo
½ t. garlic salt
1 T. parsley flakes
1 t. accent (may leave out)
1 T. dried onion
2 drops tabasco sauce
1 t. dill weed
1 t. beaumonde

Blend by hand with fork or wisk—refrigerate several hours before using

Pot O' Chili
Use 8 or 10 qt. pot

2 lb. ground beef
2-3 C. chopped onion
1 14.5 oz diced tomatoes
1 29 oz Tomato Puree (not sauce)
1-2 15 oz can each of black beans, garbanzos, kidney and navy beans – all rinsed
3 cans (14.5 oz size) Rotel zesty diced tomatoes
2 4 oz. cans diced green chilis
2-3 cups frozen corn or use 16 oz. pkg

1 ½ t. chili powder
1 T. chili powder
1 T. chopped garlic
1 t. cumin
Salt to taste
1 C. water

Cook beef and onion, drain fat. Add rest of ingredients and simmer for 30-45 min.
Share with neighborhood.

Alfredo Pasta with Shrimp

½ lb. ditalini pasta, cooked, save ½ C. pasta water
2 T. olive oil
2 T. butter
1-1½ lbs raw jumbo shrimp (peeled and tails removed)
½ C. heavy cream
¾ C. parmesan cheese
4 C. packed baby spinach
Salt and pepper to taste

In large fry pan saute shrimp in butter and oil. Add salt and pepper. Turn each shrimp so both sides are pink. Re move from pan. Put drained pasta in pan with ½ C. pasta water and ½ C. heavy cream and ¾ C. parmesan. Mix well until a little bubbly. Add shrimp back to the pan and add the spinach, stirring until spinach is partially cooked. Add shredded parmesan on top of each serving.

Chicken Noodle Hot Dish
An old-fashioned dish from
Vickie's mother-in-law
Comfort food!

Preheat oven to 375 degrees
1 C. diced cooked chicken
8 oz. wide noodles (cooked)
1 C. frozen peas
sm. can mushrooms
1 can cream of mushroom soup
1 C. sour cream
½ lb. shredded cheddar
1 lg. green pepper, diced
sm. jar chopped pimentos
¼ C. melted butter
2 t. salt
½ C. chopped onion
Mix all ingredients and place in 3 qt. baking dish or
    9 x13 pan. Bake 1 hour covered with foil.

Caramel Chews
(sinfully rich cookies-like "extra good brownies")

60 light Kraft caramels (1 bag, about 40 is enough)
½ C. evaporated milk

1 pkg. German chocolate cake mix
¾ C. melted butter or margarine
1/3 C. evaporated milk
1 C. chopped nuts
1 C. choc chips

In sauce pan combine caramels and ½ cup evaporated milk. Cook over very low heat, stirring constantly until caramels are melted. Set aside. Grease and flour 9 X 13 pan. In large bowl, combine cake mix, melted butter, 1/3 cup evaporated milk and nuts. Press ½ of dough into pan. Reserve rest for topping. Bake at 350 for 8 min. Sprinkle choc chips over baked crust, then spread caramel mixture over choc chips. Crumble or drop rest of dough over caramel layer. Bake another 8-10 min. Cool slightly, then refrigerate to set caramel layer. Cut into small squares.

Rich Lemon Bundt Cake

Preheat oven to 350
1 lemon cake mix
1 small instant lemon pudding
1 C. water
1 C. vegetable oil
1 Egg

Beat all ingredients with electric mixer for 5 minutes. Bake in greased and floured Bundt pan for 55 minutes. Let cool for 5 minutes, then invert on a cake plate. Drizzle with a thin mixture of confectioners' sugar.

You can turn this into a chocolate Bundt cake by substituting chocolate cake mix and chocolate pudding.

Vicki's Key Lime Pie

1 9" graham cracker crust or make your own
14 oz. can sweetened condensed milk
3 egg yolks
1/2 c. Key lime juice (this can usually be found at most supermarkets in bottles, see note below)

Combine milk, egg yolks and juice. Blend until smooth. Pour filling into crust. Bake at 350 degrees for 10 minutes. Allow to stand for 10 minutes, then refrigerate. Cool several hours. Top with whipped cream and decorate with key lime slices if you have them.

Author's Note: Do not make this with regular lime juice (you know, from the green limes; Key Limes are tiny and yellow) unless you want a regular lime pie, not Key Lime pie.

ABOUT THE AUTHOR

Lesley retired from her life as a professor of psychology and reclaimed her country roots by moving to a small cottage in the Butternut River Valley in upstate New York. In the winter she migrates to old Florida—cowboys, scrub palmetto and open fields of grazing cattle, a place where spurs still jingle in the post office. Back north, Back north, the shy ghost inhabiting the cottage serves as her literary muse. When not writing, she gardens, cooks, frequents yard sales and renovates the 1874 cottage with the help of her husband, two cats and, of course, Fred the ghost, who gives artistic direction to their work.

She is the author of a number of mystery series and mysteries as well as short stories. The third book in the Eve Appel murders (from Camel Press) *A Sporting Murder* was awarded a Readers' Favorite Five Star Award and her short story *Gator Aid* a Sleuthfest (2009) short story first place.

www.lesleyadiehl.com